Wishing Hearts

Plum Valley Cowboys Book Six

Emmy Sanders

Beta Reading by A. E. Madsen, C.J. Banks, Georgia Johnson, and Lauren

Editing by M.A. Hinkle

Proofreading by Ky

Cover Design by Cate Ashwood

ISBN: 9798986448381

Content Warning: This book includes situations involving the aftereffects of animal abuse/neglect.

This one is for my readers. Without you, this story wouldn't exist.

CONTENTS

CHAPTER 1

Harrison

As the cow-shaped road sign for Plum Valley, Texas comes into view, I breathe a silent curse. This sounded like a much better idea last night when I was still four hours away and the idea of returning was this vague hypothetical. But now that my wheels are rolling past that big ol' cow denoting the border of town, the reality of the situation is smacking me in the face. I can't help but wonder if I'm making a mistake, coming back here.

It's been ten years since I left Plum Valley. I never thought I'd return.

But how could I refuse? Doc Hanson called me directly and said he needed help. I wasn't about to tell him no.

It's still early morning—the ass-crack of dawn to be precise—but that doesn't mean much here. Plenty of folk are already up and about, working the ranch land or heading that way now, their trucks passing mine on the dusty dirt roads. A few wave out their windows.

Small towns.

I follow the directions on my GPS to the location Doc Hanson gave me—the address of the house where over 500 animals were discovered in a hoarding situation after their owner ended up ill. The man's daughter came into town to check up on him after he missed a visit, but what she found was more than her sick, bedridden father. Neither she, nor anyone else around here, had any idea that Amos Calhoun had been collecting—and neglecting—animals of all kinds.

And as I pull down the long driveway into Mr. Calhoun's property and get my first glimpse of the absolute mayhem onsite, the reason for my return to Plum Valley is clear. There's no way I could have turned my back on this many abused animals.

"Shit," I mutter, parking my truck behind another in a long line of vehicles at the side of the drive.

I grab my gear bag full of medical supplies from the passenger seat but stall before exiting my truck. My heart is pounding a little too heavily, and it doesn't require any guessing on my part to understand why.

My eyes dart around the clearing where countless men and women are moving about, tending to the organized chaos on Mr. Calhoun's grounds. There are cowboy hats everywhere, which makes it hard to get a good look at faces, but I wouldn't need to see his face. I'd recognize him from body language alone, the man who was responsible for my leaving town. And right now, he's not here.

Blowing out a breath, I push open the door and step out of my truck. Dust kicks up when my boots hit the dirt—must've been a while since it's rained in this part of the Texas Hill Country—and I twist to grab my hat from the backseat. I've barely placed it on my head when a voice calls out my name.

"Harrison."

Turning, I set eyes on my boss from so many years ago. "Doc."

Doctor Jake Hanson shakes his head as he approaches. His brown hair whips around his face, and his smile is the same as I remember. "Just Jake," he says for what must be the thousandth time. He grabs my hand in a hearty shake. "It's good to see you, Harrison."

"Mm," I reply, knowing my own thoughts on the matter are best left unsaid. It *is* good to see Doc Hanson again—the man was always kind to me—but everything else about being back here has my mind spun tight like a thick ball of wool. "How bad is it?"

The question is mostly rhetorical. I can see exactly how bad it is, and Doc Hanson's grimace confirms as much.

"We're still sussin' through it all, but there are a lotta animals here in need of medical attention. That's what I'd like you to help out with. Patchin' up minor injuries and whatnot. See Tilda in the blue shirt over there?" He points, and I give a nod. "She's runnin' point. Check in with her to see where you're needed, all right?"

"I can do that," I agree easily.

Doc Hanson nods, hands on his hips as he looks around the premises. The man looks older than my recollections, but it has been a decade since I saw him last. I'm sure I look older, too.

After shaking his head one more time, he claps me on the shoulder. "All right, then. Lunch'll be served around noon, so make sure you stop to take a break. And lemme know if you need anythin'. I'll be back at the clinic dealin' with surgeries, but you can always call. We've got a long couple days ahead of us."

I have no doubt. Even from a distanced glance, I can see the conditions of not only some of the animals here, but the squalor they've been living in. This won't be an easy job.

"And hey," Doc Hanson goes on, mouth tightening some. "Thanks again for comin'. I can't imagine it was an easy decision for you."

"It was, actually," I tell the man. Not a *welcome* decision, but an easy one. "And thanks, Jake. I'll let you know if I need anything."

He gives me a nod and heads off, and after one more brief visual sweep of the folks gathered around, I head toward Tilda in the blue shirt.

"Hey, hun," the woman says, eyeing the bag in my hand as I approach. "You here to help?"

"Yeah. I'm Doctor Bailey. DVM," I clarify, hefting up my bag, as if it's necessary.

"Great," she says with an abundance of cheer considering what we're here for. "I'm Tilda, your taskmaster for the day."

I huff a laugh, and Tilda smiles.

I guess maybe Tilda's cheer is a good thing. It'd be all too easy to fall into a somber mood with this many neglected animals about.

"You all right doin' some care on the ungulates this mornin'?" she asks.

"Sounds fine with me."

"Okay, then," she says. "See that old barn over there? The one with the faded red door?"

Tilda points, and I give her a nod. Looks like the barn was probably in decent condition about twenty years ago.

"Right," Tilda says. "I've got Carl sortin' sheep thataway. He'll bring the injured ones into the barn for you to take a look at. We already had somebody check the integrity of the buildin', and it's old, but it'll do. Electricity's runnin', as well."

"Sounds good. Anything else I need to know?"

Tilda shrugs a little. "We're dealin' with this as we go. If you get any animals that need more care than you can give here on the spot, let me know. We're workin' on transportin' batches to the veterinarians standin' by here and a couple towns over."

I nod, taking another look around. Someone leads a horse past. The mare's mane is badly tangled, as is her tail, and she's favoring one of her front legs. A few pigs squeal nearby, running wild in a makeshift pen, their bodies much too lean to be considered healthy. There are sheep with terribly matted fleece, dogs yipping, cattle, a few donkeys, water fowl, barn cats—every farm animal imaginable in droves. And who knows how long they've been here, not given the care they need in this tucked-away plot of land that no one but Mr. Calhoun himself has been to in ages. Even the property is in disrepair, the barns and sheds missing boards, the grasses and tangled weeds growing wild and tall. There shouldn't be a single animal living here, let alone hundreds.

It's messed up. *Totally fudged*, as Winnie would say.

"Fuck," I mutter aloud, letting loose a breath.

"That 'bout sums it up," Tilda replies, slapping me on the back. "Get on out there, Doc. And good luck."

"Thanks," I tell the woman, setting off toward the rundown red barn.

The sound of *baaing* intensifies the closer I get, and I'm just turning the corner when I set eyes on who I presume to be Carl. The man has a slipknot rope over the neck of a sheep he's leading toward the barn, and he raises his hand as I approach.

"New recruit?" he calls out.

"Guess so," I return, squinting at the interior of the barn. One side is opened up, doors thrown wide, and although it smells musty inside, it is, as Tilda indicated, lit up.

I wait until Carl is close and then hold out my hand. "Doctor Harrison Bailey," I say. "Nice to meet you."

He gives me a handshake, smiling, his other hand keeping tight on the sheep's lead. "Just Carl for me. C'mon, I'll show you 'round."

Carl leads me inside the barn, pointing out the area they cleaned up for me to use. There's an extension cord nearby, plugged in, and an exam table that looks brand new. Carl loops the sheep's lead around a nearby post before huffing a big breath.

"I'm gonna head out and look for your next patient," he says. "Ready to get started, Doctor Bailey?"

I plop my bag atop the exam table. "Ready as I'll ever be."

Carl gives me a big salute before heading back out of the barn, and I look at the sheep. The poor thing is a bedraggled mess, but she doesn't object as I step close. Noticing a new bag of feed set against the wall, I head that way. The sheep perks up at the sound of the top of the bag being torn off, and when I bring a handful of pellets her way, she races toward me, nearly reaching the end of her lead.

My heart constricts as the sheep gulps down the food in my hand. Her fleece will have to go—it's far too overgrown and matted to be healthy and is caked in a number of things I don't want to know the origins of. I can feel her ribs, much too prominent beneath the fleece, as I run my fingers along her side. And there's at least one abscess visible on her leg.

Totally fudged is right.

No, I didn't want to come back to Plum Valley, Texas. Not anytime soon. Maybe not ever. But being back here is the right thing.

That I'm sure of.

CHAPTER 2

Sammy

"I swear to God, if I ever catch this guy, I'm takin' his left nut," I say.

"Jesus, Sammy," Carl responds, eyes widening as he wipes BBQ sauce off his mouth.

"What, don't think that's fair?" I ask, shaking my head. "He had no right treatin' these animals this way."

I toss my napkin onto my plate. I couldn't stomach eating much, but the food from Nash's in town *was* dang good.

"I'm not sayin' you're wrong," Carl says.

"But?"

"No buts," my coworker replies, and I huff a laugh.

"You boys 'bout done here?" Tilda asks, coming over to our table, clipboard in hand.

"Geez, Tilly. We just sat down," I tease, grabbing my glass of water before chugging what's left. "But yeah. We're done."

"Speak for yourself," Carl says, mouth full. He holds up a BBQ rib. "I'm still workin'."

"Well, *I'm* done," I say, standing up and grabbing my trash. I toss it into the bin beside the table as a man passes by. My head swivels around in time to catch his denim-clad ass walking away, and I stop still, staring and not caring one bit about it.

Hot damn.

The man, dressed in blue jeans, a plaid shirt with the sleeves rolled up, and a well-worn cowboy hat, stops at the drink station nearby and fills a cup with lemonade. He downs the contents before taking off his hat and fanning himself with it. The motion makes the muscles in his arm ripple, *thank you very much*, and then, just when I can't take the suspense any longer, he turns enough for me to get a glimpse of his face, lit golden by the midday sun.

Good. Lord.

My heart plain swoons right inside my chest.

"Dibs!" I call out, shooting my hand high into the air.

"I'm sorry. What now?" Tilda asks, following my line of sight.

I point at the man, who's now walking away, his hat back atop his head. "That one. He's mine. I'm callin' dibs."

Carl huffs out a laugh, and I turn his way, narrowing my eyes. His own shoot wide before he holds up his BBQ-covered hands. "Hey, you know I'm straight."

"I don't care, Carl. I need you to acknowledge my dibs 'cause that man could bend a crowbar."

"All yours, Sammy," he says in a rush.

Satisfied, I turn to Tilda and raise an eyebrow.

Tilda shakes her head, a little smile at the corner of her mouth. "Gonna lick the boy, Sammy?"

"That's the plan," I acknowledge.

"Aw, geez," Carl moans.

Tilda shakes her head when I continue staring. "Hun, he's all yours. I'm married; you know that. And that man is much too young for my taste."

"Well, then," I say, dusting my hands off on my pants. "Tilly, I need information."

"Name's Doctor Bailey," she says, smile still in place. "He's workin' with the sheep."

"Who else is on sheep?" I ask, straightening my hat.

"Carl is," she answers.

I look at Carl, and he holds up his hands again in surrender. "You can 'ave 'em," he mumbles around his food.

"Tilly?" I ask.

"Sammy's on sheep," she says, scratching a note onto the papers atop her clipboard.

"Damn right I am," I mutter, walking off as Tilda says something to Carl about pig duty, to which he groans. I don't worry too much about it.

I have a Doctor Bailey to win over.

As I walk toward the red barn adjacent to the sheep pasture, I send up prayers to every deity I can think of that the doctor is queer.

Please, let me have this one. Just this one.

When I turn the corner, Doctor Bailey is at the mouth of the barn. The worn-down structure and the overgrown grasses nearby create a somewhat wild but beautiful backdrop behind him. The wind is blowing gently, rustling the weeds near his boot, and the sky is clear and blue. Doctor Bailey's hands are clasped around the back of his neck as he stands there, and his shirt is pulled tight around his biceps. He's looking out over the sheep, the lines of his face understandably drawn. His hair, dirty blonde, curls gently at his nape, and there's the most perfect smudge of dirt on his cheek.

The man is a damn rugged dream.

He notices me almost immediately, dropping his arms and straightening up. His eyes swing over me quickly—too quickly for me to make an assessment—and his brows draw in under the wide brim of his hat.

"You're not Carl," he says, heading my way.

I give him a grin. "Nope, sure aren't. I'm Sammy. Nice to meet you."

Doctor Bailey accepts the hand I hold out his way, his palm warm in my grip and a little dry from working.

"Harrison," he replies. "Nice to meet you, too."

"You're not from 'round here, Harrison," I note, following the man into the barn. He sounds like a Midwesterner.

He chuckles a bit. "Not originally, no. But I've lived in Texas for the last sixteen years."

"That so?" I ask. "What brought you here?"

He hums a little, poking through his bag and setting a few items onto the exam table we set up early this morning. "Vet school initially," he answers, glancing my way. "And then I stayed."

For what reason?

I want to ask, but I don't. I've been told on more than one occasion that I ask too many personal questions. That I'm a little too *intense*. I call it caring, *thanks*, but regardless, I don't want to scare the good doctor off before I can woo him out of his mighty fine jeans. That would be a damn shame, in fact.

So, I rub my hands together and get down to business. Or, at least I try. "How can I help, Harrison? My hands, my body, they're all yours."

He lifts a brow, gaze pinging down to said hands for a moment before he faces the exam table again. My heart patters away as I wait to hear how he'll take that. Whether or not he'll bite.

In the end, he simply says, "These sheep need to be sheared."

I look at the three matted sheep in the pen and give Harrison a nod. "Then I'm your man."

Harrison doesn't say a word as he gets the shears set up, plugging them into the extension cord nearby. I grab a lead and get a hold of one of the ewes, bringing her out of the pen and over to where Harrison is standing. He gives me a nod, and I get a firm hold of the sheep before positioning her on her rump so that her belly is exposed. Apart from a flick of her ears, she doesn't put up a single fuss as Harrison starts running the clippers up under her fleece, cutting it neatly away from her skin.

Up this close while Harrison is working, I'm able to get a better look at the man. He's a little older than me, if I had to guess. But by how much, I'm not sure. I'd put him closer to forty than my thirty-two years of age. He has a few lines around his eyes—nice lines; the kind that come from laughter—and his skin is a light tan that speaks of time spent in the sun. His hair, even though mostly obscured by his hat, is a sandy blonde, and stubble frames his jaw and those damn firm lips of his, giving me all sorts of naughty, wonderful ideas. His eyes are blue and kind, albeit cautious. And he's fit. In fact, he's very near my own size and six-foot height. We were eye to eye when I first walked up.

I like guys who are bigger, like me. Especially if they like getting tossed around from time to time.

"So, Harrison," I say, breaking our silence when I can't stand it anymore. His eyes flick up to me. "Whereabouts do you live?"

"Near Houston," he answers. "Twenty minutes out."

"No shit?" I reply, smile stretching wide. "Tilda, Carl, and me are all from Houston. We work in Animal Control there."

"Yeah?" he says.

"Mhm. Which means we're practically neighbors. If you ever need a pool boy, you can call me up."

Harrison's lips twitch. "Thought you worked in Animal Control."

"I'm a man of many talents," I say, sending him a wink.

He shakes his head just a little before refocusing on the sheep. "I don't own a pool," he finally says.

"One step at a time."

He huffs a little laugh at that, and I practically preen. The man definitely isn't shutting me down. That's something.

When Harrison is finished with the sheep's stomach, I carefully maneuver her so he can run the shears over the rest of her body. Her skin is red in places, patchy and sore from carrying over-matted fleece around for much too long. The poor thing. All the animals here are in similar condition. I swear to God, if I ever find myself alone with that Mr. Calhoun...

"What was that?" Harrison asks.

"What?"

"That sound," he says. "Were you growling?"

I smile a little sheepishly. "Maybe so. I just... There's nothin' that makes this right, y'know? This isn't a week's worth of neglect. It's years' worth."

"Yeah, I know," Harrison says softly, his voice barely discernible over the noise of the clippers.

You'd think, by now, I'd be used to this sort of thing. And I am, in a way. I'm accustomed to seeing the cruel nature of humans. Doesn't mean it ever gets easier, though.

"It's fucked up," I say, vocalizing my thoughts.

Harrison nods. "Totally fudged."

"I'm sorry, what now?" I ask, chuckling when Harrison shakes his head in response.

"Nothing. She's all set," he says, turning off the clippers and running his fingers lightly over some of those sore spots I noticed. He sighs before hefting the mound of dirty, oily fleece off to the side. "Let's do the next one."

Harrison and I get through all three sheep with minimal fuss. There are dozens more outside in their small pasture—and probably *all* of them will need to be sheared—but it's progress, at least.

"This is gonna take days," I note.

Harrison nods, features pinched.

"Well, look at the bright side," I say. "It'll give us plenty of time to get to know one another. Neighbors really should be friendly, after all."

Harrison's lips press together, all pouty and cute, but his eyes are sparkling. "Is that what you are?" he asks. "Friendly?"

"Mhm." I give him a big smile. "The friendliest."

Harrison loses his battle not to laugh, and I have to bite my lip to keep from propositioning him outright. The man's smile has me feeling all sorts of weak in the knees.

But I have time. Days, in fact.

"Get me another sheep, Sam," Harrison says, trying to hide his amusement by turning back toward the exam table.

"Yessir," I reply happily, backing away. "And it's Sammy."

Grabbing a lead, I turn and head out of the barn. The sun blasts me the moment I step outside, making me realize just how much cooler it was in the shade. A little more stifling, though, without the breeze. The pen around the rest of the sheep is worn down, the wood splintering and broken in parts, but the sheep are too docile to care much about escaping. They do scatter a bit as I approach, but I move slowly, sweeping my gaze around the flock and looking for injuries.

I spot an ewe with a limp right away. Pulling a few food pellets from my pocket, I approach at an even pace, and although her eyes are wide and frightened, she doesn't move away as I hold out my palm and wait. Her nostrils flare, sniffing out the food, and then she takes a step closer, snatching it up as I slip the lead over her head. The sheep doesn't object to being led toward the barn after that, but I still go slow, not wanting to exacerbate her injury.

Harrison looks up when we step inside the barn, eyes dropping immediately to the sheep. His gaze is so soft, so compassionate, and it makes that empathetic part of me flare in response.

"Leg," I say unnecessarily. The man can tell.

He nods, gesturing me forward and dropping to a crouch in front of the ewe. He palpates her leg gently before lifting her foot back and checking her hoof.

"Foot scald," Harrison says with a sigh. A bacteria that causes inflammation. "We'll need to check the rest of the flock and separate out the diseased."

"Christ," I mutter. "This just keeps gettin' better."

"Yeah. I think I'm going to need a drink when this day is over," Harrison says, letting the ewe's foot go.

A smile tugs at my cheek. "Is that an invitation? 'Cause I love a good stout."

Harrison huffs, lips twisting as he looks up at me. "Is this you being friendly again?"

"Lemme ask you this," I say in response, gaze running down to where Harrison's jeans are pulled tight around his crotch and thighs because of his crouched position. When I return my slow perusal to his face, his eyebrows are raised. "How much honesty do you appreciate?"

Harrison doesn't answer for the longest time, and I start to wonder if maybe I *am* reading him wrong. But then his eyes track down my chest in a way that is most definitely not passive, and my hope flares bright.

"Sam."

"Yeah?" I ask eagerly.

Those eyes flick back up to my face. "Get me another sheep. Please."

I puff out a breath before flashing a smile. "Whatever you need."

"You're my man?" he asks wryly, leading the ewe with foot scald over to a separate pen.

The brightness of my grin could rival that big ol' Texas sun. "You're catchin' on." I'm halfway out of the barn before I call back, "And it's Sammy."

CHAPTER 3

✦

Harrison

Sam is an incessant flirt.

I should discourage the man, seeing as I'm here to work, not play *whatever* this is. But honestly, I can't bring myself to do it. Not only because it's a welcome distraction from the tragedy of this situation, but the simple fact of the matter is Sam is damn fine.

It's been a long time since I've had someone interested in me the way he so clearly is. I'm not under any delusions that Sam is after more than a quick fuck. But I haven't gone out, haven't hooked up or dated, in years. It's been too hard with everything else going on. And it feels good, being wanted again. Having someone look at me the way he does.

I used to be like Sam. A flirt. A little more carefree with my smiles. Ten, fifteen years ago, I wouldn't have hesitated to return his interest. I might have even suggested slipping inside the storage room at the end of the barn for a quickie.

But I'm not the same man I was back then.

Sam sure makes me tempted to forget all that, though. At least for a night.

We've been at it for several hours when my phone rings from inside my pocket. Excusing myself, I make my way outside to answer.

"Hello?"

"Grandma and Grandpa don't have the good crackers," a small voice says in lieu of a greeting. "They have the off-brand. And Grandpa said it's 'cause they were cheaper, but more doesn't mean better, Daddy."

I huff a laugh. "No, it doesn't, Pumpkin."

"I want you to come home."

My chest seizes tight at the sadness hidden away behind the pluck in my daughter's tone. I blow out a slow breath. "I know, but it's going to be a few days."

"Why do you gotta be gone so long?"

"Oh, Winnie." I walk over to the nearby fence, setting my hat atop a post and leaning on the rail. The wind feels cool against my sweaty hair, and I breathe in the musky animal-scented air before answering. "Remember what we talked about?"

"Yes," she says with a huff. "I'm ten. I've got a good memory, not like Grandpa."

My lips twitch. "Right. Which means you remember me telling you about the animals that need my help."

Winnie sighs in exasperation in only the way a child can. "Yeah," she finally says.

"And we agreed my helping was a good thing," I go on.

"Yeah," she says again, a little more glumly.

"It'll only be a few days," I say gently, even as my throat burns. "You can call me again at bedtime if you want a story."

"If it'd make you feel better," Winnie says sagely, and I crack a smile.

"Definitely would," I agree. "So give me a call in a few hours. And until then, try the other crackers. Maybe you'll like them."

"They're not even goldfish, Daddy. They're penguins. *Penguins*."

I snort a laugh. "Love you, Pumpkin."

"Love you, too," she mutters. "Grandma wants to say hi."

"All right. Put her on."

"Sorry, Harrison," my mom says a moment later.

I shake my head, even though she can't see it. "It's no problem. Is she having a rough time already?"

"Seems so," she replies. I sigh, and my mom adds, "We knew this might happen."

"Yeah."

Winnie has never done well with my being gone. It makes me feel guilty for leaving her, even though, realistically, I know we have to work on her separation anxiety at some point.

"It's only a few days," my mom says.

"Yeah, well. Let her call for a story, okay?" I say, looking off toward another barn on the property, where a few folks are tending to some pigs. Off near the driveway, a couple horses are being loaded onto trailers, either for medical attention or to be relocated.

I can't even imagine the amount of work involved in finding homes for all these animals.

"Of course we'll let her call," my mom answers. "Don't fret too much, okay, dear? Your dad and I can handle things."

"Thank you," I say around the lump in my throat.

"Love you."

"Love you, too," I reply before hanging up. As I'm slipping my phone back into my pocket, Sam steps out from the barn.

"Everythin' all right?" he asks, squinting against the sun. His hat is off, leaving him in his worn-to-hell jeans, a dusty red shirt, and brown cowboy boots. Not to mention the honest-to-God bull-shaped belt buckle he's sporting. I mean,

Christ. The man looks like all the things I haven't let myself want in a very long time. He has big, brown eyes. Stark cheekbones and a stubble-lined jaw. Brown hair buzzed short in a way that looks sexy as fuck, making him just as appealing without the cowboy hat. And I guarantee he's hiding a six-pack—at the very least—under his shirt. The man's a fox, and he knows it. I *know* he knows it.

And yet here he is, looking concerned over whatever he sees on my face after that phone call.

"Yeah, everything's fine," I mutter, grabbing my hat and kicking off from the fence. "Let's get through as many of these sheep as we can before we have to call it quits."

Sam nods, expression drawn for a moment before he grins. "And then that beer?"

I shake my head a little, doing my best not to crack a smile.

"One step at a time," I shoot back, using his words from earlier.

If possible, he smiles wider. But then he gets back to work, hopping the fence into the sheep pen.

And *that's* the other reason I haven't yet told the guy to bug off. Because he, like me, is here for a purpose. And I admire the man's work ethic.

I tend to some minor wounds on the sheep inside the barn as Sam brings a few more ewes in. We check them for foot scald before separating them accordingly. Luckily, none have been as bad as the first sheep, which makes me think the infection spread recently.

Of course, the flock could have been vaccinated against such a thing. But clearly, that wasn't a priority of their former owner's.

"Things'll be better now," I tell the sheep nearest to me, smoothing my hand over her side as she nibbles up some high-energy pellets.

Footsteps draw near, and then a throaty hum follows, pulling my gaze. Sam gives me a rakish grin. "I sure do like that."

"What? That I talk to the animals?" I ask, dusting off my hands and standing up.

"Mhm," he answers. "Shows you have humility."

And, what, humility is sexy now? I've been out of the game way too long.

"Animal folk are the best folk," Sam goes on, expression soft.

"You won't hear me contradicting that," I say.

"Doctor Bailey?" a voice calls from outside. A moment later, Tilda walks in, eyes flicking from me to Sam. "And our Sammy. How's it goin' in here?"

"Okay, all things considered," I tell her. "We've pulled out a few infected ewes, but the ones in the bigger pen are clear to go."

Tilda nods. "We found a rancher up near Austin who can take half the flock. I figure we'll start packin' up the healthy ones. Should be able to get a handful on the road tonight."

"Make sure he knows to keep 'em in quarantine for at least two weeks," Sam says before I have a chance to.

"Will do, Sammy," Tilda says warmly. "Now supper'll be delivered shortly, so make sure y'all go eat. And then we're kickin' everybody out at seven. Folks need their rest before we start again tomorrow."

"Sounds good. Thanks, Tilda," I reply.

"You betcha, Doc." Tilda gives me a nod, Sam a smile, and then heads from the barn.

"Have you worked together long?" I ask once she's out of sight.

Sam smiles. "Nearin' eight years now. That woman is the mother I never had." Then, as if he hadn't just dropped *that* loaded statement, Sam claps my shoulder and says, "C'mon. Let's get through a couple more before food arrives."

I nod, watching the man walk back out the door, my shoulder tingling.

When trays of enchiladas, tacos, and burritos are delivered from Nash's restaurant in town, Sam and I clean ourselves up as best as we can and join the others for food. Everyone looks a little harried, a little worn down from the events of the day. I'm feeling it myself, but for some reason, the emotional drain I usually get after dealing with such difficult cases is absent.

I think I may have the distraction named Sam to thank for that.

"Christ, this is good," Sam says, licking his finger clean. He shifts his gaze my way as he tackles the next, sucking his pointer finger almost obscenely. I should absolutely tell him to stop.

I don't.

"Aw, c'mon now," Carl mutters from across the table.

"All right, Carl?" Sam asks, swinging his gaze over to his coworker.

Carl shakes his head dismissively, cheeks a little ruddy, and Sam huffs a laugh.

"You stayin' 'round here?" Sam asks me, grabbing a napkin.

"Mm," I answer noncommittally before shoving my last sweet potato fry in my mouth.

"One of Loretta's places?" he presses.

I look over at him in surprise. "You know Loretta?"

Sam shrugs a little. "I know of her. I used to live near those rental houses she owns."

"When was that?" I ask.

Plum Valley is a small town. If we'd crossed paths, I'm fairly certain I would have remembered the man.

Sam's smile is a little crooked. "For just a year when I was nine."

That explains it. He was long gone when I arrived. "Well, yeah," I answer. "That's where I'm staying."

"Lucky you," he says, bumping me lightly with his elbow. "I'm all the way outta town at a motel that's seen better decades."

Sam goes quiet for a moment, and I finish my lemonade. His silence doesn't last long.

"Hey, Harrison?"

I huff a laugh. "Yeah, Sam?"

"Sammy," he corrects with a lopsided grin.

I shake my head. "I can't call you that. You're not my lover," I all but mumble. The nickname feels much too personal. Much too affectionate, even though Sam's own coworkers have been calling him such.

But Sam's eyes twinkle like I just gave him the winning lotto numbers, and I realize my mistake far too late. He leans a little closer, speaking under his breath. "I could be."

Oh, Christ.

Carl mumbles something and makes a swift retreat, and I clear my throat, raising a brow pointedly. "What was your question, Sam?"

"Well, Jesus, Harrison. I ain't got a clue anymore. My mind is stuck elsewhere."

"Okay. Well." I stand up and collect my trash. "If you think of it, let me know."

Sam hastens to follow me as I dump my trash and head toward the barn where my gear bag is. His footsteps reach me before long, and he falls into stride beside me. I already know what's going to come out of his mouth before he opens it.

"Wanna hit the bar in town?" he asks, expressive brown gaze flicking to me, ever-present smile on his face. "My treat."

God, it's tempting. *So* tempting. I know Sam's offer is for more than a drink. What would it feel like to forget all of my responsibilities for a little while and let myself get lost in the company of this man?

Could I do it? Could I be that Harrison from a decade ago?

"No," I say, catching a flicker of disappointment cross Sam's face as we enter the barn. "Meet me at my place instead."

He perks up as if I'd electrocuted him, and that smile of his stretches wide. *Fuck*, he has a nice mouth.

Am I really doing this?

"It's the green house," I tell him before I can lose my nerve. "Do you know where—"

"Yeah, I know where it is," he says, cutting me off in his excited haste.

A few of the sheep baa as I collect my things and close my bag, and all the while, I can feel the weight of Sam's gaze on the side of my head. My heart beats rapid-fire inside my chest, and when I turn, Sam is watching me unflinchingly.

The *confidence* he has. I've always liked that in a man.

"Harrison," he says, taking a step forward. His previous humor washes away, and in its place is a startling intensity I'm unprepared for. "Just so you know... I would metaphorically kill for a go at your ass. But whatever it is you want? Whatever you need? I'm here for it."

Jesus.

"That's a bold statement, Sam," I respond, shifting my weight as my cock plumps.

Sam grins, raking his teeth over his bottom lip in a way that has my gaze dropping. "I'll get you callin' me Sammy yet."

"You're a cocky fucker, aren't you?" I mutter, heading toward the barn doors. Sam stays at my side.

"Mm," he rumbles. "I like that word comin' outta your mouth."

"Which one?" I ask, knowing I'm only egging him on at this point. But my pulse is firing, and for the first time in a *long* time, I'm excited about the prospect of some uncomplicated fun. I want to *feel* again. It's been too damn long.

"*Cock*," he says, answering my question. "And *fuck*."

I clear my throat. He has a point. Those words coming out of *his* mouth in that Southern drawl are downright sinful.

"Meet you there?" Sam asks as we round the corner of the barn, heading side by side toward our vehicles.

I'm about to say yes when I realize... "Shit. Give me an hour."

I check the time on my phone. Yeah, an hour should work. Winnie will be going to bed soon, which will give me plenty of time to read her a story before Sam arrives.

Sam nods, not questioning me, even though I can tell from his expression he's curious. I don't think he knows how not to be.

When we reach my truck, Sam stops with me. I plop my bag inside the vehicle and climb in, and he takes a hold of my door, as if getting ready to close it for me.

"Hey, Harrison?"

My lips twitch. "Yeah?"

"Please don't change your mind."

"Pardon?" I ask, surprised by the sudden vulnerability in Sam's tone.

He steps closer, putting his body right beside the cab of my truck. So close his chest brushes the side of my arm.

"You can always say no," he says quietly. Seriously. "I'm not gonna push you on somethin' like that. But, fuck... I just really hope you don't change your mind."

Is this because I asked for an hour? Does he think I accepted just to placate him, and I'm going to beg him off as soon as I'm gone?

"I'm not changing my mind," I tell the man, chest simmering with something warm when Sam exhales in clear relief.

His smile is back in full force as he retreats a step, hand returning to my doorframe. "Good. In that case, see you in an hour."

With that, Sam shuts my truck door and steps away, cocky grin in place as he swaggers backwards. And I realize, even if I wanted to change my mind—which, to be clear, I don't—I wouldn't be able to anyway.

I never got Sam's number.

CHAPTER 4

Sammy

I'm whistling on the drive over to Harrison's rental. I swung by the motel first to clean myself up, considering how filthy I got, but it was a quick trip in and out before I stopped at the small grocery store in town for some beer. Main Street wasn't terribly busy, but there were a few people going in and out of Nash's restaurant-slash-bar just down the road from the grocers.

When I pull around the little looping driveway to Loretta Olroy's rental properties, I spot Harrison's truck right away. It's parked out in front of the green house, and I pull up behind it, cutting the power. Checking myself in the mirror, I smooth a hand over my short hair and then hop out of the truck.

The lights are on inside the rental, a soft glow filtering through the drawn curtains. The porch stairs creak when my boots land on them, but the place otherwise appears to be in good condition. I knock on the door, beer at my side, and wait.

What feels like twenty minutes later—but in all likelihood is probably twenty seconds—Harrison pulls open the door. A phone is held down at his chest, and he looks stressed, the lines of his face pinched. My gut sinks, but Harrison waves me in.

"Make yourself at home," he says. "I just need to finish this phone call."

I nod, and with an audible sigh, Harrison turns and walks off down a short hall. A door closes a moment later, and then his voice filters gently through the walls. Not loud enough for me to make out his words, but loud enough to hear the concern in his voice.

Well, dang. That's not a good sign.

As Harrison talks to whoever is on the other end of the call, I kick off my boots and take a look around. The inside of the place is decorated heavily with tones of green to match the exterior. I take a seat on the olive-colored leather couch and set the beer I brought onto the coffee table. There are a couple agriculture magazines nearby, so I flip through those as Harrison's call goes on and on and on. Surprise, Texas loves its beef cattle. When I've run out of magazines, I scroll through my phone for a bit, but nothing holds my attention.

I'm putting some serious consideration into popping one of those beers open when the door clicks down the hall. I drop my feet to the floor, and a moment later, Harrison steps into view, looking exhausted.

"Hey," I say, standing up.

"Sorry," he replies, shaking his head as he comes over to the couch. He plops down onto it so hard air rushes over my skin. The man looks the very definition of defeated as he kicks his feet onto the coffee table and rubs his eyes.

"Everythin' all right?" I ask, sitting down beside him. Stupid question, I know. But I don't know what else to lead with.

"Yeah," Harrison says, looking over at me. His eyes are creased at the corners, and I can tell he's about to say *Sorry, Sam, but I'm not up for this anymore.* But I don't want to go.

Even if nothing happens here tonight, I don't want to leave Harrison alone while he's so clearly down.

So, I head him off and make a grab for the goods I brought. "Beer?" I ask, holding up a bottle. It's still a little cool to the touch.

Harrison huffs a laugh, and it takes him a moment, but he finally answers, "Sure."

His fingers touch mine as I hand over the bottle, and I try not to let my eyes linger on those hands, but it's hard not to. They're big and a little roughened, same as mine. Hazard of the jobs we hold.

"I'm not going to be good company tonight," Harrison says after a single swallow of his beer.

"Why don't you let me decide that for myself?" I reply, twisting the cap off my own bottle of stout. The grocery store didn't have a huge selection, but they did have Guinness. Harrison seems okay with the choice.

Harrison lets out a little sigh in response, and I settle more fully against the couch cushions, kicking my feet up beside his.

I tap him lightly with my toe. "Wanna talk about it?" When Harrison stiffens, I touch his arm and add, "There's no wrong answer."

He relaxes slightly, and I pull my hand away, idly turning my beer bottle. Finally, he says, "No. Tell me something. Anything."

I huff a laugh. "Okay. I can do that." I think for a moment before something comes to mind. "All right, so you met Carl." Harrison nods, and I grin. "Carl and me have worked together for years. We were on this call 'bout a year ago, checkin' up on a report of a loose dog, right? Well, the dog comes runnin' out of nowhere, slippin' right past us, and Carl takes off after it. There was this short garden fence, maybe two feet high, between a couple houses, and Carl, tryin' to head off the dog, vaulted it. Except he didn't make it over. His foot caught, and Carl fell flat on his face."

Harrison chuckles, taking another swig of his beer. His blue eyes twinkle a little. "Was he okay?"

I wave my hand in the air. "Pft. Yeah. Carl was fine. Got the dog, too. The bully mix came right over and proceeded to lick every inch of Carl's face while he was hangin' halfway upside-down." I shake my head at the memory. "He adopted that dog."

"Yeah?"

"Mhm. Named her Rosie," I say.

"'Cause there were roses along the fence?" Harrison asks, lips hiked up at one corner.

I point a finger his way. "Bingo."

Harrison is quick. I like that.

He looks off across the room, a small smile on his face. "I have a dog."

"Yeah?"

He nods. "When my, uh..." He cuts off before starting again, and I can't help but wonder what his original sentence was going to be. "I got her five years ago. She's smart as a whip. But gentle. So gentle."

"What's her name?" I ask, shifting toward Harrison a little more and bending my knee up onto the couch between us.

"Tigger."

I cock my head. "Like the Winnie the Pooh tiger? She particularly bouncy?"

His eyes twinkle again. "No, she's not. She is orange, though. At least, partially. She's a Brittany Spaniel."

"Oh, no shit? Yeah, I bet she's a smarty-pants, then."

Harrison nods, relaxing more of his weight into the cushions behind him. He takes another sip of his stout before laying his head against the back of the couch.

He looks more at ease now, and I'm glad for it. I can't help but feel fond as I gaze at him.

So of course I open my big fucking mouth. "Are you in a relationship, Harrison?"

"What?" he asks, head turning my way.

"That phone call," I say. "It seemed...personal."

He sighs lightly—something he's been doing a lot of today—but his eyes don't hold any upset as they stay trained on my face. "It was personal. But no, I'm not in a relationship, Sam. I wouldn't have asked you here if I was."

I nod, relieved to hear that.

"But I don't think I—"

"No, I know," I say, cutting him off. "I'm not expectin' anythin', Harrison. Your turn. Tell me somethin'."

He hums at that, eyes flicking over my face for a moment. "Technically, I did. I told you about my dog."

I roll my eyes, shoving his leg. I resolutely do *not* think too hard about the firmness of his thigh beneath my fingertips.

"Gonna be like that, huh," I say. "Fine. I've got a tattoo."

Harrison's head cocks slightly against the couch-back. "Really? Where at?"

"Oh, nuh-uh. You gotta earn that information."

He presses his lips together, eyes running lazily down my chest and stomach. "Hm," is all he says.

Trying not to fidget—and failing—I take another sip of my beer before aiming the neck his way. "Your turn."

"Fine," he says, a little smile dancing at the corner of his lips. "I used to be a stripper."

"I'm sorry. What now?" I cough out, sitting upright.

Harrison laughs, rubbing his hand down his face before giving me a genuine smile. "For two months while I was in college. Just for some extra cash. It didn't last."

"Not any good at it?" I ask.

Harrison grabs a pillow and smacks me in the chest with it.

"Hey," I complain, beer held out of the way.

"Why wouldn't I be any good at it?" he asks, voice sullen.

"I don't know, Harrison," I say with a laugh. "Honestly, I'm just tryin' not to picture it too hard."

"I bet that is *hard*," he says, the bastard.

"On second thought," I amend. "Maybe you should show me how good you were. I don't believe it."

"I'm not falling for that," he says, draining the rest of his beer and then leaning forward to place the empty bottle on the coffee table.

"Fallin' for what?" I ask. "I'm a genuinely concerned citizen here. I have only your best interest at heart."

I place my hand over my chest for emphasis, and Harrison shakes his head.

"Somehow, I believe that last part," he says, nearly making me lose my breath. "Your turn."

As Harrison resettles against the couch, turned fully toward me now, my mind runs wild. "I've never broken up with any-one," I blurt.

Harrison's eyebrows rise. "How many people are you dat-ing?"

I bark a laugh, and Harrison grins. "None," I answer. "They've always broken up with me."

His grin turns into a frown. "Why?" I open my mouth, but Harrison goes on quickly. "Never mind. That was too person-al."

I shrug. To be honest, I wouldn't have minded answering his question. I've never had much of a filter. But Harrison yawns, and I'm distracted away from the topic.

"C'mon," I say, standing up. "Let's go lie down."

Harrison eyes me a little dubiously, mouth parted like he's trying to figure out how to politely decline.

I roll my eyes. "I'm not in the habit of fuckin' unwillin' men, Harrison. You look beat. I just figured you might wanna rest."

It's not all that late, but after the day we had, my body is feeling the exhaustion, too.

But... I don't want to go. Even though sex is off the table, I want to stay. And I'm hoping Harrison will let me.

Finally, he stands, giving me a nod. "All right."

With a smile, I set my empty beer bottle aside and follow Harrison down the hall to the bedroom. The walls are light green in here, like celery, and the comforter is a deeper sage. Harrison swings up and over the top of the mattress, plopping down with zero finesse whatsoever, and with a happy little grin, I follow.

He bounces lightly when I jump onto the bed, and I lie down next to him. Harrison is on his back at first, but he shifts to his side, mirroring my pose, and for a minute, we stay that way: watching each other, neither of us saying a word.

When Harrison exhales deeply, tension leaches from his frame. "Do you ever feel like...like you're watching your life from the outside?" he asks quietly.

"Like as a bystander?"

He nods against the pillow. "Yeah."

I think about what I told him earlier. About how I've always been the one to be broken up with. The one to be left. I think I understand a little of what he means. How it feels for things to be out of your control.

"Maybe," I answer. "A li'l."

He nods again, slowly, his brow creased.

"D'you feel like that?" I ask softly.

He blows out a breath. "Sometimes. It's like...life just keeps moving. It just keeps moving forward down this path I never signed up for in the first place, and there's nothing I can do but hold on and pray I don't fall off the tracks."

Well, fuck.

"I'm sorry," I tell him because what else can I possibly say?

His lip quivers for a moment, and if I hadn't been looking directly at his mouth in the first place, I would have missed it. But then his face is stoic once more.

"There's so much in my life I love," he goes on, eyes intent on me, as if he's trying to get me to understand. "So much I wouldn't change even if I could. But sometimes it feels like I'm not living my own life. I'm living someone else's. And every time I think that—every time I feel a little resentful toward the curveballs I've been thrown—I get hit with so much damn guilt, it's a miracle I stay upright. There's no one I can tell that to, Sam. I can't say it aloud to anyone in my life, and I'm sorry for putting it on your shoulders—"

"Hey," I say gently, reaching forward and grabbing Harrison's hand. He latches on tight, and I swallow around the thickness in my throat. "It's all right. You can tell me. I'm a good listener."

"I don't even know you," he says with a wet laugh.

"Which is why it's perfect," I respond. "You don't know me. So what's the harm? You can tell me whatever you want. Get it off your chest."

He shudders out an uneven breath, and then he starts to talk. There are no details. No specifics. Just the weight of the world on his shoulders and the feel of his hand held tightly in mine.

CHAPTER 5

Harrison

When I wake up to my phone alarm going off, I groan a little weakly. I reach toward the nightstand where it's resting, but a weight around my chest keeps me from going far.

"Hrm," Sam grumbles, tightening his grip.

And *oh*. Oh.

"Sam," I say quietly, running my hand over the bristly hairs on his forearm. He's warm beneath my fingertips and oh so firm. Real. *Tempting*.

But then I remember the venting words that poured from my mouth last night as if I were nothing more than a broken faucet, and I let my hand slip away.

"My alarm is going off," I point out.

Sam grumbles again, sinking his face against the back of my neck. I squeeze my eyes tight. It feels too good, having someone near. Someone like Sam.

I shouldn't get used to it.

This time, when I reach forward, Sam relaxes his grip. I shut off my alarm and sink back against the mattress.

"Sorry about last night," I say.

"Nothin' to be sorry 'bout," Sam says.

His arm is hanging loosely around my middle now, and it'd be easy for me to slide away. Put some distance between us.

But I don't.

"Still," I say, feeling guilty for ruining what was headed in the direction of being one heck of a hookup. "That wasn't what you came here for."

No, the reason Sam came here was T-boned by my own dejected attitude after I spent an hour and a half soothing my crying daughter.

Fuck.

"Harrison," Sam says gently, his lips brushing the back of my neck. The sensation makes me shiver. "I had a good night."

I huff a little. Can't help it. "Right. Because finding out how much of a mess I am was a good time for you. Very attractive, I'm sure."

Sam hums a little, tightening his hold. "If you think last night made me want you any less, you'd be sorely mistaken," he says, sliding his hand to my stomach and anchoring there, fingers splayed wide.

My pulse kicks up, and thank God for the shirt I'm wearing, or I'm not sure I'd have the willpower to shift away. If his skin were against my own...

"We need to go," I say, sliding out of Sam's grip.

He groans, and when I look back at him, his eyes are still sleepy and hooded. "Yeah, all right," he says around a yawn, rolling over and swinging his legs out of bed. He stretches his arms high in the air, and my eyes track every single muscle that ripples and pops beneath his skin.

Sam looks over his shoulder at me, catching my ogling. He doesn't say a word, just drops out of bed and heads to the dresser, where his jeans are hanging over a drawer. He tugs them on silently, and I do my damndest to tear my gaze away from his brief-covered ass.

Good grief.

I'm tempted to say *fuck this day* and pull Sam back into bed for more than just sleepy cuddling, but a ding from my phone pulls my attention. It's a text from my mom.

Mom: She's doing better this morning. Eating pancakes now.

Me: Thanks. Keep me updated.

When I look up, Sam is watching me. He doesn't ask what was on my phone.

"Ready to go?" he says instead.

"Bathroom," I mutter, grabbing my own jeans and passing Sam as I head into the hallway. I stare at myself for a good long minute in the mirror, seeing the bags under my eyes and the lines in my face that weren't there even five years ago. I run a hand through my dark blonde hair but don't bother styling it, seeing as I'll throw my hat on anyhow.

I look tired. Older than I used to. More worn down than a guy like Sam deserves.

Heading back into the bedroom, I change out my shirt for a clean one. Sam is waiting in the living room, thumbing through his phone. He looks up when I enter, a smile leaping to his face. He has that belt on again—the one with the bull-shaped buckle. Or maybe it's a Longhorn. Lord knows there are plenty of them around here. I don't know why, but the sight of that buckle makes my throat dry up in an instant.

Yes, you do know why, my brain scolds. I've always loved a cowboy. And while Sam isn't one in actuality, he looks the damn part.

"Ready," I say, grabbing my keys and hoping there's coffee waiting at Mr. Calhoun's.

Sam follows me out the door and heads to his own truck. He gives me a salute before saying, "See you soon." And then he's driving away, and I'm following him down the dirt roads of Plum Valley.

Sam pulls into an empty spot among the vehicles already parked along Mr. Calhoun's long drive, and I follow suit. Tilda is standing near what looks to be a breakfast buffet, and I thank my lucky stars when I see a big metal coffee carafe. After grabbing my gear bag and putting on my hat, I head that way, trying not to focus on the fact that I can see Sam in my periphery, heading the same direction as me.

"Mornin', Doctor Bailey," Tilda says cheerfully as I approach. A moment later, she adds, "Sammy."

"Good mornin', Tilly," Sam returns with equal cheer. He grabs two waxy paper cups at the coffee carafe, handing one to me without even looking my way. "Any news to report?"

While Tilda briefs Sam on the progress with the animals here, I fill up my cup with steaming black coffee and then discreetly look around the property. All I see are strangers.

It's odd to think about how that might not be the case had I stayed. If I still lived here, I might recognize some of these people. So much would be different.

I push the thought away, focusing on the conversation as Sam sets his gaze on me.

"Ready to get back to work?" he asks. "I'm on sheep with you again."

Sam's warm brown eyes sparkle in the early morning light, and I can't help but huff a laugh.

"Oh, you are, are you?" I shoot back. "Wonder how that happened."

"I ain't got a clue," Sam says, refilling his coffee as Tilda shakes her head.

"All right," I mumble, topping off my own cup. "Let's get out there."

Sam and I are quiet as we trek the short distance to the faded red structure. There are a few other barns on the property, too, as well as a myriad of other buildings. Sheds, lean-tos, even a pavilion that could have once been beautiful. Now, the wood is splintering apart, and the white paint is almost completely peeled away.

It's a pretty good representation of this place, actually.

"You know what I don't get?" I say as Sam throws the barn doors wide.

"What's that?" he asks.

"If he had all these animals here, how didn't anyone know? I get that he's set far back from the road, so if he didn't have visitors and if his neighbors were too far away to hear them or distinguish them from others nearby, I can understand how it slipped unnoticed in that regard. But didn't he have to buy enough feed and straw to draw someone's attention in town?"

Sam gives me a sad little look. "I actually have an answer for that," he says, checking in on the sheep we left quarantined inside the barn last night while I set my tools on the exam table. "He visited his daughter every week. That's why she checked in on him in the first place. He missed their usual get-together, so she came lookin'. Found 'im and these animals. Anyways, she said he'd always come with his trailer in tow. He claimed he liked to haul his trash to a dump in her town 'cause it was cheaper, and he was already in the area, so why not?"

"But he was buying supplies before he left?" I guess.

Sam nods, dumping some pellets into a big rubber bowl for the sheep. They converge right away to mow down the food. All of the animals here will have to be steadily introduced to a more nutrient-rich diet. They're far too skinny as is.

"Why go through all the trouble?" I wonder aloud. "Why keep these animals if he wasn't going to take care of them?"

"'Cause sometimes," Sam says slowly, "folks don't care as much about what's best for the animals. Only for themselves. Mr. Calhoun liked havin' these creatures around, for whatever reason, and he didn't care that he was hurtin' them in the process."

I shake my head. "That's fucked up," I mutter.

"Totally fudged?" Sam says.

I look at him in surprise, and there's a smirk resting on his lips. It takes me a moment to remember he heard me say the same phrase yesterday, and for a good couple seconds, my heart is beating so fast I can barely breathe.

"Yeah," I finally manage. "Totally fudged."

Sam grabs a lead rope. "Ready to get started?"

"You see a lot of this, don't you?" I ask, instead of answering his question. "Neglect."

It's not the same for me. Yes, I see animals in poor condition, but I'm involved because their owners called or brought their pets in. It's not because they don't care.

But Sam works in Animal Control. It's different.

"Yeah, I do," he says simply.

"I'm sorry."

His lips twitch into the slightest smile as his eyes drift along my face, down and then up again. "Thanks, Harrison," he says, and it's so simple and so pure that I can't find a single retort.

Sam turns without another word and heads out of the barn. I see him vault the worn fence around the sheep pasture and can't help but chuckle. The man has boundless energy.

Sam comes back a few minutes later with an ewe in tow. She looks healthy enough, but I won't know for sure until I examine her. As I check her over, Sam leaves to grab another sheep, and for the next few hours, that's what we do. Sam brings me animals to examine; I clean up minor wounds and separate those with foot scald away from the rest. And for a solid hour before lunch arrives, we work together to shear the overgrown, matted fleece off the animals he brought in during the morning.

We're washing up in the big double sink inside the barn when Doc Hanson shows up, looking as if he hasn't slept a wink in the past forty-eight hours. I wouldn't put it past the man. He always did work himself to the bone.

"Heya, Harrison," he says before giving Sam a greeting and a nod. "How's it goin' over here?"

"Not bad, all things considered," I answer. "We're through—what? About half the sheep?"

"That's right," Sam says.

Doc Hanson nods. "Good, good. I'll send Cooper your way once he's done with surgeries."

"Cooper?" I ask.

"My new employee," the doc says. His lips twist into a smile. "The new *you*."

I huff an acknowledgement, and Sam looks over at me in clear curiosity.

"Havin' an extra hand should help speed things along," Doc Hanson says just as a shout rings out.

"*Jake.*"

"Oh, Lord," the doc mutters before flashing a wide smile. "What is it, Nash?"

Nash, the restaurant and bar owner in town—and the doc's best friend as of the last time I was here—strides into view at the opening to the barn. "You needa eat somethin'."

Doc Hanson rolls his eyes, but Nash simply steps closer, bracketing his hand along the doc's neck.

Well, that's new.

"I mean it, Jake," Nash says, softening his tone. "You haven't taken a proper break since this started, and I don't want you fallin' on your face."

Doc Hanson's lips twitch, and he notches his head our way. "Nash, you remember Harrison." Nash looks over at me in surprise as the doc adds, "And that's Sammy."

"Oh," Nash says, dropping his hand. It doesn't go far, however, finding a home on the doc's lower back. "O'course. Hey, Harrison. It's good to see you."

"You, too," I reply as Nash gives Sam a nod of greeting.

"I hope you don't mind, but I'm stealin' Jake away," Nash goes on, none too gently steering the doc in the direction of the food. "He needs to eat."

Doc Hanson shakes his head a little, but his eyes are bright as he lets Nash tug him along. "I'll check in with you before you go," he says, and I give him a nod a moment before he and Nash disappear from sight.

The two bicker in soft tones that quickly grow too quiet to hear, and Sam turns to me.

"You used to live here," he says, more statement than question.

"I did," I answer. Just like him.

"When?" he asks, standing opposite me, hands on his hips in a casual pose.

"After vet school. I left ten years ago."

"Hm." I can see the gears turning behind his eyes, and my lips twitch when it only takes Sam another couple seconds to ask his next question. "Why'd you leave?"

My burgeoning smile falls away. "That's a long story."

"You could tell it to me over beers tonight," Sam says, falling in step beside me as we head from the barn.

I huff a little laugh, looking over at the man. His grin is more dazzling than the sun hanging high in the sky. "You're still on that?" I ask.

He cocks his head, looking at me incredulously. "Of course. Didn't think I'd quit that easily, did you?"

Something flutters inside my stomach, soft and tumbling and *scary*. Even so, a smile finds its way to my lips.

Who wouldn't want to be coveted by a bright, handsome man like Sam?

And he still wants me, even after last night. That's what I don't get. I don't *understand* it, but I like it.

But then those soft, fluttery feelings inside my stomach fall like lead. Because while I'm here, entertaining ideas of this cowboy beside me, my daughter is back home, upset over my absence. And there's no reason to expect tonight will be any different. She'll still be upset. She'll still need to hear my voice. I'm the only parent she has. She needs me, and my daughter will always—*always*—come first.

Sighing internally, I force a smile I don't quite feel. "We'll see," I tell Sam of his suggestion for drinks, even though I know the answer will be no.

It has to be. I was only kidding myself, thinking I could forget about my responsibilities for a little while. I'm a father, and the moment that became true, my priorities shifted. They had to.

And when I go back home in a few days, men like Sam will continue being a fantasy I never get to entertain. Because no one wants to come in second.

I know that for an absolute fact.

CHAPTER 6

Sammy

Something shifted between me and Harrison. It was subtle, but I felt it, like the man had powered down. He was still perfectly friendly with me, and he even flirted a bit, but it lacked any real conviction. And when I asked if he wanted to get together again, he said no.

It's our third day working together now, and the man has been particularly quiet this morning. I don't know what to do to make him happy again, but I'm desperate to see one of those genuine smiles. The ones that make his blue eyes twinkle.

"So, Harrison," I say, delighted when he gives me an amused look instead of being annoyed by my many questions. We're taking a quick water break in the shade beside the barn, and a slight breeze ruffles Harrison's hair now that his hat is off. "If you had to choose, would you rather walk naked down your street or eat a cockroach?"

He tilts his head. "What kind of question is that?"

"A fun one," I reply, giving him a nudge. "What's your answer?"

He shakes his head, biting his lip before looking me in the eye. "I'm not eating a cockroach."

"Hmm," I say happily. "Nudity it is, then. All right."

He huffs a laugh, and I internally pump my fist.

After Harrison drinks the remainder of his water, he shakes the empty canteen. "I need to refill this."

"I'll come with," I say, walking with him toward the tables where lunch has yet to arrive.

We're halfway there when Harrison stutters to a stop quickly enough that some dust floats up around his boots.

"What is it?" I ask, looking from his wide-eyed gaze to the area he's staring.

He shakes his head quickly, turning and heading in a different direction. "Nothing," he mutters, even though it's obvious that's not true.

"Harrison," I say, jogging to keep up with him.

He doesn't once look over his shoulder, but when I reach his side, placing my hand on his arm, the expression on his face makes my gut clench.

"I can't," he says, shaking his head again. "I have to..." His eyes search the nearby buildings, roaming frantically, before they land on me, pleading. "Get me out of here."

I don't hesitate. I grab Harrison's arm and tug him toward a small shed. Motes of dust billow out when I throw the door wide, and sunlight illuminates the interior for all of a second before I'm shuffling Harrison and myself inside and closing the door.

It's cramped in here, the inside of the shed filled with gardening equipment I doubt has been used in years, as well as a riding lawn mower and a roll of chicken wire. There's a broken board along the side of the shed, which lets in a slanted sliver of light, but otherwise, now that the door is shut, it's dark.

Harrison's breathing is audible in the small, dusty space, and his chest heaves against my own. We're pressed tightly together, having nowhere else to go. There's barely enough room for the two of us to stand.

"Harrison?" I question gently.

"Thank you," he replies, voice whisper-soft. "I wasn't ready."

"Wasn't ready for what?" I ask, bringing my hands tentatively up his arms to his shoulders. He's firm under my grip, muscles tensed.

Harrison is quiet for a long moment before he answers. "To see my ex."

Oh. His ex. From a decade ago?

"Are you still in love with 'im?" I ask before I can filter my mouth even a little. I'd slap myself if I had the space to do it.

Harrison shakes his head slightly, a movement I can feel more than see, although my eyes are starting to adjust to the dimness inside the shed.

"No, I'm not," he answers around a rough laugh. "I'm really not. I just... I haven't seen him since..."

He doesn't say since *what* or *when*, but it's easy enough to guess. Since they broke up.

"I'm sorry," I say gently.

He lets out a breathy chuckle before leaning into me, and I don't hesitate to wrap my arms around him. This is the closest we've ever been, cuddling aside, and as Harrison's cheek brushes lightly against my own, his stubble coarse and prickling me like static electricity, my heart takes off at a gallop.

It'd be so easy to turn my head. So easy to find his lips in the dark and taste this man who has revved my engines since the moment I set eyes on him.

But I don't. I don't because Harrison hasn't given me any indication that would be welcome.

"Sam," he says quietly, my name a sigh.

I hum a little. "I'll get you callin' me Sammy one of these days," I say. Even though we only have a couple days left.

The thought is a strangely disappointing one.

Harrison lets out a little huff, and his breath hits my neck. "You're not a dog," he counters.

That makes me chuckle, and before I can think about it, I reply, "No, but I *would* come if you called out my name."

Harrison goes still against me. Even his chest stops moving, as if he's holding his breath. I open my mouth to apologize for the poorly timed joke—which wasn't really a joke—when Harrison turns his head slightly. His lips touch my cheek.

"Would you?" he asks, and this time, it's my breath getting caught in my chest.

I nod. One quick, short movement.

Harrison inhales, as if he's scenting me. As if he's breathing me in. And even though we're surrounded by the smell of animals and motor oil hanging in the air inside the shed, I wonder if he can find me underneath it all.

"Sam," he says again.

My heart starts to pound.

"Whatever you want," I tell him, repeating the words I said two days ago, when all *this* was was trying to get a gorgeous man into bed. I'm not sure what, exactly, it is now, but it feels like something else. "Whatever you need."

"I..." he says before cutting off, but he doesn't move away. In fact, one of his boots knocks into mine as he moves an inch closer. "I shouldn't."

Shouldn't. Not *can't*. Not *don't want to*.

"Who says?" I ask.

He doesn't answer.

"Harrison," I say gently, slipping my hands over the broadness of his back, rubbing a little but not venturing too low.

"D'you want me to convince you? Or d'you want me to back up and open this door?"

He takes four breaths before muttering, "Convince me."

Oh damn. All right, then.

Sliding my hands lower, I run my fingers over his work shirt and then his jeans. I stop on his ass, palming him and tugging him closer. Harrison gasps, breath on my neck.

"Lemme make you feel good," I say, digging my fingers into his cheeks and turning my head. Mouth at his ear, I all but whisper, "I wanna hear you call my name."

A sound catches inside of Harrison's throat, only half-formed. His hand moves to my side, fingers skating over my shirt, barely touching.

"This isn't because of him," he says. *The ex.* "I wanted you before."

I nod, lips skimming Harrison's neck. I know he did.

"I don't want you to think I'm using you," he adds.

"Use me," I say, opening my lips and swiping my tongue over Harrison's skin.

He groans, head falling back, fingers digging into my side. "Kiss me."

Grin on my lips, I turn my head. Harrison does the same, connecting our mouths in an instant. And *ho-ly shit.* I was not ready. I was not prepared for the way my body would light the moment Harrison's lips touch mine. It's incendiary, and suddenly, my back is against the shed door, and Harrison is crowding me into the wood.

I groan, the sound eaten up and swallowed down between us, lost to this temporary void we've found ourselves in, where nothing—and no one else—matters but *this.*

Harrison reaches for my belt, and I do the same to his, our hands fumbling between us as our lips remain locked. He tastes like salt from our sweat. Like hard work and something I want to call my own.

When he gets my jeans open and his hand wraps around my erection, my whole body jolts.

"Sam," he says. "Do you have a condom?"

And, oh fuck, is that a question.

I nod hastily, pulling my wallet from my back pocket as Harrison's tongue tangles with my own. His hand tugs me rhythmically, sending waves of bliss rolling up and down my shaft as I quickly snag a condom and packet of lube from my wallet.

I have never been more grateful for the optimism leading me to be prepared for such an occasion.

When I shove the packets Harrison's way, fumbling for his hand in the semi-dark, he hands them right back. His grip leaves my cock a moment before he turns, and then he's pushing his pants down to his knees and bracing his hands on the hood of the riding lawn mower, his ass inches in front of me.

Oh fuck. *Yessir.*

I fumble with the lube, tearing it open clumsily as my hands shake. The strip of sunlight coming through the broken slat at the side of the shed runs perfectly over Harrison's ass, lighting up the taut swells at a slanted angle, and I can *not* look away. Can not think of anything but what it will feel like to be buried inside that ass.

"This is what you want?" I ask Harrison. Because even though the man all but shoved his consent in front of my dick, I'd still feel better hearing the words.

I tuck the condom back into my pocket for now and lube two of my fingers, palming Harrison's ass cheek as he says, "Yes. I don't want to think, Sam. I just want to feel. Feel *you.*"

Ah, fuck.

My gut simmers. Burns.

I kick Harrison's feet further apart and step in close. He curses, dropping his weight more fully onto the hood of the lawn mower, his ass stuck out with his bent position. He looks obscene. Perfect. A wet dream come to life inside this shabby little shed where powdery dirt flits through the air like fairy dust.

When I bring my lubed fingers to Harrison's ass, he pushes against me. He chokes out a moan as I slip two digits inside, his body tight and hot. I start to slow as his rim strangles me, but Harrison shakes his head.

"Don't be gentle," he says. "I don't want gentle."

I think you're perfect for me, I want to shout. *I think you're mine.*

Instead of saying a thing, I press my fingers as far inside Harrison as they'll go. He grunts, dropping his head forward as I stretch him roughly. I reach my other hand between his legs, finding his heavy balls and rolling them in my palm. Harrison moans, the sound reedy and nearly a whine.

"Good, darlin'?" I ask, turning my hand so I can rub along his prostate.

Harrison's knee buckles before he quickly rights himself, but he shakes his head, turning to glare at me in the dark. "Don't," he says, voice surprisingly harsh. "Not that word."

I falter as I run over what I said. *Darlin'?*

Shit, was that what his ex called him?

"All right, stud," I say instead, feeling better when Harrison huffs a laugh. It quickly turns into a moan when I run my fist over his cock. He's looser now, but I don't want to hurt him any more than he wants. "Tell me when."

"When," he says immediately.

My cocks kicks, and I grab the condom from my pocket, keeping my fingers inside Harrison's body and opening the packet with my teeth. When I finally pull away to roll the condom on, Harrison shuffles his weight, getting a better grip on the hood of the lawn mower. That tells me everything I need to know.

I quickly spread the remaining lube onto my cock and get into place, one hand on Harrison's hip, the other on the base of my shaft. As soon as my crown is inside the hot press of his body, I shove forward, and Harrison keens so loud I move my hand to cover his mouth. He nods his head rapidly as I stall, bottomed out, and when he mutters out a muffled "*Please*" against my palm, I lose it.

I grab Harrison's hips and make him *feel*, just like he asked. His hands scramble against the lawn mower, trying to find purchase, and he meets every single one of my thrusts, even more so once he finally finds a place to hold onto. His breath punches repeatedly from his lungs, and our bodies slap together as dust rolls violently through the sliver of sunlight racing over the space above Harrison's ass.

It's fast and hurried and beautiful, in a way, but I shove every single one of my sentimental thoughts down as I focus on Harrison. On his sounds and the tightening of his body. On making him feel good.

"Hey, Harrison," I huff out, our bodies making a particularly loud slap as my groin meets his ass.

He chokes on a laugh. "Sam."

"Are you still thinkin'?"

His breath saws out. "I..."

"Okay, good," I mutter, running one of my hands up Harrison's back to his shoulder. I grip him there, pulling him back on me as hard as I dare, and his leg gives out. He slips forward, chest against the mower, but he doesn't bother pushing up. His hand leaves a sweaty print on the dusty hood as it slips away, and Harrison's body starts to clamp down on me.

"Sam," he says, voice half breath. "I'm gonna—"

I reach down, tugging Harrison's hips away from the mower so I can stroke his cock, and he splinters apart in my hands.

"Sammy," he calls out, fluttering around me as his cum coats my fingers.

My chest freaking *sings*.

"Knew it," I grit out, my orgasm barreling down on me fast. "Knew I could get you to call me by my name."

"Be smug," Harrison says between breaths, "after you come."

"Already comin'," I fire back, slamming my eyes shut as I grind against Harrison's ass. The man squeezes me *hard*, and I grunt, my hips jerking, my cock unloading deep inside his body. "Fuck. Fuckin' fuck."

"So damn eloquent, Sam," Harrison says, although there's laughter in his voice. And something else. Something floaty and satisfied.

"*Nooo*," I groan out regardless, resting my weight along Harrison's back as I come down. "Go back to callin' me Sammy. We're lovers now."

"Are we?" he asks, turning his head.

"Yeah, stud. Can't take that back."

He hums, a little smile gracing the corner of his mouth.

When I pull out of Harrison's body, taking care to go slow, he sighs. I lean down, tugging his briefs up over his soft cock, and then I pull up his jeans. He has to shift his legs closer together for me to get them over his hips. He looks back at me after I'm done, arms under his head.

I pull off the condom, tying it quickly, and then look around. Spotting an old, oily rag, I grab it off the shelf and crouch down. Harrison chuckles as I reach through his legs to clean his cum off the mower and floor.

When I stand back up, Harrison finally pushes upright. He turns in the tight space of the shed, putting us toe to toe.

"Sammy," he says, grabbing the back of my neck.

I *oomph* into his mouth but grab him back just as quickly with my unsoiled hand. Harrison is all spit and vinegar and fluffy white clouds as he kisses me just as intensely as he did before we fucked. It startles me in the best possible way.

And it's over as quickly as it began.

"Thank you," he says, eyes dark in the dim light but intense and focused on my person.

And even though I know he's being serious, that he needed that release for whatever reasons that are his alone, I can't help but grin.

"You don't gotta thank me. I've been beggin' for it, and you know it."

His lips twitch into a smirk, and he finally lets go of the back of my neck. "And?"

"You really gotta ask?" I retort with a scoff, but I answer his question nonetheless. "And *Halle-fuckin'-lujah.*"

Harrison's body shakes with his chuckle. "Now for the fun part. Get us out of here, Sammy."

I don't respond to Harrison once again calling me *Sammy*. I don't want to draw attention to it, afraid if I do, he'll stop. Instead, I give him a swift nod and turn around.

"Here we go."

Chapter 7

Harrison

Sam opens the shed door and walks out without a care in the world, although he closes the door behind him so I can't be seen. Not ten seconds later, he reappears, grin wide as the sun frames his body.

"All good," he says, waving me forward. "Carl's the only one around."

As I step out of the shed, Carl's blush-red face disappears as the man walks away, and Sam rolls with laughter.

"I think we might have scarred your coworker," I say, eyes pinging about, even though Sam already told me it was all clear.

He waves me off. "He's fine. Should we get some lunch? Might still be somethin' left."

I look at the old rag in his hand. The one smeared with my cum and folded around his used condom.

"Good point," Sam says, veering off toward our barn.

Our barn. Funny how quickly I started thinking of it that way.

It's quiet for a moment as we walk, apart from the soft sounds of the farm animals, and then Sam says, "Harrison?"

I huff a laugh. "Yeah, Sam?"

"You got a li'l..." He reaches toward my head, and I stop walking. He does, too, threading his fingers up into the hair along my temple. My eyes flutter closed until Sam pulls his hand away. He brushes his fingers off on his jeans. "Cobweb, I think."

Heart beating a little too fast, I nod, and we continue on our trek to the barn. Sam heads inside as I walk around to where my hat is still waiting on a fence post. I plop it back on my head, and when I get inside, there's another man there. One who's not Sam, but he's shaking Sam's hand. Sam, I notice, isn't holding the rag any longer, so he must have cleaned up.

"Nice to meet you, Sammy," the other man is saying. He's young, with a wide smile and a voice devoid of the Southern accent prevalent here. When he catches sight of me entering the barn, his smile shifts a little. "And you must be Harrison."

"That's right," I say, curious about his tone. "You know who I am?"

The younger man scratches the back of his neck, wincing slightly. "I'm one of Will's partners."

"One of?" jumps out of my mouth before I can process the implication of what he just said. *Will.*

"Yeah," he answers simply. "The name's Cooper."

This is Cooper. Doc Hanson's new veterinary employee. He must be just out of vet school. And, apparently, he's dating Will. Will, who's all grown up now. He must be, what...twenty-two?

I shake myself loose. "Nice to meet you, Cooper. Sorry for my rudeness. Was just a little surprised, is all."

"I get it," he says, nonplussed. "Jake said I should head over here to help you two out now that the major injuries have been taken care of. What can I do?"

"Well," I say, sharing a look with Sam. I think our little bubble has just burst. "Let me wash up real quick, and I'll fill you in."

Cooper nods, walking over to one of the pens where some of the ewes are, and Sam follows me to the sink.

"Will?" he asks quietly as I wash my hands.

I glance at him sideways. "Wyatt's son." At his continued expectant expression, I explain, "My ex."

Understanding lights Sam's eyes, but he doesn't say anything on the topic. Instead, he sticks by my side as we rejoin Cooper. And, as I explain what we've been dealing with thus far and what else there is left to do, Sam at my side is a constant reminder of what I found today.

For a handful of minutes in a dusty shed in Plum Valley, Texas, I was reminded of the man I used to be. The one I thought I'd lost.

And I don't know if I can go back to forgetting he ever existed in the first place.

———————————★———————————

I was right that Sam and I would lose the privacy we'd enjoyed our first few days here. Cooper stayed with us the rest of the afternoon, and now, a day later, Carl is back on our team, too. The four of us have run through the flock of sheep more efficiently than just Sam and me, and there's no doubt in my mind we'll be finished by the end of the evening.

The realization sits like a heavy stone in my stomach, and I wish I could say I don't know why that is, but I'd be lying.

My eyes seek out Sam across the barn. He's laughing at something Cooper is saying, his brown eyes twinkling and his handsome face bright with joy. It's infectious, that endless optimism he seems to have. I wish I could bottle it and take it home.

Sam looks my way after a moment, as if he felt me staring. He shoots me a quick smile and a wink before focusing on the sheep he's helping Cooper with.

He's so *open*. So unabashed about conveying whatever it is he's feeling or thinking in the moment. There's something sexy about that. About that sort of transparency. It feels good being wanted the way Sam wants me. Seeing it on his face. Hearing it in his voice.

I'm sad that I'll be giving all that up in just a few short hours.

Sad. What a simple, incomplete word. I feel like Winnie, when she tells me she's sad about something, and I know there's so much more she's feeling that she's unable to articulate. The word isn't enough, and yet I know this feeling is about more than just Sam, a man I've known for only a matter of days. It's about the temporary lightness he's gifted me with. The way I feel warm and a little bit weightless in his presence.

I wish I could hang onto that.

When we break for dinner, Sam lopes my way, all the eagerness of a puppy in his step.

"Look at that," I can't help but say, giving him a little smirk. "I didn't even call, and you came."

Sam bites his lower lip, tucking it away between his teeth. "I'll always come for you, Harrison."

My body flushes hot.

"How old are you?" I ask as we head toward the food tables. I'm almost certain he's younger than I am.

He barks a laugh. "Worried 'bout the legality of what we did?"

I snort. "No. Please, you're not *that* young."

He clutches his chest, as if wounded, and I huff in amusement as he pretends to stumble. "Ouch. Y'know, when the guy you're wooin' says you don't look that young anymore, it hurts."

I shake my head, cheeks aching with my smile. "I know your ego isn't that fragile, Sam."

Sam stops faking his death, but the look he gives me isn't the cocky one I was expecting. It's more hesitant, and I'm not sure what to make of it.

I stop still, chest feeling hot. But not in a good way. "Sam," I say.

The man stutters to a halt, turning toward me. He cocks his head, and I take a step closer, speaking low.

"I'm glad you don't look young. Because the thoughts I have about you? They're entirely adult in nature."

"Yeah?" he replies, hand brushing mine lightly.

"Mhm. And I still have the twinge in my backside to prove it."

With that, I keep walking, and Sam hastens until he's in step next to me. I can feel the heat of his stare on the side of my head.

"Still?" he asks, voice low and raspy.

And *damn*. I like that sound a lot.

"Mm," I answer, catching his gaze. But I don't say anything more because we're at the buffet table now and no longer alone.

Sam is quiet as he dishes up a plate beside me, but that only lasts until we're seated at a table with Carl and Tilda, and then Sam is talking a mile a minute, catching up with his coworkers in a way speaking of familiarity. Even though I don't know Sam well, I'm glad he has that in his life.

I let my eyes wander as we eat burgers from Nash's. I don't see Doc Hanson, although he did stop by earlier to thank me again for coming. Cooper is nearby, chatting with a few people I don't recognize. But the one person I've been keeping an eye out for since I arrived in town is gone.

In fact, I haven't caught sight of Wyatt since that one brief glimpse the other day... Right before I fled like my ass was on fire. As far as I could tell, he didn't spot me.

I don't know what to think about my reaction. I'm not in love with the man anymore—I haven't been for a very long time—but I didn't expect it to hit so hard, seeing him again. I thought I'd be more composed. I didn't think I'd run and hide in a nearby shed.

Part of me is relieved that it's looking more and more like I'll leave here without a confrontation with my ex. But part of me... Part of me is disappointed. And that's the feeling I'm unsure what to make of.

It's not like I want to get back together with Wyatt. I truly don't. But he hurt me. Plain and simple. And maybe, I don't know...maybe I wanted a chance to yell or scream or say nothing at all. Maybe I wanted a chance to face my old ghost.

"Hey," Sam says, elbowing me lightly.

I look his way, wondering what I missed.

"All right?" he asks, eyes squinted a little against the early evening sun.

I give him a smile. "Sure."

"D'you think..." he starts, looking uncharacteristically nervous. And isn't that something? That I already know what constitutes uncharacteristic behavior for Sam.

"What is it, Sammy?" I ask, hoping the nickname will help set him at ease.

His responding smile makes me warm. "D'you think we could meet up sometime? Near Houston, I mean, since we live so close. We're practically neighbors, after all," he teases.

"Right," I say, my gut swooping a little.

My house pops into my head. The blue siding and the white shutters. The paved stone path up to the front door and the big, golden knocker in lieu of a doorbell. Winnie's face and her laugh and the twirly dresses she likes to wear. My dog, Tigger, and the orange and white hair she leaves all over the house. My bed, so big and empty.

All the facets of my life that make things like *this* so much more complicated than it ever used to be.

I open my mouth to tell Sam I don't think it's a good idea. Because frankly, I think a clean break would be best. I already care about Sam. I don't want to disappoint him. I don't want to tie my baggage to his hands.

But he's looking at me in such a hopeful manner that I can't bring myself to do it. I can't tell him no. So, instead, I say, "Maybe," even though it holds little conviction.

His smile widens regardless. "Okay," he replies, tucking a bite of burger into his mouth and chewing.

"Hey, uh." I clear my throat. "You never answered my question."

Sam's brows draw in for a moment before his expression lightens. "I'm thirty-two," he answers. "And you? How old is the incomparable Doctor Bailey?"

I huff a laugh, shaking my head. "Thirty-eight."

Sam hums, nodding. "And what's it like up there?" he jokes, cheeky as ever.

Lonely.

The thought stops me cold.

But it's the truth, isn't it? I'm lonely, even though I'm surrounded by people I love and people who love me. I'm still, somehow, alone.

I don't have a partner. Someone I can lean on. Someone I can laugh with. And it's been years since I've even tried. My last relationship ended shortly after Winnie's sixth birthday. I remember because the guy—Hank—was upset that he had to spend his entire day at a kid's party. He never said as much, but I could tell. He liked me, but Hank never liked my daughter, and that was a fucking deal-breaker.

That short six-month relationship ended four years ago, and there's been no one since. And before that? Similar situations. A couple guys I dated. One when Winnie was two years old. That relationship folded before it ever really got a chance to start. And the other lasted close to a year before I realized I never *saw* the guy. He was hardly around, and that's the only reason we hadn't broken up yet.

Needless to say, the last decade has been one miss after another for me. And hookups? Yeah, those don't happen anymore, Sam aside. Because when would I even manage it? When my daughter is in school and I'm on my lunch break? Over the weekend, when there are so many other things I need to do around the house?

There's no time. No time and, honestly, no energy once the day is done. Being here in Plum Valley has been the closest thing I've had to a vacation in the past ten years, and even still, it's been riddled with guilt and nightly crying episodes from my daughter, who's four hours away and doesn't understand why I can't be with her *always*.

And what could I tell her? What could I tell my daughter who just wants the assurance someone is there for her? That I have more important things to do? Because I don't. She's the most important, always. I thought a few days would be okay. I thought I could come here, and she'd be okay. But she's not. And that's my fault.

So dating? It's not happening. Not anytime soon, and maybe not ever. That ship has sailed. Guys like Sam with their good intentions and wicked fucking cocks aren't for me. It's a pipe dream. A passing wish.

So what can I say to Sam, who wants to know what it feels like being thirty-eight and resigned to a loveless life?

I shoot the man a smirk I don't feel. "At least my knee tells me when a storm is coming."

Sam barks a laugh, big and bright. And *God*, for a moment—just a moment—I let myself wonder... *What if?*

CHAPTER 8

Sammy

Harrison is quiet as he packs away the rest of his gear. His head is tipped down, focused as he works, and his hat blocks most of his face from view. We're the only two left in the barn now, apart from the sheep.

"Are you headin' back tonight?" I ask. The sun is getting low in the sky, and it'd be a late night if Harrison drives the four hours home now instead of waiting for the morning. But something about the way he's rushing slightly makes me think he's antsy to get out of here.

He nods before looking up at me briefly. "Yeah."

I try not to let my disappointment show. Harrison said we could get together again, so it's not like this is goodbye.

I kick off from the pen where a few sheep are busy eating their meal of pellets and hay. "Are you safe to drive?" I check.

His lips twist slightly, and he zips his bag closed. "I'll be fine. I'm not that tired."

"All right," I mumble, walking closer. "Good."

Harrison lets go of his gear bag, watching me as I close the gap between us. I'm not sure what my intention is, but as soon as I'm near enough to touch, I reach for Harrison's side. He doesn't stop me, but there's a wariness in his expression I don't like.

I want him to look at me the way he did before. With a smile. Or a laugh hanging at the corner of his mouth. With those blissed-out, sated eyes that sparkled blue in the low light of the shed.

I twist my fingers in Harrison's shirt, and he sighs, eyes fluttering half-shut.

"Sam," he says quietly.

I don't reply. I just bring my lips to his, knocking Harrison's hat up and off his head in the process. There's no hesitance as he kisses me back, as if whatever trepidation he might have been feeling before snapped away the moment my mouth met his. He's warm, and he's soft, and I'm goddamn *hungry* for him. I want to devour him. I want to kiss him until our mouths are raw. I want to fuck away whatever troubles he has, until all he can think about, until all he knows, is *me*.

For a brief moment, I think he might let me. I think I might get my chance, right here, right now.

But then Harrison tears his mouth away, turning his head as he sucks in air. "*Sam*." My name is a croak.

"Whatever you need," I remind him, bringing my lips to his jaw. His throat. The sliver of neck available above the collar of his shirt.

He groans, hands tightening on my shoulder blades. "I need to go home," he rasps.

My lips stop still on his skin. *Damn*.

Inhaling through my nose, I suck him in. The smell of animal dander is there, sure. But there's also something soft and sweet, like melon. Why does he smell like melon? Fuck, I want to lick him all over.

"Sam," Harrison groans again, and I pull my face out of his neck, putting a few inches between us. He looks tortured.

"You really gotta go tonight?" I ask.

He nods once. Slowly.

I force my fist to loosen its death grip on his shirt and take a full step back. "All right."

"God, Sammy," he says, and I can't get too excited about the use of my name because the tone is plain sad.

"What is it?" I ask softly.

"You just... You look like a kicked puppy," he answers, smoothing his palm down my chest and stomach, as if righting my shirt.

"'Cause I'll miss you."

I don't mean to say the words aloud. I really don't. But there they are.

Harrison makes a soft sound, almost a plea. "Sam, we just met."

"So?" I counter.

"So it shouldn't be this hard," he says. And the fact that he's including himself in that statement makes my hope spring.

"Go out with me," I say.

Harrison looks taken aback, and he drops his hands off my body. They hang at his sides. "I..."

"Let me take you on a date, Harrison. A proper one when we're back home. I still have a few days left here"—I'll be helping transport the rest of the animals away—"but after that, lemme take you out."

"I don't know, Sam," he says, scrubbing his hand along the back of his neck. "My life is...complicated."

"That's all right."

Harrison shakes his head, his blue eyes sad. "I just... I need to think about it, okay?"

I nod, even though every fiber of my being wants to press. Wants him to acquiesce before he leaves.

Tucking my fingers into his belt loops, I say, "Okay. You think about it. But Harrison?"

"Yeah, Sam," he breathes.

"Just keep in mind that if you say yes... If you're mine"—I bring my lips to his stubbled cheek—"I will fuckin' worship you. I will make you feel good."

His hands land on my abs, trembling.

"Every inch of you," I promise. "Your lips, your cock, your pinkie toes, even, if that's what you want." Mouth at his ear, I nip gently. "There won't be a single day where you don't know what you mean to me."

Harrison lets out a shaky breath. "You've got a mouth on you, Sam."

"Mm," I answer, leaning back. "So lemme make good use of it."

Harrison holds my gaze for two beats before stepping back somewhat reluctantly. I let go, watching as he snags his gear bag off the exam table. He rubs his hand over his mouth before eyeing me.

"I have to go," he says.

"All right," I answer, knowing I've said my piece.

Harrison grabs his hat off the ground, holding it in his hand as he simply stares at me for a moment. It feels like a lifetime, those brief few seconds. And then he plops his hat back on his head and strides away.

I turn, watching him go, eyes running all over the back of his neck where his blonde hair curls gently, his broad back, and his ass in those jeans. When he turns the corner out of the barn, I let out a sigh, shoulders slumping.

It wasn't a yes. But it wasn't a no, either.

It's not until a good three minutes later that something clicks in my brain, and I take off running after him. Harrison is nowhere in sight—not him or his truck—and the dust in the driveway has already settled.

"Shit," I yell, hands landing on my knees as I try to catch my breath after the brief sprint.

"Everythin' all right?" Carl asks from about ten feet away.

I push upright. "No. No, it ain't all right, Carl. I didn't get the man's number."

There's a beat of silence, and then Carl hiccups a laugh. He covers his mouth, doing his best to hide his amusement, but he fails spectacularly.

Pointing his way, I warn, "Not a word." He holds up his hands, still laughing, and I groan, looking up at the dusky evening sky. "Unbelievable. Of all the goddamn stupid things."

I forgot to get his *phone number*.

"What are you gonna do?" Carl asks.

I sigh, meeting my coworker's gaze. "He's a vet who lives within twenty minutes of Houston. I'll find the damn man."

And I will. I didn't get nearly long enough with him. I'm not ready to let go. Not until Harrison tells me to.

"C'mon," I tell Carl, heading toward Tilda, stationed not far off. "The sooner we finish up here, the sooner we can go home."

And the sooner I can find one Doctor Harrison Bailey.

--------------------★--------------------

It's midweek when Carl, Tilda, and I get back to Houston. We spent several days hauling animals across the state, relocating them to new homes in singles, doubles, or larger groups.

Luckily, our Animal Control unit approved the allocation of resources, so it's not like any of us got in trouble for being away so long.

As soon as we're back, though, Carl and I get inundated with a stack of animal cruelty reports that built up in our absence. We spend an entire day driving around, looking into the claims. Unsurprisingly, no one wants to admit to neglecting their animals. It's often slow going, making progress in these cases. But we get the ball rolling, and then we head back to fill out all the necessary paperwork.

It's late when Carl takes off. I stay a while longer, heading into the area of the building that houses adoptable pets. We're closed to visitors at this time of night, but I walk along the rows of cages, stopping to say hello to the dogs we have on site. Some of these animals were picked up from abusive situations. Some were abandoned. And some were found and simply never claimed.

"I wish we had homes for all y'all," I say quietly, rubbing behind the ears of a German Shepherd who's leaning up against the wire door at the front of her run. All of the cages in here are open at the top and separated by cement blocks with chipped yellow paint. They're long and spacious enough, but it's no cozy house. "I'd take you all if I could."

"That'd be a neat trick in that tiny apartment of yours," Tilda says, surprising me with her presence.

"And what're you doin' here this late?" I ask, turning to my coworker.

"Could ask the same of you," she retorts.

"Just catchin' up," I say, giving the German Shepherd one more scratch behind her ears before walking on. Tilda follows along.

"Why're you still in that apartment, Sammy?"

I huff, looking over my shoulder at the woman. Tilda is in her mid-sixties, her bobbed hair sleek and silver-gray, and her face has a good many wrinkles. She works in this division of Animal Control, with the adoptable pets.

I've always liked Tilda, ever since I got this job and she swooped me under her protection as if I were hers. As if I had been all along. The woman has invited me over for every holiday and special occasion in the past eight years, and I've accepted more often than not. Her family is as familiar to me as, well... I'd say my own, except I don't have one.

Tilda and Carl—they're my family now. And Tilda, for as sweet as she can be, is not afraid to get tough with me at times.

"You know I've been savin' up," I tell her in regards to my living situation.

Yes, my apartment is tiny, but it's not a shithole. And yet it's also...not really a home.

"You've set aside enough by now," she replies, stopping to coo over a terrier mix who's wiggling in excitement. The little thing can't hold still long enough for her to give him a good pet through the wire.

Sure, I have. I've banked a good savings at this point. But...

"Sammy," Tilda says, equal parts stern and tender. "It's all right to set down some roots. You know that, don'tcha?"

I swallow around the ball in my throat. I never had roots. Never had a home that lasted longer than a year and a half.

I guess, maybe, I'm still waiting to plant my own. Waiting for it to feel right.

Or maybe I simply want someone to help me dig into the dirt.

"I'm in no hurry," I tell Tilda, avoiding the heart of the matter. "My apartment is fine." For now.

"Yeah, well," Tilda says, sighing a little. "If you had a place of your own, you could bring a few of these cuties home with you." She scratches behind the little terrier's ear, and he practically vibrates. "Isn't that right, honey?"

"Prob'ly best I don't, then," I joke. "You know I've got no impulse control. I'd be up to my eyeballs in fur."

Tilda chuckles, standing upright. We head out of the adoptable dog wing, and the sound cuts off a little when the door shuts behind us.

"What about that Doctor Bailey?" she asks. "Bet he's a dog person."

I snort. "I see what you're doin', Tilly. You're not subtle."

"Not tryin' to be, hun," she shoots back. "He seems like a nice man. Gonna call 'im?"

"I'm gonna do one better," I say, not bothering to mention I *can't* call him. At least, not yet. "I'm gonna pay him a visit."

Tilda hums at that, patting my shoulder. "I wish you the best, Sammy boy."

"Thanks, Tilly. Have a good night, you hear?"

"You, too," she replies, giving my shoulder a squeeze before letting go.

I watch Tilda head into the parking lot, and once she's secure in her car, I grab my things from the employee lockers and make my way to my own truck. It's a short drive to my apartment, and once I'm inside, all I want is to strip out of my navy-blue uniform and drop into bed. But there's something I have to do first.

After scarfing down a granola bar, I grab my laptop and spread out atop my mattress. It only takes a single Google search to find the information I'm looking for. There's exactly one Harrison Bailey, DVM who works near Houston. *Jackpot.*

With a smile on my face and the memory of heated skin under my fingertips, I fall asleep, dreams spinning webs inside my head.

CHAPTER 9

Harrison

"He's at it again," my coworker, Deborah, whispers.

"Oh, Christ," I mutter, following her line of sight to where Abbott, the oldest veterinarian at our practice, is scolding the copy machine. "I'll go help."

Abbott scowls at me when he sees me coming. The man has been working here since the eighties, and although he's by no means a *bad* veterinarian, he's stuck in his ways, and his techniques and practices—as well as his understanding of modern technology—are out of date. But Doctor Abbott Fry owns a prominent majority of this practice, which means, until he decides to retire, the rest of us have to make do with his more-than-occasional bad tempers and propensity for yelling at the electronics.

"Can I lend a hand?" I ask Abbott.

He grunts, his white hair matching his lab coat. He's one of the only vets here who wears one all the time. "Damn thing won't print the copy."

The vet techs, I notice, have made themselves scarce. I don't blame them. Abbott isn't easy to deal with on a good day.

"The original needs to go inside," I say, lifting the top of the copy machine to show him where.

Abbott grumbles, grabbing his paper from the feed tray in back and slapping it over the scanner. "I got it," he says, waving me off.

I nod and walk back over to Deborah, who's shaking her head.

"That man is a dinosaur," she says under her breath.

I huff a laugh, which I quickly dispel. "He's trying."

"He is *not*," she responds. "You're just too damn sweet to say a bad word 'bout anyone. You and I both know he doesn't *wanna* learn. He doesn't want help."

I shrug because while that may be true, part of me feels bad for Abbott. He's been here for decades, and everything has changed around him. Sure, I think he could have put in more effort to evolve over the years. To learn and grow. But he didn't. He's held onto what he knows, and there's something sad about that. About watching a person fade into the background of their own world.

The sentiment hits a little too close to home.

"Deb, I'm going to take my break," I tell my coworker.

She nods. "Headin' to lunch?"

"Yeah, I..." My words die off as the front door opens and a familiar figure I'm not expecting in the least comes strutting through the lobby. His head swivels around, taking everything in with bright eyes, and when his gaze lands on me, a slow smile spreads across his face.

My heartbeat trips.

"Can I help you?" one of the vet techs asks, having headed back to the front desk.

Sam flicks his gaze to her for only a moment, but then he nods at me. "I'm here for him."

Oh damn. *Damn.*

"Yum," Deborah mutters too quietly for anyone but me to hear.

I swat her arm before stepping out from behind the big curved reception desk. "Sam?"

His grin doesn't let up, but something in his gaze softens as I approach. He's wearing a dark blue uniform with a shiny silver badge on his breast pocket, and the effect has my mouth drying up in an instant.

I didn't think he could get hotter than when he was in his cowboy getup. Guess I was wrong.

"I see you already forgot my name," Sam teases. Right, because I didn't call him Sammy.

I huff a somewhat strained laugh, coming to a stop in front of him. "What are you doing here?"

"Isn't it obvious?"

Fuck. Somehow, in only a matter of days, I forgot what it felt like to be in the presence of this man. How intoxicating he is. How his very words possess the unique ability to wrap around me and *tug*.

The man is temptation personified. At least, he is to me. And I so badly want to let him pull me in.

"Y'know, I realized somethin'," Sam says quietly, taking a step that puts us nearly toe to toe. "It's hard to call somebody for a date when you don't have their number."

I wince, and Sam raises an eyebrow. As soon as I left Plum Valley, I realized we never exchanged numbers, but I thought it was for the best. I figured my fling—if you could call our storage shed hookup that—had flung. It's what I wanted.

At least, it's what I *thought* I wanted before the man decided to waltz back into my life. I didn't expect Sam to go through the effort of tracking me down. I didn't expect to be so *thrilled* he did.

"Walk outside with me?" I ask before glancing over my shoulder. A few of my coworkers are watching us with rapt attention. Deborah, in particular, has a massive smile on her face. I know she won't hesitate to grill me later, but none of them need front-row seats to my personal life as it's unfolding.

"Sure," Sam says easily.

Sam follows me out and around the side of the building, where we have a fenced-in area for the boarding dogs to go outside. There's a picnic table nearby for the employees to use when the weather is nice, and I take a seat. Instead of sitting across from me, Sam plops down on the same bench, straddling the wood plank so close that his knee touches my thigh. He's not wearing a hat at the moment, and his brown eyes sparkle with golden flecks in the sun.

He's beautiful.

"Sorry about the phone number," I start.

But Sam leans forward, halting me with a hand on my leg. "Were you tryin' to blow me off?"

"No," I admit, even though I wasn't sure whether or not I intended to follow through on a date should Sam call. But it wasn't my intention to ghost him.

"Then nothin' to be sorry 'bout," he says. "Now, when can I take you out?"

I huff a laugh, running my hand through my hair. "God, Sam."

"What?" he presses.

"It's just... You're relentless."

"Yes."

"And that's really what you want?" I ask.

He cants his head. "What d'you mean?"

"You want to *date* me? Not just fuck me?"

Sam's lips twitch, and his hand tightens briefly on my thigh. "Are the two mutually exclusive?"

My breath punches from my lungs. "Why?" I ask. *Why me?*

Sam blinks once. "You know why, Harrison."

"You want me that much?"

"Again, yes," he says. The wind ripples through the trees around us, and even though Sam's hair is too short to flutter in the breeze, his shirt billows open slightly at the collar. "Say you'll go on a date with me."

It's a plea or a demand. I'm not sure which.

I open my mouth, but nothing comes out. I've tried this before. I've tried, and I've failed. What reason is there to expect it'd be any different with Sam?

I don't want to fail him. I don't want him to fail *me*.

Sam's fingers continue to draw lazy, intentional circuits on my leg. "What do I gotta do to get a date with you, Harrison? To get you into bed?"

"You had me in bed," I say weakly.

Sam's lips spread into a smile. No, not a smile. A *smirk*. "Y'know what I mean."

My body flushes hot. Not only at the memory of Sam's arms around me in Plum Valley when all we did was cuddle. But at the recollection of what he felt like against my body—*inside* my body—in that dusty, old shed.

What would Sam be capable of in a bed where he could really let loose?

"Cake," I blurt.

Sam's fingers still, and his smile goes a little crooked. "Cake?"

"Yeah," I say, swallowing. "Dinner at my house. Six o'clock. And bring cake."

Sam's grin is blinding. "I can do that."

"Okay," I manage.

"Okay."

We're silent for a beat, and my heart pounds like a drum.

"I, uh...need to grab some lunch," I tell Sam, realizing my break time is running out.

He nods, fingers drawing over my leg once more before he pulls his hand away and stands. I do, too.

"I should get back to work," Sam says. "But, uh, Harrison? Can I get your number this time?"

I huff, nodding, and Sam pulls his phone from his pocket. I give him my digits, and he enters them into his phone. A moment later, my own buzzes.

"Now you've got mine, too," he says with a wink. "You'll send me your address?"

"Yeah," I reply, wondering what the hell I'm doing. This is bound to crash and burn.

Sam nods, looking around for a moment before he gives my arm a little tug. I follow, unsure why he's pulling me toward the edge of the building. But the next second, he wordlessly answers that question, backing me up against the wall where we're out of sight. He boxes me in, chest to chest, eye to eye, hands in my hair.

And then he's kissing me.

I moan long and low, broadcasting my pleasure plain as day as Sam's tongue greets my own. I flash back in an instant to the inside of that shed. To the way Sam simply *took*. He took everything I was so willing to give, and he gave back in equal measure.

I want more. More of that. More *Sam*.

Except—*Christ*. We're at my workplace, where anyone could come outside and stumble upon us. And that reminder is what has me gently pushing the man back.

Sam doesn't protest. He never has, I realize. Any time I pump the brakes, he's quick to back off, same as now. He stops kissing me the moment I give him a little shove, and he eases away, lips shiny, eyes bright.

My gaze roams over those shiny, puffed-up lips, and I nearly forget my resolve. "Shit, Sam," I groan. "Is this how you always say goodbye? Because if so, we might have a problem."

Sam smirks a little, eyes drifting down my body and landing on my crotch, where said problem resides. He raises a brow. "I'm good at solvin' problems."

I groan again, giving him another little shove. "Don't you dare tease me right now."

"Who says I'm teasin'?" he replies. "Say the word and I'll drop to my knees right this instant."

I close my eyes tight, pulling in a few centering breaths. *My God*. When I blink my eyes open, Sam is watching me with an unrepentant gaze. I'm not even convinced that was a joke.

I clear my throat pointedly. "I'm thirty-eight years old, Sam. I'm much too young to have a heart attack."

He laughs loudly before finally stepping away. The air feels cooler when he goes, and I don't like the reprieve nearly as much as I should.

A foot away, he says, "Hey, Harrison."

I huff a laugh. "Yeah, Sam?"

"See you tonight."

With that, Sam walks off, and I wonder if somewhere in Plum Valley, Texas, my common sense is waiting for me to come pick it back up.

———————— ★ ————————

When I get to my parents' shortly after four-thirty, Winnie rushes me as if she hasn't seen me in days. It breaks my heart a little. She's been extra clingy ever since I got back.

"Hey, Pumpkin," I say, bending down and wrapping my arms around her slim shoulders. Winnie has always been a petite thing, and even with her recent growth spurt, the top of her head only just reaches my chest.

She gives me a squeeze around the middle before stepping back and grabbing her backpack from beside the door. "I'm ready," she says before rushing outside.

I sigh a little as she goes. She always tries to act so strong—until she can't. Until she cries at night and tells me not to go.

"Everything okay today?" I ask as my mom comes around the corner from the kitchen.

Winnie takes the bus to my parents' after school, and I pick her up once I'm done with work. It's a routine that's worked well for us for years.

My mom nods, her gaze following Winnie out the open front door. She chuckles a little. "Boundless energy, that one."

Reminds me of someone else I know.

My heartbeat kicks up as I roll over the implications of that. Sam will be coming over tonight. In less than two hours, he'll find out exactly how complicated my life really is.

"I should go," I tell my mom. "Before Winnie decides to try her hand at driving."

My mom chuckles and gives me a quick hug. "Love you."

"Love you, too," I reply. "See you tomorrow."

When I join my daughter inside the truck, she's already buckled up in the back, tall enough now not to need a booster seat.

"How was school?" I ask, backing out of my parents' driveway.

Winnie kicks the passenger seat in front of her. "Fine."

"Just fine?" I ask, lifting a brow. That's a pretty short answer coming from my ten-year-old.

She sighs before saying, "Janey said my drawing looked like a little kid scribble. It wasn't a scribble, Daddy. It was our family. So I told Janey her face looked like a Picasso, and Mrs. Turner said that wasn't appropriate. She put a note in my folder."

I keep my initial reactions to myself—the sadness followed by amusement and then resignation—and check my daughter in the rearview mirror. She's looking out the window, her blonde hair—so much like mine...and Danielle's—falling messily around her face. It never does stay inside her ponytail.

"I'm sorry Janey said something uncomplimentary about your picture, Pumpkin. I'd love to see your drawing of our family." I wait a beat before adding, "But just because someone isn't nice to us, that doesn't mean it's okay to be not-nice back."

"Yeah, I know," Winnie says sullenly. "But it's so hard to be nice to Janey, Daddy. She's a very difficult person."

I huff a laugh, clearing my throat afterward. Maybe I should discourage Winnie's ball-buster attitude, but the truth is I love it. I'm glad she's not afraid to speak her mind and defend herself, and I don't want that to change. Even if it does get her into occasional trouble at school.

When I turn onto our short driveway, I remember the news I still need to share and steel my nerves. "Hey, kiddo. We're going to have company tonight, okay?"

"Who?" Winnie asks.

"Someone I met when I was away helping the animals."

She's quiet for a moment, digesting that as I park the truck inside our garage. "Are they nice?"

A little smile sneaks onto my lips. "Yeah, I think so."

Winnie hums and then unbuckles her seatbelt. "We'll see."

Oh boy.

Winnie rushes inside the house, promptly tearing all of the cushions off the couches in the living room to build a fort, and Tigger appears in front of my feet, stubby tail wiggling in excitement. I greet my dog before letting her out into the backyard, and then I head into the kitchen to start dinner. My gut twists a little as I think about Sam arriving.

What will he think? What will he say? Will he turn right back around and leave once he finds out I'm a single dad with a perpetually messy house and an even messier life?

Am I making a mistake?

CHAPTER 10

Sammy

As I take the short stone walkway up to Harrison's front door, my stomach somersaults. I haven't been this nervously excited for a date since...well, I don't know when. It's been so long.

In fact, I haven't been on a real date in over six months. Hooked up a few times, sure. But it's not remotely the same thing. And while yes, I absolutely want to see the man inside this house spread out naked across his bed, I also want to *know* him. I have since the moment he started venting his insecurities at that little green rental house in Plum Valley.

Do you know how many guys open up like that? How many have the ability to get vulnerable with a veritable stranger? The list is damn near zero in my experience.

But Harrison did.

For whatever reason, Harrison trusted me to listen when he needed to let off some steam. And yeah, maybe it was because he thought I was a safe bet. Someone he wouldn't see again after last week. But the ability to be unguarded is a rare quality in a man.

Harrison is a rare man, I can tell.

I'd be honored to share his bed. And a little sliver of space inside that busy head of his, if he'd let me.

When I knock on the door—using the big gold knocker shaped like a lion—it takes maybe fifteen seconds before Harrison appears. When he does, he looks much stiffer than I'm expecting. The *tense* kind of stiff. Not the just-been-kissed-behind-work kind.

"Hey," I greet, offering Harrison a wide smile.

"Hi," he replies, one hand on the door but making no move to let me in.

I hold up the grocery bag with the cake he requested. "Brought the goods."

That gets me a nervous huff of laughter, and he finally steps back.

"How're you doin'?" I ask, eyes quickly sweeping the entrance to his home. "I know it's only been a few hours, but... Woah." I eye the towering construction of cushions and sheets inside Harrison's living room with some confusion. The...fort?...spans a good ten feet wide, but even more surprising than the existence of a fort in Harrison's house in the first place is the small blonde head that pops suddenly out of it. "Oh, fff—udge."

I barely manage to correct my slip, and the small blonde human narrows their eyes my way before disappearing. I swing my gaze to Harrison, but he's avoiding eye contact and looking sheepish.

"Winnie," he calls softly. "Would you come out, please?"

The blonde slowly reappears, exiting the fort and walking our way. An orange-and-white dog who must be Tigger follows, slipping past the sheet that denotes the front of the fort and trotting after the small human.

"Uh, Sam," Harrison says, scrubbing the back of his neck before blowing out a breath. When the tiny blonde stops at his side, he finally meets my eye. "This is Winnie, my daughter."

Oh, wow.

"You can call me Winifred," she says primly, her pale blue eyes meeting mine. She looks so much like Harrison, down to the straw-blonde hair and the way her jaw is set, as if she's forcing a bit of stoicism into her exterior.

"Nice to meet you, Winifred," I say, holding out my hand. "I'm Sammy."

"I'll call you Sam," she decides, accepting my handshake. Her hand is petite and warm inside my own, and something inside my chest cracks. A tiny fault line.

She's just like her father.

My eyes meet Harrison's, and he no longer looks nervous. He's steeled himself.

"Can I go now?" Winnie asks, letting go of my hand and shifting her weight, as if ready to bolt.

"Go ahead," Harrison answers. Winnie is already halfway to the fort when he adds, "Dinner in ten."

Tigger's stump tail wags once before she follows Winnie, and Harrison waves me forward.

"Come on in," he says, waiting as I slip off my boots. He leads me down the hall and around a corner, into a bright, airy kitchen. "I, uh... Here, let me take the cake."

I pass him the bag, and Harrison sets it onto the counter. He fiddles with the plastic for a moment, the lines of his back taut.

"Harrison," I say gently.

He looks back at me.

"I'm fairly certain I already know the answer to this, but you're not married, right?" I check. Because yes, he told me he wasn't in a relationship, and I don't think he lied to me about that. But it's possible he could be in the process of separating with someone.

Harrison shakes his head. "No."

"Okay." I nod, rubbing over my chin. "Is there a reason you didn't tell me you have a kid?"

Honestly, I'm shocked. Why wouldn't Harrison mention his daughter before inviting me over?

He winces, body language still closed off, and that just won't do. Letting out a little breath, I approach, and Harrison watches me steadily. When I touch his arm, he turns toward me.

"I can tell you're expectin' me to react badly," I say. "So let's clear that up first. I'm not pissed. I'm not scared that you've got a daughter. But I don't like bein' lied to, Harrison."

He looks down, gently touching my hand. "Shit, Sam. I'm sorry. I don't know why I didn't tell you."

I think I do. I think he was scared.

And suddenly, him talking about his life being complicated makes a lot more sense.

"That's all right," I tell him, running my knuckles over his stubbled jaw. "Although I think we needa have a good long conversation later."

"Christ," he says, huffing a little laugh. "I feel like I'm in trouble."

"I can spank ya, and we'll call it good."

"Jesus, Sam," he says, eyeing the doorway. His cheeks brighten some, and *damn*, I love the sight.

"How old is Winnie?" I ask, redirecting us to safer ground.

"Ten," he answers.

Ten. Didn't he leave Plum Valley ten years ago?

"And her mom?" I ask as evenly as possible.

His eyes meet mine, imploring. "It's..."

"Complicated?" I guess.

He nods. "She's not a part of Winnie's life. She never has been." Harrison pauses, mouth open like he's debating how much to say on the matter, when the timer dings. "I need to..."

He points to the oven, and I take a step back, giving him space. Harrison puts on oven mitts before grabbing a pan out from the heat. He places it atop the stove. "I hope mac and cheese is okay?"

I cock a little smile. "Considerin' I'm still a kid at heart, yeah, mac and cheese is definitely okay."

His lips turn up at that. *Finally*, a smile.

"Winnie," Harrison calls out. "Dinner's ready."

Half a minute later, as Harrison is setting food onto the table, little feet pad into the kitchen. Winnie looks up at me, eyes light and hair all in disarray. "That's my seat," she says matter-of-factly.

I look over at the chair I'm standing beside before pulling it out. "All right, li'l miss. So, where's my seat?"

Winnie thinks this over as she gets into her chair. Finally, she points to a spot across the table. "You can sit there."

Harrison snorts quietly, and I round the table, sitting down where Winnie deemed appropriate. Tigger settles on the floor next to Winnie's chair, out of sight, and Harrison sits at the end of the table between Winnie and me. We all look at one another before Harrison says, "Dig in."

Winnie goes straight for the bowl of fruit while Harrison holds the spoon for the mac and cheese my way. I dish some up as Harrison helps himself to salad.

"So, Winifred," I say, glancing at the little girl. "D'you go to school?"

She looks at me like the question is preposterous. "Of course."

Hey, at least she's talking to me. That's a start, right?

"What grade?" I ask as Harrison dishes more food onto his daughter's plate.

She shoves a strawberry in her mouth. "Fifth."

I whistle. "Next, you'll be on to middle school."

She blinks at me, not saying anything else.

"Winnie, did you get your homework done at Grandma and Grandpa's?" Harrison asks.

She nods, poking her fork into her mac and cheese, trying, I think, to separate the specks of green broccoli out from the noodles.

I, on the other hand, love it. I've never had mac and cheese with broccoli. There's even some sliced tomatoes and crispy bread crumbs on top.

"This is really good," I tell Harrison.

He gives me a little smile. "Thanks, Sam."

"Sam," Winnie speaks up, sounding quite serious. "Do you have kids?"

Well, shit.

"No, I don't," I answer.

Winnie hums. "Why not?"

I huff a laugh. "Never had the chance, I guess."

I'm not about to explain to Winnie that with the type of partners I choose, pregnancy isn't even an option.

She eats another piece of fruit. "Do you like kids?"

I finish chewing my bite of food slowly, eyeing the small human. She's staring right back. Harrison, I note, is staying quiet.

Finally, I answer, "No, hate 'em."

Winnie looks affronted. "Why?"

"They're always sticky, and they don't like vegetables," I say, spearing a piece of my broccoli.

Winnie's brows draw together as she looks down at her plate. "*I'm* not sticky," she says sullenly, adding, at a mumble, "and I like veggies."

"Do you?" I ask.

She nods resolutely before poking the tiniest-ever broccoli floret onto her fork and stuffing it in her mouth.

"Well, dang," I say. "Maybe I'm wrong about kids."

"I think you are," she says, making a face as she chews. "I mean, some aren't all that great. Some are *difficult*."

Harrison huffs a laugh, and I barely refrain from glancing his way, just to see his smile.

"But *I'm* not," Winnie goes on. "And I'm never sticky. Daddy can tell you that."

"Is that so?" I say, finally looking over at Harrison. His eyes are already on me, full of something vulnerable that makes my chest twinge. Returning my gaze to Winnie, I ask, "Even after cake?"

"Huh?" Winnie asks, perking up, as I knew she would.

I give her an exaggerated shrug. "Well, see, I brought cake. But I dunno if it's the kind for kids."

"*All* kinds of cake are for kids," Winnie says, turning in her seat and popping up on her knees. She scans the kitchen until she finds the cake box, and then her head whips Harrison's way.

"Not until after dinner," he says.

Winnie huffs, but she sits back down, quickly shoveling more fruit into her mouth.

"And some veggies," Harrison says, brow raised.

She looks incredibly disappointed but eats a cucumber from the mostly untouched salad on her plate.

As Winnie races to finish her food, I ask Harrison a little more about the practice he works at, finding out he deals with small animals at the hospital but is the only veterinarian on staff who also does large animal house calls. He asks a little about my job, too, and I fill him in on what my typical day looks like working for Animal Control.

By the time my plate is empty and our conversation comes to a lull, Winnie is bouncing in her seat.

"Okay," Harrison says, answering her unspoken question.

Winnie shoots up off her chair, sending it screeching back. Tigger jumps up in surprise, but Harrison gets up at a more sedate pace, chuckling slightly as he follows his daughter over to the counter.

I watch, insides doing all sorts of funny little things, as Harrison helps Winnie cut a portion of cake. He's so much bigger than her, his body broad and tall and hers slight and almost delicate. And yet there's no doubt in my mind they're part of the same whole. A matching set, and they always will be.

It makes me wonder if there's room for anyone else.

When Winnie shuffles back to the table, a frosting-covered finger in her mouth, I can't help but smile.

"Want a piece, Sam?" Harrison asks.

"Please."

Harrison comes back with two small plates and sets one in front of me.

"Winnie," Harrison says pointedly, interrupting his daughter's absolute annihilation of the cake on her plate. Girl's got style.

Winnie slows her eating and looks at me. "Thank you, Sam," she says politely before going back to her food.

Harrison gives me a small smile. "Thanks, Sam."

"'Course," I say, chest warm as I eat my own slice of vanilla cream cake.

When our desserts are finished, Winnie jumps right up and makes her way to the sink, washing her hands for a particularly long time. I can't help but wonder if it's because of my sticky comment. I help carry dishes to the counter, but before the table is fully cleared, Winnie bounds over.

"Can I show Sam my fort, Daddy?" Winnie asks, much to my, and I think Harrison's, surprise.

Harrison looks at his daughter for a moment before saying, "Sure, Pumpkin."

Winnie grabs my hand, giving me a strong tug, and, slightly bewildered, I follow her out of the kitchen. I glance back before we turn the corner, and Harrison is wearing some sort of expression I'm not sure how to decipher.

When we get to the entrance of the fort, Winnie drops my hand and climbs inside. I hold the sheet open, following her as Tigger brushes past me. The dog settles immediately on a big, flat pillow, and I let loose a "*Woah.*"

Inside the patchwork of strung-up sheets is a night-light of sorts, projecting soft yellow stars all along the walls and top of the fort. There are pillows and blankets covering the ground, and a few books stacked in one corner. Winnie takes a seat, legs crossed in front of her, and grabs a book.

"Do you like stories?" she asks me.

"I do," I answer, deciding to lie down on my back instead of staying hunched over. The fort is pretty wide but not that tall. The pillows are plenty soft beneath me, though, and the stars flicker above as Winnie opens her book.

Without hesitation, she starts to read. She stumbles on a word every once in a while but always manages to correct herself, and I watch the little blonde girl, wondering how, in the span of a single evening, I've managed to find myself in such unexpected company.

"Sam," she says, stopping suddenly.

"Yeah?" I ask, hands folded on my chest, head turned her way.

"Are you and Daddy friends?"

I don't know exactly how to answer her. I want to be more than that, and I think there's a good chance Harrison and I are headed that way. But this *does* complicate things, the fact that Harrison is a single parent. The fact that he didn't tell me.

In the end, I answer her as truthfully and simply as I can. "Yeah, we're friends."

Winnie nods slowly at that, eyes on her book. "Does that mean we're gonna be friends?"

My lips pull at the corner. "Well, I dunno. D'you wanna be?"

She ponders that for a long moment. "I'm not sure yet."

"That's all right," I tell her.

After a moment, she says, "If I'm your friend, will you bring me more cake?"

I huff a laugh. "I could do that."

"Okay," she replies, voice like a whisper.

"Okay, then." When Winnie doesn't say anything else, I bop her knee. "How about we finish that story? I wanna know how it ends."

Winnie nods and continues to read, and I look up at the blanket of stars shimmering all around us. Spotting one that's brighter than the others, I make a wish.

CHAPTER 11

Harrison

When I find Sam and Winnie in the living room, they're inside Winnie's fort. Sam's feet are sticking out of the end, and the sight is so damn endearing, I have to cover my mouth, lest I let some sort of sound escape.

My hands are shaking slightly, adrenaline still heightened like it's been ever since Sam arrived. The moment I saw him on my doorstep with that big smile and those warm, brown eyes, my gut swooped, and I knew I'd made a mistake.

Just not the one I thought I had.

I'm glad Sam wasn't upset that I didn't warn him about Winnie. Glad he didn't hoof it out of here the moment he found out. But most of all, I'm glad he called me on it. Because it was an insensitive fucking thing to do, inviting him over here without preparing him for what he'd find.

He has every right to be mad at me. Maybe that's even what I wanted. I can't lose the man if we're never in a relationship to start with, right?

But Sam... No, Sam is inside my daughter's fort, feet sticking out because he's too tall, voice quiet and rumbly as he tells Winnie he liked her book. He didn't run.

I clear my throat. "Winnie, it's time to get ready for bed."

She whines, as I knew she would. "Five more minutes."

"One," I counter.

"Ooh, he sounds serious," Sam says, bringing a smile to my lips.

Winnie says something too quietly for me to hear, and I wait while she milks every last second of her final minute. When I clear my throat again, she reluctantly emerges from the sheets.

"Cleanup, first," I remind her, heading to one corner of the fort.

Winnie nods, grabbing an end and tugging. Sam's face appears below me, and he grins. Right before the rest of the fort comes toppling down on his head.

Tigger rushes from the mess of blankets, sheets, and couch pillows, tongue out, and Sam groans in a theatrical manner, his feet kicking feebly.

I snort. "Oh no," I deadpan. "We've squashed him."

"It's just blankets, Sam," Winnie says, entirely unconcerned about Sam's apparent peril. But she does climb onto the mess to try to pull the sheets off his face, and that's when Sam groans for real.

I cover my mouth again, holding in my laughter at what I'm assuming, based on the shape of the Sam lump, was an unintentional knee to Sam's groin.

When Winnie frees Sam's face, his lips are pressed tightly together.

"Okay, Sam?" I ask, a little laughter bleeding through my tone.

He nods a tiny bit, opening his eyes and blinking up at me. And *oh*. Damn, do I want to kiss that man. I want to throw myself down on top of him, blankets and all, and thank him for staying. I want to tell him he'll probably regret it. I want to warn him and beg him in equal measure because it's been a long damn time since I've felt like this.

It's not even a monumental feeling, what's stirring inside. It's this tiny seed, sun-starved and dehydrated. It's hope and *want*. And I'm scared to feed it. Scared to let it grow.

Sam gives me a look as he sits up, brushing sheets and pillows off his body. I wonder if he can read whatever is on my face. I focus on helping put the couches back together as Winnie stores her books and night-light on the toy shelves. Sam folds blankets and sheets, and before long, we're done.

"Winnie," I say. "Why don't you head upstairs and pick out pajamas? I'll be up in a minute, okay?"

"Okay, Daddy," she says, hopping off and taking each stair one at a time, thumping in a way that tells me she's jumping from step to step.

I wait until Winnie is firmly up the stairs before facing Sam. He's watching me with far more patience than I deserve.

"I know we need to talk," I say, feeling a curl of guilt, once again, in my stomach. "But this might take a while with Winnie."

"I'll wait," Sam says. "I don't mind."

I puff out a breath, eyes stinging a little. Now that there's a very real chance I might actually lose this man I barely know, I'm dreading it. I wasn't looking for *more*. I'd resigned myself against it.

But then Sam burst into my life, not once, but twice. For whatever reason, he *wants* me. And I want him, too. I can't even deny that. I want to *try*. I want to latch onto that hope inside my chest and see where we could go.

But Sam might choose to pass on all of this. It's not what he signed up for, and I wouldn't blame him if it's not what he wants. I wouldn't blame him for leaving, especially after how I acted.

I fucked up.

"Harrison," Sam says gently, walking close. He takes my hand, such a simple, soft gesture. "It'll be all right. I'm not goin' anywhere. We'll figure it out."

Could it really be that simple?

"Can I kiss you?" he asks.

My breath hitches. "You really want to?"

That smile of his turns up at the corner. "Yeah, stud. I really do."

I grab the back of Sam's neck, tugging him in, and his arms come around me, locking me in place as his mouth meets mine. He tastes like vanilla, like everything that's good and sweet in the world. He tastes like a million wicked, perfect promises, and I drink them down, begging for more.

How? Why this man? Could we work? Is it too much to ask for?

Am I only setting myself up for disappointment?

Shoving every single doubt away and telling them to fuck off for good measure, I grab a hold of what's in front of me—literally. I run my hands over Sam's short, sexy hair, wishing, for the briefest of moments, that I could feel it on the insides of my thighs. He hums, as if he knows what I'm thinking, and I damn near whine, desperate for this man to make me *feel* again.

But I have Winnie's bedtime to do. And I'm not quite ready for Sam to spend the night. It's too soon for that.

So, easing back, I force myself to let go of the temptation named Sam, and I blow out a little breath. "I need to..."

He nods, giving my arm a gentle, playful push. "Go on."

Turning, I head toward the stairs. When I glance back, Sam is plopping onto the couch. Tigger jumps up next to him, and Sam strokes her fur as he coos over my dog.

Winnie is already in her pajamas when I get to her room. She's lying in bed, flipping through a book, and when I give her door a little rap, she looks up.

"Come on, Pumpkin," I say. "Teeth and hair."

She nods, rolling out of bed and following me to the bathroom. After detangling the billion knots in her hair and brushing her teeth, we head back to her bedroom. Winnie already has a stack of three books picked out for me to read, and I huff a little laugh. It's scary how organized my child can be when it comes to her getting the things she wants.

"Which one first?" I ask, taking a seat at her headboard. She sits beside me.

"Is Sam your boyfriend?" she asks.

Well, shit. Should've known that was coming.

"Right now, we're just friends," I answer. I know it's an incomplete truth, but I'm not ready to get Winnie's hopes up before I know where Sam and I stand. I don't want her getting attached only for things to end.

Although she never much liked any of my boyfriends in the past. Sam, though. Sam is damn likable.

"Okay," Winnie says simply before pointing to one of the books.

Conversation over for now, I start to read. Tigger joins us soon enough, like she always does, but it takes all three stories, ten minutes of reassurance that I'm not going anywhere tonight, and another thirty minutes of staying by Winnie's side before she's finally asleep. I ease out of her bedroom slowly, avoiding the floorboard that creaks.

Once I'm out the door, leaving it cracked enough for Tigger to get through should she need to, my shoulders relax. When I get downstairs, Sam is right where I left him on the couch. The TV is on, sound low, but he turns it off, angling my way as I approach.

He's always so...tuned in. Body language open and inviting. Expression welcoming. It makes it easy to take a seat directly beside him, close enough to touch. Sam takes that opportunity, placing his hand gently on my bent knee.

"I'm sorry that took so long," I say, readying myself for a lengthy apology.

But Sam shakes his head. "D'you always apologize for bein' a good father?"

Well, shit.

"It's fine," Sam goes on. "She's asleep now?"

"Yeah," I answer. "It takes a while sometimes. She...she's scared of me leaving. Scared I'll be gone when she wakes up."

Sam's eyes soften at that.

"It's part of why we got Tigger in the first place," I say. "I thought having company at night would help."

"Does it?" he asks.

"I think so? Sometimes? She doesn't wake up as much in the middle of the night as she used to. It's just getting her down that's hard. And maybe me staying until she's asleep makes it worse—"

Sam squeezes my knee, gently cutting me off. "No. It makes her feel safe, and that's most important. She knows her dad will be there when she needs him."

My eyes sting, and I blink a couple times. "You don't hate kids," I state, recalling our conversation at dinner when Sam told Winnie that very thing.

Sam snorts, fingers drifting idly over my leg. "No, I don't. I like kids a lot."

I nod. I can tell.

And there goes that little feeling inside my chest again.

"Did I pass your test?" Sam asks, the words a shock. "That's what it was, right?" He watches me closely, eyes intent on my face, and I don't know what to say.

"I..."

Maybe it was, but not intentionally. I didn't set out to put Sam to the test when he showed up here tonight, and yet that's exactly what I did, didn't I?

"Y'know what I find interestin'?" Sam says softly, lips twitching a little. "You didn't want me to fail. You told me to bring cake."

Fuck, I did.

"You wanted her to like me," he adds.

I can't deny it. Any of it. Can't deny I set Sam up to be surprised tonight, even though it wasn't conscious on my part. Can't deny I wanted to see how he'd react to the reality of my life. Can't deny part of me wanted him to fail because that'd be the easy way out. You can't get hurt if you never *try*.

But what I can't deny the most is that I'm so very glad Sam stuck. And that yes, I told him to bring cake because it's Winnie's favorite.

"I think," I say slowly, throat clicking when I swallow. "I think you see me, Sam."

He grins like that's the best thing I could have said. "I like what I see, Harrison," he responds, voice rumbling in a way that *does* things to me. *Sam* does things to me. He has from the beginning. "I'd like to date you."

"Still?" I ask. "After tonight?"

"Still."

"I'm a package deal," I point out.

"I know that," he says with a little huff of laughter.

I rub my neck, chest feeling hot. "My life is messy, Sam. Really fucking messy. I can't go out at night and miss family dinners. I have to drop my daughter off at school early and pick her up again right after work. There's homework and bake sales and play dates and making goddamn volcanoes in the kitchen. Do you know how much baking soda I keep in stock? Our dates would include Winnie, and we'd have to be careful. We wouldn't be able to fuck around whenever we want. Not like in Plum Valley. It wouldn't be easy. Nothing in my life is *easy*. It's one big mess."

When I finish my rant, Sam's brown eyes are soft. My pulse is still skipping a little wildly, but Sam's lips lift into a gentle smile.

"I like messy, Harrison," he says evenly. "What you just described? I never had that. I was in foster care my entire childhood. I never got to make volcanoes in the kitchen. Never had suppers with family that was my own. I don't need easy. Nothin' in my life has been easy, either. But... I think I could help with the mess if you'd let me."

Fuck. *Fuck*.

My throat is tight when I speak. "This might be a bad idea, Sam. I'm fragile."

It's hard to admit, but it's the truth, and he needs to know it. Because if we do this—if we *try*—and I get attached to this beautiful man who keeps pulling back layers and making me want him more, it could end badly for me. I've had my heart shattered before. And now, it's a patchwork of mended lines that don't quite fit together the way they once did.

Entering a relationship isn't a decision I can afford to make lightly. Not only because I'm a single parent whose child is always going to come first. But because of that glass heart inside my chest.

Sam hums a quiet sigh of sorts. "I'm fragile, too, Harrison. I think I'm a little more like Winnie than you may realize. I don't... I don't take abandonment well."

My chest clenches. It's not hard to guess why. Sam didn't have parents.

He's more similar to Winnie than he realizes.

"What if we hurt each other?" I ask softly.

"What if we don't?" he counters.

"My daughter..."

"I know, Harrison," Sam says gently, shifting a little on the couch. He comes closer, threading his fingers through the hair at the side of my head. "I'm not askin' you to pick me over Winnie. I never would. All I'm askin' is that you don't push me away." He's quiet for a moment before he adds, "And that you're honest with me."

I blow out a breath, nodding. "Exclusivity?" I ask. I don't want to worry about potential STIs on top of everything else.

Sam's face spreads into a slow grin. "Yeah."

"And, uh...I'm not ready for overnights yet," I say. "We need to go slow around Winnie."

He nods, fingers toying with my ear. "Mkay."

"And, uh..." My eyes drift shut. "Um."

Sam's lips ghost over my own. "One step at a time," he says.

He gives me a soft kiss before leaning back, and I open my eyes. How does he make it feel so easy?

"Tell me something," I say. Because even though I'm not ready for Sam to stay over quite yet, I'm not ready for goodnight, either.

Sam grins, hand falling back to my leg. "I've never broken a bone."

"No?" I ask with a chuckle, grateful for the levity.

He shakes his head, toying with my thigh casually, fingers running over my jeans. "No, which is a miracle, really. I was always movin', always gettin' into trouble as a kid. Fell from a couple trees. Crashed my foster carer's bike. All sorts of stuff. But never broke a bone."

"Well, I hope Winnie has your luck. I'm just waiting for her to break something," I admit.

"She a little daredevil?" he asks.

"Like you wouldn't believe," I answer. No fear, that one.

Sam smiles, and it feels nice to be able to talk to him about my daughter. To share that part of my life.

It's a little surreal that he wants me to. I wouldn't have anticipated that this happy-go-lucky guy I met in Plum Valley would be here with me now. That he'd be so unexpectedly even-keeled and compassionate—and a little vulnerable himself—under all that cheery glow.

I never would have guessed that one missed hookup could have led to all...this.

"Your turn," Sam prods gently after a moment.

I think about it before answering. "My sweet tooth might be worse than Winnie's."

Sam barks a laugh, and I grin with him. "I'm gonna have to keep you two stocked in treats, aren't I?" he says. "All right, stud. Good to know."

Sam keeps talking about cake and sweets as he settles against the couch, giving me a little tug to settle in with him. And as I lean against Sam's chest, feeling his laughter and words vibrate through me like a gentle quake, I let that little seed inside my chest grow.

CHAPTER 12

✦

Sammy

"You hummin' again, Sammy?" Carl asks.

I shrug, a grin on my face. "Maybe. Gotta problem with that?"

He glances at me from the driver's side of the truck. We're on our way back to Animal Control, and despite the temperate day, I'm a dirty, sweaty mess. Our afternoon was spent digging up an underground pipe to rescue the little peeping chick trapped inside.

Some days, I tell ya.

"No problem," Carl answers. "Just curious about the good mood. Does it have somethin' to do with that Doctor Bailey?"

My grin widens as I remember the way Harrison sent me off the other night. Despite the relatively serious tone of our first date—and the unexpected complications—I consider it a success. Plus, the way he kissed me before I left? How he pressed me up against his front door, hands cradling my face as if I were something precious he'd found and didn't want to part with?

I sigh wistfully. "I swear, Carl. I'm gonna do so many dirty things to that man."

Carl sputters, and I thump him on the chest.

"Respectfully," I clarify, in case my coworker wasn't sure.

He huffs, shaking his head. "Jesus, Sammy. The things that come outta your mouth sometimes."

I snort. Harrison said nearly the same thing.

"He's somethin' special, Carl. He's so good and kind and gentle. But also strung tight, y'know? I wanna help him unwind. With the dirty things," I explain.

Carl groans.

"But beyond that," I add. "I dunno... I really think there could be somethin' there."

Harrison is also scared and cautious, and now I understand why. He has a daughter to think about. An entire life, structured just so before I came into it. I'm essentially a stranger, and I could mess up his already messy existence.

But I don't want to do that. I don't want to make things any harder for Harrison than they currently are. I just want to be there. With him. For him, if he'll let me. True, I barely know the man. But we're getting there, one step at a time. And each step makes me want more.

Carl pulls into a spot in our parking lot, but he doesn't move once he shuts off the truck, instead staring out the window.

"Somethin' wrong?" I ask.

He turns toward me, expression pinched. Serious. "It's just... You have a tendency to rush into these things. And I don't wanna see you get hurt."

I give my friend an understanding smile. Carl and I may goof around a good bit of the time, but he always has my back. I have his, too.

"I appreciate that," I tell him. "I really do. But you gotta understand. I don't know how *not* to try with everythin' I've got."

He sighs a little. "I know. I know that, Sammy. It's admirable. It is."

"But you think it's foolish, too."

"Not foolish," he says quickly. "But you could...I dunno, ease into your relationships a li'l slower, y'know? Feel the person out more before you get too attached."

He winces a little after he says that, but I don't mind his honesty. I do get attached. And I have a history of falling faster than my partners do. Maybe Carl's right, that I should take things slower. Walk instead of run. But...

"If I hold back, I'm not givin' them my true self. One day, I'll find that man who loves me for me. And until then, I'm gonna give it my all. They deserve that. I do, too." I blow out a breath, and Carl watches me patiently. "Doctor Bailey might not be that man," I concede. "But what if he is? He *could* be. And I wanna find out."

Carl nods before squeezing my shoulder. "Yeah, Sammy. I hear you. I just hope this Doctor Bailey treats you right."

I give Carl a little grin. "Gonna give 'im the talk for me, Carl? A li'l *you hurt my boy, and I'm comin' for ya?*"

Carl shakes his head before pushing his door open and getting out of the truck.

"No?" I ask after him. "What about the safe sex spiel? We're definitely gonna be needin' condoms. Lots of 'em. Y'know, 'cause of all the dirty things!"

Carl groans, slamming his door shut and walking away. I chuckle as I follow him out of the vehicle.

"Seein' him tonight?" he asks as we approach the building.

"Mhm. Goin' over for supper." After a pause, I add, "He's got a daughter."

Carl's head whips my way fast, eyes wide in surprise. "He does?"

"Yeah," I say, puffing out a laugh as I think about Winnie. "Her name is Winifred. Ten years old. She's a tiny spitfire."

But cautious, like her dad.

Carl nods, opening the door, and I follow him inside. He stops in the empty hallway, turning to me. "Be careful, Sammy."

There's that concern again. That crease in his brow.

"I'll try," I tell him. It's the best I can do.

He sighs but doesn't say anything more before pushing into our employee break room. As Carl clocks out near the lockers, I head to the shower inside the small, adjoining bathroom to wash up so I don't have to make a trip home. That lets me get to Harrison's a whole half hour early, and when I arrive at five-thirty on the dot, I use the big gold knocker at the front of his house to signal my arrival. Not ten seconds later, the door opens, and a pair of light blue eyes stare up at me.

"Sam," Winnie says seriously, appraising me.

"Hi, Miss Winifred," I reply, giving her my best smile. "Can I come in?"

"Suppose so," she mutters before taking a step back.

I hold in my chuckle. "Where's your daddy?"

Oh, shit. Yeah, no. I don't think I can call Harrison that.

Winnie points toward the kitchen just as Harrison's "Sam?" rings out from that very direction. He peeks around the corner not a moment later. "You're early."

"Hope that's all right," I say, eyes tracking over his form. He has a small towel hanging over his shoulder and some flour dusted on his hands. His shirt is plaid again today—he seems to favor those—and the sleeves are rolled up to his elbows. *God*, he looks good.

"Sure, that's fine," he replies, a small smile lighting his face.

Nails tap against the floor as Tigger emerges from the kitchen, rounding Harrison. The dog comes right over to me, stubby tail wagging, and then she sits and waits patiently for some lovin'.

"Aren't you just the best girl," I say, going down on one knee to give her some rubs. Her tongue lolls out, doggy breath fanning over my face as I scratch over her neck and down her sides. "Such good manners. Your humans taught you well, huh?"

I give her a few more pats, and when I pop back up onto my feet, Harrison is watching me. As is Winnie.

"So, uh," I say, clapping my hands together. "What's goin' on? Anythin' I can do?"

Winnie turns, heading for the back door. "I'm gonna play outside with Tigger," she announces before stepping through the door at the end of the hall. The Brittany Spaniel takes off after her, abandoning me for greener pastures.

"All right, then," I mumble when the door slams shut. I turn my focus back to Harrison. "Did I do somethin' wrong?"

He licks his lips slowly. "No, Sam. You didn't." Giving me a little curling wave, he beckons me to follow. "Come on, I'm making dinner."

Harrison heads back into the kitchen, and I trail after him. A pile of dough is resting over a generous sprinkling of flour on the counter, and when Harrison stops in front of it, I can't resist stepping up right behind him. Hands on the counter to either side of his body, I tuck my face against his neck, and Harrison deflates, his body melting on a sigh as I pepper a kiss against his skin.

"Mm," I hum. He smells like melon again. Delicious.

"I'm making biscuits," he says, although he doesn't move an inch, except to lean his head more to the side.

I take up his unspoken offer, drifting my lips over the column of his neck. I'd slip my hand to his crotch if I thought it would be welcome. But I know Harrison wouldn't want me to do that. Not right now.

So, instead, I settle for swiping my tongue against his skin. I can't taste the melon, unfortunately, but Harrison sure is sweet. He shivers a little, a simple "*Sam*" leaving his lips.

"I like biscuits," I say, stepping back and putting a little space between us.

Harrison nods, hands held in front of him for a moment. After a beat, he seems to shake himself off, and then he starts to work the dough, flattening it and then folding it over on itself several times. I settle beside him, watching him work and taking in the space a little better than the first time I was here. The walls of the kitchen are a warm, sunny yellow, and the cabinets and countertops are white. A big window looks out over the backyard, where I can see Winnie and Tigger playing, and the evening sun slants in at an angle, giving the room a gentle glow.

I like it in here. It's bright and worn in a touch, and it feels welcoming. Like a place for family.

"I haven't done this in a long time," Harrison finally says, looking my way.

"Haven't what?"

"Dated," he answers. He rubs his nose with the back of his wrist, leaving a small white spot behind. "It's been years."

"All right," I say, hoping my tone lets him know I have no problem with that.

"Sex, too," he adds, pressing the dough down with the heels of his hands.

That gives me pause, and Harrison senses it. He looks over at me again.

"You're the first person I've been with in four years," he says.

Oh wow. That's...wow. I can't deny I get a little thrill at that fact, and yet...

"Damn it, Harrison," I mutter before sparing a glance out the window to confirm Winnie's whereabouts. "I wasn't gentle with you."

"I didn't want you to be," he replies.

I groan, rubbing my eyes. "I fucked you over the hood of a goddamn ridin' lawn mower. It was dusty and dirty and smelled like motor oil. There's nothin' romantic about that." *Christ.* "We're doin' it in a bed next time."

Harrison's eyes are full of mirth when I drop my hand from my face. "You won't hear me complaining about that," he says. "But Sam? You're doing just fine romancing me."

"Yeah?" I ask, a smile blooming over my face.

Harrison nods, patting the layered biscuit dough flat. He grabs a knife and cuts it into squares instead of circles. "Get me a sheet pan from below the oven?" he asks.

I nod and do as he says. Harrison rounds the pieces of dough with his hands before placing them on the sheet pan, and then he washes up in the sink. I know Harrison said our dates would be like this most of the time—fit into his lifestyle with Winnie. And I don't mind that one bit. I *like* that. But it does leave me wondering what Harrison would choose to do if he could.

"Hey, Harrison?"

He turns off the faucet, back shaking the tiniest bit before he lets out a happy hum and turns my way. "Yeah, Sam?"

"If you had one night to do anythin' you wanted, no responsibilities in your way, what would you do?"

Harrison thinks that over for a long moment, chewing his lip as he stares at a spot over my shoulder. Finally, those light blue eyes meet my gaze, and he says, "I'd go get a beer."

"Really?" I ask with a laugh.

"Yeah," he says, chuckling with me. "I haven't gone out to a bar in so damn long. And I would've with you in Plum Valley if we hadn't, you know..."

I nod. If we hadn't gone back to his place instead.

"It sounds so simple," he goes on. "But... You become a parent, and everything in your life rearranges. There's always this other person whose priorities come first. When Winnie was a baby, I couldn't even pee when I wanted to. I didn't dare chance it if I was feeding her or rocking her to sleep because if I stopped, all hell would break loose. It wasn't worth it, so my bladder came second, not first. I never realized, before becoming a dad, how much of my own independence I would be sacrificing on a daily basis. It's all the tiny things you take for granted that you can never get back."

Harrison licks his lips, and I can tell there's more he wants to say, so I keep quiet, watching him gently.

"I wouldn't erase my daughter," he says vehemently, even as his voice shakes a little. "I would never undo Winnie. But I'm no longer just Harrison. The moment she came into my world, I became a dad, first and foremost. That's who I am now. My needs, my wants, they come second to her. So yeah, a beer isn't much, but it's the simplest things I miss the most. Using the bathroom when I want to. Eating the last slice of cake. Going to the bar." After a moment, he adds, quietly, "Sex."

My throat clicks when I swallow, and Harrison's eyes track me as I close the distance between us. I take his face in my hands, fingers curling at the back of his neck. Harrison's mouth pops open the tiniest bit.

"I think," I say gently, placing a kiss on his cheek, right above my thumb, "you are a wonderful father." I move to his other cheek, kissing there, too. "I also think you deserve to come first every once in a while."

Harrison's hands encircle my wrists. "I can't," he says.

My breath stutters a little, and I pull back to look Harrison in the eyes. "If you can't put yourself first, let me."

He sucks in a breath. "Sam—"

"Daddy," Winnie calls out a second before the back door slams.

Harrison stiffens, and I let him go, taking a step back as his ten-year-old mini-me comes racing into the room, dog beside her. Both are caked in dirt, and I cover my mouth to keep from laughing.

"We got a little messy," Winnie says, "but it wasn't my fault, I swear. Tigger wanted to investigate some chirping behind the bushes. I just followed to make sure she didn't get into trouble." She pauses. "Are we in trouble?"

Harrison's lips twist, and it looks like he's battling his own laughter. "You're not in trouble, Pumpkin. What was the chirping?"

Winnie lets out a big gust of air before throwing her arms up. "I don't even know! It was gone when we got there."

"All right," Harrison says, crossing his arms casually, a little smile on his face. "Why don't you and Tigger head upstairs? You can give her a bath first. Then yourself."

The little blonde groans. "Why do I gotta—" At Harrison's raised brow, Winnie sighs. "*Fine*."

She tromps off toward the stairs, calling for Tigger to follow, and dirty human and dog disappear from sight. I swear I hear "*not fudging fair*" as footsteps hammer up the stairs.

"Oh my God," I mutter, eyes wide. "There was dirt in her ear. Her *ear*, Harrison. She was outside for ten minutes. How the heck did that happen?"

"I don't know," he says, shaking with laughter. "I really don't. It's a talent."

"I'd say," I agree.

Turning, Harrison grabs the tray of biscuits and pops them in the oven. He sets the timer before grabbing a pan and putting it on the stovetop. He pauses then, looking toward me. "I'm sorry."

"For what?" I ask.

"For freezing when she came inside."

"Harrison," I say gently, heading back his way. "You're not ready for PDA in front of your daughter. You already told me that, and I respect it. I'm not gonna push."

He sighs a little, reaching for my hand. Much to my surprise, he tugs me closer and then curls his fingers through my belt loops, holding me in place. "You make it so easy, Sam."

"It doesn't have to be difficult," I reply.

Harrison's brow crinkles at that.

"It doesn't," I say, resting my weight against his body, hands on the counter beside his hips. "I like you, Harrison. You gave me boundaries, and I heard you. So I'm not gonna kiss you unless we're alone"—I punctuate my point with a featherlight brush of my lips against his—"and I'm not gonna stay the night until you ask me to. But, stud?"

"Yeah?" Harrison asks a little breathily.

"I really hope you let me into your bed soon. 'Cause I want my mouth on you, every piece of you. I wanna suck down your cock. I wanna hear your moans. I wanna bite your damn ass until you muffle your cries into the pillow."

Harrison curses, eyes on my lips.

"Your needs and wants?" I tell him softly. "They matter."

I'm not a parent, no. But the idea that this man has felt alone for so long... That he hasn't had anyone to care for him, even in the smallest of ways, while he's been taking care of his family? It makes me damn sad.

"*You* matter," I add. "It doesn't have to be all or nothin'. You can have things that are just for you, too. Lemme give you that."

He lets out a big, shuddering breath. It takes a moment before he speaks. "Sammy?"

"Yeah?" I ask brightly, stomach flipping.

He runs his thumbs along the top of my waistband, right near my hipbones. "You can bite my ass. So long as I can bite yours, too."

My cock kicks up, and I'm positive Harrison feels it. He smirks a little.

"Bite my ass anytime," I tell him.

He hums before letting go. "Dinner first."

Insides fizzing, I step back so Harrison can start cooking bacon on the stove. And as I whip up some eggs the way Harrison requests, my mind runs over all the ways I can help this man let go of his burdens.

At least for a little while.

CHAPTER 13

Harrison

When I ease Winnie's door partway shut, I listen for a couple seconds to make sure she doesn't wake up. My heart is pounding, making it hard to hear anything else. But after I'm sure she's well and truly down for the night, I make a pitstop in the bathroom, and then I head downstairs to find Sam.

He's on the couch again, posture relaxed as he flips through a magazine, but he looks up immediately when I step into the room, giving me an easy smile.

So transparent.

"Sam," I say, cocking my head toward the stairs.

He doesn't have to be told twice. Sam drops the magazine, swings off the couch, and passes me by, jogging lightly up the stairs. I huff a laugh at his retreating form.

When I get to my bedroom, Sam is already inside, standing in front of my dresser and looking at a picture of me holding a baby Winnie. There's a soft smile on his face, and it makes my throat close up a bit. When I lock the door, Sam's head swings my way.

"Hey," he says quietly, walking right into my space. I lean against the door as Sam lifts his hands to my face, cradling me for the briefest of moments before his lips press to mine.

I make a sound, the tiniest kind, and Sam rumbles in response, kissing me as if it's all he wants. As if it's all he's wanted since the last time we were connected this way. It's sweet and coaxing, but after Sam's impassioned words this evening, I don't need any coaxing. Not in this.

Grabbing a hold of him, I walk Sam backwards until he hits the bed. He *oofs* in surprise when I shove him flat, but there's a grin on his face as I climb over his body, reconnecting our mouths in an instant. He moans against me, the sound turning into a grunt when I pin his wrists flat to the bed.

"Mm-hm," he says against my mouth, voicing his approval as I rut against him. He meets my movements, our crotches rubbing together, both of us chasing friction on our cocks through the material of our clothes.

Abandoning Sam's wrists for his fly, I lean up enough to open his jeans. His eyes are dark and wide in excitement, and the moment I get him undressed enough to close my hand around his cock, he groans.

"Shh," I remind him, giving him a couple slow strokes. The weight of him in my hand is heady, and heat settles in my stomach as Sam hitches his hips into my grip.

I could take him apart just like this—slowly, methodically—but part of me is worried we won't have the time. That this will be the night Winnie wakes, looking for me. The other part of me... Well, the other part is desperate to see this man fully naked before the night is over. We didn't get the chance during our quickie in the shed.

With that in mind, I grab Sam's waistband and tug. Sliding off the bed, I take his pants and underwear with me, pulling them neatly down his legs. His socks go next, and by the time my gaze rises to take him in, Sam has removed his own t-shirt, leaving him stark naked, up on his elbows on my bed.

I drink him in. The smattering of dark hair on his chest. The trail that leads down his stomach. The damn six-pack I just knew was going to be there. His cock, standing hard and flushed a beautiful pink. And... Oh. The tattoo sitting along his hip.

"Told you I had one," Sam says as I step closer.

"What is it?" I ask, tracing the seven small, irregular dots that remind me of stars.

"The Big Dipper," he answers, giving me a slight shrug when I look at him questioningly. "I like lookin' at the stars."

I hum, a million questions entering my mind, but Sam reaches for me. "Get undressed, Harrison," he practically pleads. "I'm dyin' over here."

Huffing a laugh, I shuck my clothes. Sam watches all the while, his gaze on me hot. He rumbles when I finally drop my briefs, and *God*, I love that sound. I want to hear this man purr for me. I want to hear him *growl*.

When I climb back over Sam's body, the both of us naked, he watches me carefully. I can tell he's waiting to see what I'll do. He's sizing me up after the way I manhandled him onto the bed. He's ready to let me lead, and I know he would do just that if it's what I wanted.

I grab his wrists again, slowly, wrapping my fingers around him tight. He grunts slightly as I rub our bare dicks together. He's hard against me—hard everywhere. His dick. His stomach. His thick fucking thighs.

"Sam," I say gently, leaning down to nip at his ear. "You're letting me win."

His hands twitch. I can feel it in the way his muscles bunch under my grip. He's still for a moment, processing, and then he tugs his arms down. He gets pretty far, too, nearly loosening my hold, but I slam his wrists back against the mattress, pinning him down tight as I rub against him.

"Thought you said you wanted your mouth on me," I taunt, sliding my lips down his neck. I inhale greedily, and Sam infiltrates my lungs. He smells like sunshine. Like fresh air and an honest day's work. I give his skin a kiss. "What are you waiting for?"

Sam takes and expels a breath. And then he moves.

Before I can count to two, I'm flat on my back, and Sam is claiming my mouth like he has every right to it. It's hungry and near bruising, and I don't know that I've ever felt anything more perfect. The startling thought lasts only a moment before Sam is moving down my body, one of *his* hands holding my wrists tight, his other sliding to my neck as he trails his mouth lower. My heart thumps a heavy, thrilling beat as he licks against the hollow of my throat.

"Stud," he drawls, the word gravelly. "I wanna do so many wicked things to you."

God, yes.

His thumb presses up against the underside of my jaw, lifting my head, and Sam licks up the length of my neck. He closes his teeth gently over my chin, and I instinctually tug my hands, but Sam simply tightens his grip.

"Not done," he says, running his thumb along my neck as his lips travel lower. My pulse hammers, and I wonder if he can feel it. I wonder if he can tell exactly how damn turned on I am right now.

Sam detours down my chest, laying little kisses across my pecs, flicking the skin with the tip of his tongue. Even his torture is playful. And goddamn *filthy* with the way that tongue of his moves. With one hand holding my wrists, the other wrapped possessively around my neck, Sam pulls my nipple into his mouth, and I damn near shoot off the bed.

"Shh," he reminds me, chuckling darkly as I muffle my moan against the side of my arm. Sam flicks my nipple with his tongue, draws a circle around it, and then blows against the skin.

"*Fuck*," I mutter, squirming. "*Sam*."

"Hm?" he hums, dragging his lips to the other side of my chest. He gives that nipple a closed-mouth kiss. "You wanna fight me some more, or are you gonna let me worship you?"

Shit, what can I even say to that?

I know he's giving me the choice, too. They're not idle words. I can tell Sam isn't the type of guy who *needs* dominance in the bedroom. But he's happy to have it, and he'll do all sorts of wonderful things to my body if I just let him.

Sometimes I like the fight. But sometimes, I just want... I just...

My hands relax against the bed before I've made the conscious decision, and Sam rumbles against my nipple, the vibration of it sending a shock of energy down my spine.

"Good choice," Sam mutters before rolling me swiftly onto my stomach.

I gasp out as Sam's hand presses down on the small of my back, fingers splayed wide to hold me in place.

"Look at you," he says, the words so quiet I wonder if I'm meant to hear them.

Sam does nothing for a beat, and my heart pounds. I have no idea what he's planning, so when his teeth clamp onto the meat of my ass, I nearly shout in surprise. I grab the nearest pillow, stuffing it against my face, and Sam chuckles, his fingers skimming over the mark he surely left on my skin. Both of his hands drag down my thighs next, and his mouth follows, skipping leg to leg as he peppers me with kisses. When he gives the back of my thigh a slap, I'm glad for the pillow between my teeth.

"Up," Sam says.

Scrambling, I get my knees under me, and then there's Sam's stubble, drifting across my ass cheek.

"Rimmin'?" he asks.

A whine precedes my, "*God*, yes. Yes, yes."

Sam must hear me through the pillow because he spreads my cheeks. My breath comes short. Anticipation. Excitement. It's been *so long* since I've had someone—

Ahh.

Sam's tongue drags bluntly across my rim, and I moan loudly into the pillow. He rumbles again, fingertips digging into my ass cheeks, and then, he sets to work. I have never had to try so damn hard to keep my noises in check before, but it's all I can do not to scream my appreciation for Sam's wicked fucking tongue as he reduces me to a puddle of needy, aching mush.

"Sammy," I groan, not sure whether I want *more* of this torment or less. Whether I want to come right now or have Sam's face buried in my ass for the next seven days. His bristle has started to burn along my skin, but I don't even care. I'll wear his beard burn like a badge of honor. Seems like a small price to pay for the rimming of a lifetime.

Sam pulls back. "Whatever you want," he says, sounding entirely serious. "Whatever you need."

I move the pillow off my face. "I want... I need..." God, I don't even know.

Sam laves his tongue over me again, slowly, before he gives my ass cheek a little kiss. The next moment, I'm being spun onto my back. I roll easily, no resistance left in my body, and Sam presses my legs wide, his big hands against the inside of my thighs. My chest heaves as he crawls forward, his eyes intent on me all the while. I'm no blushing virgin, but *shit*. Sam's gaze makes me feel like one—like all of this is new. Like I'm young again, experiencing something I just know will rock me to my core.

Sam hooks my legs over his arms, and with a little tug, my knees settle atop his shoulders. I know what's coming a second before Sam acts, but it doesn't make it any less shocking when his tongue licks broadly up my cock. My head hits the mattress, and I stare, blinking up at my white ceiling as Sam engulfs my crown.

"*Ahh, Sam.*"

A pillow lands on my face, and I'd laugh if I wasn't so thankful to have something to muffle my moans because Sam draws more of me into his mouth, and I am *not* quiet. He chuckles against me, the wicked, wicked man, but good grief, I don't care. His mouth feels so good. *So* good. All that heat and pressure surrounding my cock. His tongue deserves an ode for what it's doing to me. *Sam* deserves an ode. The man is... He's...

Mine.

Throwing the pillow off my face, I tell him, "Gonna come."

He doesn't move off my dick, and as I look down at the dark-haired man who spun into my life like a whirling dervish of optimism and filthy promises, my orgasm takes me by force. Sam's cheeks are hollowed as he sucks on the head of my cock, his hand stroking my base, and with a stuttered inhale and the realization that I *want* what this man is offering—that I want to believe, for once, it *could* be this easy—I come blissfully down his throat.

Sam's gaze darkens as he swallows my release, his hand working me all the while, and as soon as I finish shooting, he reaches for his own dick. I'm not having any of that.

"Get the fuck up here," I tell him hoarsely.

Sam's eyes meet mine, and then he drops my legs from his shoulders and crawls up my body. Grabbing the back of his neck, I stare at this man—this lovely, light-souled man—and I bring my mouth to his. He kisses me back feverishly, and I can taste remnants of myself on his tongue as we tangle and dance.

When I can finally feel my legs again, I hook one over his. "Your turn," I tell him, flipping Sam onto his back. He grins, and I press his wrists firmly into the mattress, a demand to stay put. As I move down his body, stomach gliding over his cock, Sam groans. He leaves his arms lax above his head, and it's a gorgeous sight, one I greedily take in as I settle between his legs. His dick is long and curved gently upwards, flushed at the tip, and I take it in hand, running my thumb along the underside.

"Sam," I say gently.

"Yeah," he breathes, head lifted off the bed to look at me.

"What do *you* want?" I ask, pumping him slowly. A bit of precum is smeared over his cockhead, and I spread it down his shaft. It's not enough moisture, though, so I keep my ministrations light.

"I'm not a complicated guy, stud," he says, chest rising and falling. "All I want is you."

My stomach heats as Sam's words settle inside of me, and I know—a sudden, overwhelming realization—that Sam was right. I'm not the only fragile one in this relationship, and despite my own reservations about my readiness for something *more* in my life right now, I can not treat this lightly. I can't be flippant when it comes to Sam.

He's in this. This man is *in* this, and that's as terrifying as it is wonderful.

"Well," I say before swiping my tongue over the tip of Sam's cock. "One thing you should know about me is that I really like dick."

Sam huffs a laugh. "Yeah?"

"Mhm." I wrap my lips around him, sucking just a bit before retreating. Sam puffs out a breath, hips following me. "And you've got a great one. We're going to become well acquainted, me and your dick."

Sam grins at me. "I like this plan. I like it a lot. But, uh, Harrison?" He stutters out a breath when I lick up his shaft. "I'm real damn close, so you might needa do get-to-know-yous another time."

I bite my lip against a laugh. "All right, Sammy. You hold on tight."

He groans out an affirmative as I suck half of his length into my mouth. One of his hands flies to my hair, fingers anchoring in the strands, and my eyes flutter closed, head going all hazy as Sam's carefully restrained noises fill my ears. I open my eyes before long, not wanting to miss a thing. Not wanting to miss the way Sam's abdomen bunches. How those soft brown eyes of his light as I bob up and down on his dick. And certainly not wanting to miss him fall apart, which he does a moment later, his cock thickening in my mouth and his eyes rolling up as he arches and shoots down my throat.

"*Fuuuck*," he groans out quietly before slumping flat.

I give his head one more lick before letting him go, and Sam's fingers rub gently against my scalp. When I climb up

Sam's body, he opens his arm wide, and I settle there at his side, head resting against his bicep.

"Y'know," Sam says, still sounding a little winded. His arm wraps around me. "Anytime you wanna become better acquainted with my dick, you just lemme know. He'll be happy to see you."

I chuckle, insides feeling light and bouncy. "So selfless of him."

"Yeah. He's a good guy."

I slap Sam's chest, and he laughs.

"Roll over," I tell him. "Forgot something."

Sam gives me a curious look, but when I scoot off his arm, he does as I ask, rolling onto his stomach. I take a moment to enjoy the view, in particular the swell of Sam's ass, before leaning down and biting that very thing. Sam half-shouts, half-laughs, and I give him another swat.

"Shh," I say, laughing myself.

He rolls back over, making a grab for me. I let him tug me against his chest, not at all complaining about the landing pad. Sam gives me a grin, and my heart does a funny little jig. Sighing, I relax against Sam's solid chest, letting my fingertips drift along the constellation at his hip.

"Tell me something?" I say. "Before you go?"

Sam exhales, fingers toying with my arm. "I was calf-ropin' champ three years in a row."

"Really?" I say around a laugh. "You did rodeo?"

"Sure did," he answers. "One of my foster carers worked the fairground. I picked it up quick. Was damn good at it, too."

I hum a little, imagining Sam on horseback, roping a calf and then jumping down for the tie-off. He had to have been fast.

The thought makes my heart race.

"Your turn," Sam says.

"Right. I, uh. I think I have a cowboy kink."

Sam barks a laugh before immediately slapping a hand over his mouth. "Seriously?"

I nod, chuckling at Sam's amused expression. "The first time I saw you with that belt buckle and the cowboy hat? Damn near popped a boner."

"You're kiddin' me," he says incredulously. "You sure didn't let on. I had to work hard to get an invite back to your place."

"I know," I say with a huff. "I won't make you work for it anymore, Sam."

He rumbles a little. "I don't mind, Harrison. You're worth it."

Shit.

I kiss Sam's pec. "Tell me something else."

He does, launching into a story about him and Carl rescuing a baby chick just earlier today, and as I listen to his voice resonate up through his chest, I wonder how long I can justify telling my daughter the two of us are just friends.

CHAPTER 14

✦

Sammy

"You again?"

"*Winnie*," Harrison reprimands lightly, jogging down the stairs. He gives me a swift grin that makes my stomach go all gooey before he squeezes his daughter's shoulder. "Let the man in, please. He brought breakfast."

Winnie's eyes dart down to the bags in my hands, calculating. "Cake?" she asks.

"Close," I admit, toeing off my boots. "Waffles."

The little girl perks up immediately, spinning and skipping off toward the kitchen. Tigger stops to give me an enthusiastic hello before chasing after her.

"Morning," Harrison says, stepping in close. Much to my surprise, he gives me a quick kiss.

"Mornin'," I respond cheerfully, happy to see the man again so soon after our date a few days ago. And *really* damn happy Harrison suggested breakfast with his daughter. It feels like he's letting me in.

When Harrison steps back, his gaze drops to my bags, much as his daughter's did. His lips quirk a little to one side. "Did you really bring stuff for waffles? I don't have a waffle-maker."

"Brought mine," I say, holding up the bag in my left hand.

"'Course you did," Harrison replies lightly, shaking his head. "In that case, feed us, Sammy. My daughter has been complaining for a solid ten minutes because *it's taking forever, Daddy*."

My grin stretches wide. "Well, shoot. Can't have y'all starvin'. Let's do this."

Harrison and I find Winnie in the kitchen, sitting sideways on a chair, legs kicking. She's wearing a light blue dress with tutu material along the bottom, and there's a book in her lap. She barely pays us any mind as we unload my bags onto the countertop.

"So what d'you think?" I ask the room at large. "Fruit or chocolate on top?"

Winnie's head whips our way. "I can have chocolate for breakfast?" she asks her dad skeptically.

Harrison shrugs a little, but when his gaze meets mine, his eyes are twinkling. I love that damn twinkle. "Suppose so," he says. "If Sam says it's waffle protocol."

"Oh, most definitely is," I agree with a nod. "Everybody knows waffles are basically just breakfast cake. And cake and chocolate go together."

"They do," Winnie says with all the confidence of a ten-year-old dessert chef. "But cake also has frosting. Did you bring frosting, Sam?"

Harrison's lips press together, and I flourish a tub Winnie's way. "I'll do you one better, li'l miss. I brought whipped cream."

Winnie's chair nearly topples over as she clambers out of it. Tigger chases her to the counter, blunt nails tapping the floor as her little stub wiggles.

"Daddy," Winnie says in all seriousness, her eyes raking over the ingredients I brought. She picks up the chocolate shavings first, examining the package. "We should have waffles more often."

Harrison rubs his smiling mouth. "That so?"

"Yep. Eggs are boring," Winnie declares. "Waffles are *awesome*."

"Well, in that case, we'll have to have Sam come by again, huh?" Harrison says.

Winnie seems to ponder that, checking the tub of whipped cream next. "That might be okay."

Feeling mighty proud of myself, and a touch choked up, I go searching Harrison's shelves for a large bowl. The man himself helps me before long, hand along my lower back as he opens the correct cupboard door. Tingles race over my skin when Harrison drags his thumb against me slowly.

"Bribing my daughter, hm?" he asks under his breath, not sounding remotely upset about that fact.

I turn to him, matching his quiet tone. "I seem to recall a certain veterinarian tellin' me *he* was the one with the biggest sweet tooth."

Harrison pulls down the bowl, eyes flitting to me after a moment. "Bribing *me*, then?" he asks.

"Spoilin' you," I amend, brushing his lower lip before I draw my hand away, cognizant of Harrison's established boundaries. "'Cause I like seein' this smile."

Harrison lets out a slow breath. "You're an angel, aren't you? That's what this is."

"What?" I ask around a laugh.

He nods, like it's all settled. Voice nearly a whisper, he says, "An angel of cock and cake. Two of my very favorite things. I must've died and gone to Heaven."

Dang, Harrison is being *cheeky*. I like this side of the vet.

"Well, if I'm an angel, what does that make you?"

"One lucky bastard," he retorts before turning away, bowl in hand.

My insides swoop, and grin on my face, I follow Harrison as he grabs a whisk from beside the stove. He holds it out to me, and, taking the hint, I set to work making waffle batter.

Fifteen minutes later, Winnie is back at the kitchen table, carefully portioning cut strawberries, chocolate shavings, and whipped cream onto her waffle. Her tongue sticks out the side of her mouth as she concentrates on getting the proportions just right, and when my gaze swings to Harrison, I nearly bust out laughing because he looks exactly the same. *His* pile of chocolate and whipped cream, I note with some amusement, is even bigger than Winnie's.

"Bon appetit," I declare, settling into my own seat.

I've just added strawberries to my waffle when the front door opens and closes, and a voice calls out, "Harrison? Winnie?" I look to Harrison, whose eyes are wide, and have just enough time to wonder at who arrived before Winnie is calling back.

"Kitchen," she yells.

"Oh Lord," Harrison mutters, shooting me a little wince. "It's—"

"Well, there you are," a woman says, entering the room. She's tall and whip-thin with short, gray hair, and when her eyes land on me, she freezes. A man steps into the room not a moment later, looking from the woman to where we're sitting, and when his gaze finds me, he cocks his head. Clearly, they weren't expecting Harrison to have company.

"Hey," Harrison says, standing up and heading toward the duo, who I'm assuming at this point are his parents. "I didn't know you were coming."

He gives both a quick hug. Winnie hasn't bothered coming up for air and continues scarfing down her dessert breakfast.

When Harrison steps back, he gestures toward me. "Uh, Mom, Dad, this is Sam. Sam, my mother, Cordelia Bailey. And my father, Frank Bailey."

I stand up quickly, smile in place as I step toward Harrison's parents. "Sammy Cox," I say, holding out my hand. Harrison coughs harshly as I shake hands with his mom and then his dad.

I never did tell him my last name.

"Excuse me," Harrison says, retreating for a glass of water.

Keeping my amusement to myself, I wave toward the table. "Y'all hungry? We made waffles, and there's plenty extra."

"There's chocolate, too," Winnie puts in, that very thing at the corner of her mouth. "Sam said chocolate goes with waffles. It's a rule. That's why Daddy let me have it for breakfast. *I* said we should have waffles every day, but Daddy doesn't think that's a good idea, even though eggs are *boring*."

"Nutritious, though," Cordelia puts in, a smile on her face as she takes a seat at the table. She redirects her attention to me. "We already ate, but thank you, Sammy."

"What are you doing here?" Harrison asks. In a gentle way, not criticizing.

Frank sits next to his wife, whistling for Tigger and then scratching behind her ears as he talks. "Well, our plans with the Morgans fell through, so we figured we'd stop by and offer to hang out with our favorite granddaughter."

I retake my seat as Winnie says, "Only granddaughter."

Frank snorts. "Favorite and only granddaughter. You've been mentioning wanting to start that treehouse," he says, aiming his gaze at Harrison. "We thought you could do that today, if you wanted."

"Oh, can you?" Winnie asks her dad. "I wanna bring all my pillows and blankets outside. Tigger can come, too, although she'll have to wait at the bottom, since she can't climb ladders. And then we can watch the *stars*. Real ones. But not Janey. She's not allowed in my tree fort."

"I..." Harrison blinks a couple times, his gaze snapping to me quickly before he looks away. "I don't know, Pumpkin. It's going to take more than one day to finish, and I don't have any of the supplies picked up."

Frank shrugs, snagging a waffle from the table and eating it plain. "Need to start sometime."

"I know, but..." Harrison doesn't seem to know how to finish his sentence.

"I could help," I cut in.

"I can't ask you to do that, Sam," he responds gently, sinking back into his seat at the end of the table. "You didn't come over here to be roped into manual labor."

"And, on that note," Cordelia says, aiming for nonchalant, "why *did* Sammy come over here?"

"He and Daddy are friends," Winnie says, book open on her lap now that her waffle is gone. She doesn't look up from her reading. "This is his third time coming over. He and Daddy smile at each other a lot. I haven't decided if me and Sam are going to be friends, too, but Sam said that's okay. I might let him in my tree fort, though. Can I be excused?"

Cordelia and Frank share a look as Harrison shakes his head a little, eyes closing in an extended blink.

"Yeah, Pumpkin," Harrison says. "Just wash up first. There's chocolate on your cheek."

Winnie jumps up and heads over to the sink. Wetting a washcloth, she wipes her face and then flees the room, book tucked under her arm. Tigger jumps up from beside Frank's seat and takes off after her.

As Winnie's footsteps stomp up the stairs, Harrison says, "We met in Plum Valley. We're taking it slow."

My heart thumps. I didn't know if Harrison would want his parents to know about us, but here he is, stating things plainly. No excuses. No skirting the topic. Just the truth.

I reach over beneath the table, squeezing his leg.

"Is that so?" Frank says casually. The man's hair is blonde, intermixed with gray, and his face is boxy. He doesn't look much like Harrison apart from the eyes and hair color. "Spending the morning together doesn't sound all that slow."

Cordelia smacks her husband's arm. "Frank," she admonishes.

I'm guessing Harrison's dad is where he gets his wry side.

"We're taking it slow around Winnie," Harrison clarifies, looking off toward the entrance to the kitchen. "It's just..." His gaze settles on me, something apologetic there.

It's not hard to guess what he was going to say. We're new to each other, and Harrison wants to be cautious about telling his daughter we're a couple. I get it, and it's something we've already discussed.

"Hey, it's all right," I tell him, giving his wrist a squeeze and leaving my hand there atop the table. "You don't have to justify it. We already talked this through, and I'm on board. I don't mind waitin' to tell your daughter."

Harrison whooshes out a breath, looking relieved.

"You live close by?" Frank asks. He clasps his hands together, gauging me, if I had to guess.

"I do, sir," I tell him. "I have an apartment in Houston."

"Yet you two found each other in Plum Valley," Cordelia cuts in, smiling. It's a smile that reminds me of Harrison. "How interesting."

"Fortuitous," I agree.

Harrison gives me a soft look before nodding down at my plate. Breakfast, right. I dig back into my waffles as Frank and Harrison start talking logistics of the treehouse.

"I need the lumber still," Harrison is saying. "Cement, too. And some hardware."

"Then go get it," Frank says. "Your mother and I will stay here with Winnie."

"You're sure?" Harrison responds. I don't know why he looks so guilty about the idea. It seems like his parents are happy to help.

"Absolutely," his mom says. "We'll have a great time."

Harrison looks to me next. "And you're sure you want to stay? You don't have to—"

"I'm stayin'," I tell him, setting my fork down. "Honestly, it sounds like a blast. You know I've got energy to spare."

Harrison huffs a laugh at that.

"Might as well put me to use," I add, giving him a wink.

I didn't *intend* any double meaning with that comment, but by the way Harrison looks at me, I can tell he took it as such.

"You're my man?" he asks.

My pulse fires, and I shoot him a grin, rolling the words I want to say around inside my head. *My hands, my body, they're all yours.*

Instead, I tell him, "You're catchin' on, stud. So, are we doin' this?"

Harrison pushes out of his seat. "Guess so. Come on, Sam. Let's go build a treehouse."

CHAPTER 15

Harrison

It's late morning by the time Sam and I get back to my house, the bed of his truck loaded with lumber. The first thing he does once he parks is settle his cowboy hat atop his head. The second thing is lower the tailgate and heft a bunch of boards onto his shoulder.

I watch, more than a little tongue-tied, as Sam hauls the wood toward my backyard, his navy t-shirt stretched taut around his back and arms. *I* want to be stretched around his back and arms.

Great, now I'm jealous of a shirt.

Grabbing a few boards myself, I follow Sam through the open gate into my backyard. The tree we're building around is an oak, big and sprawling with a thick trunk and plenty of shade to offer. It's the only large tree in my backyard. The rest of the space is open or filled with lower bushes and flowerbeds.

Sam is beside the oak when I arrive, appraising the tree. When he sees me approaching, he gives me a grin.

"This is gonna be great," he says.

"You really don't have to do this, Sam," I tell him for the dozenth time. "I don't want you to feel obligated—"

"Stud, I'm gonna stop you right there," he says, facing me as if he's squaring off. His hands are on his hips, shiny silver belt buckle flashing in the sun. It's not the Longhorn-shaped one, but it's still big and decorative, and I want to rip it right off his body. "Spendin' time with my..."

"Exclusive dating partner?" I suggest.

Sam huffs a laugh. "Spendin' time with my exclusive datin' partner is not a goddamn obligation. I *like* spendin' time with you. I want more of it. And, if you haven't noticed, I like gettin' my hands dirty. This is gonna be fun for me, all right? Stop treatin' yourself like a burden."

His words stop me still. Is that what I'm doing? Assuming I'm a burden?

"Besides," Sam says, eyes tracing over my body, lingering. "Watchin' you is gonna be a treat. I just know it."

I huff a laugh. "I think you've got that backwards," I tell him, heading toward the front yard. Sam stays in step beside me, and I glance at his hat and then his boots. "You're a sight."

Sam practically preens. "Well, somebody told me he's got a—" He looks left and right before whispering, hand at his mouth, "*Cowboy kink.*"

I bite my lip. "Somebody, huh? Well, then somebody is really lucky you're here today."

Sam rumbles at that, looking mighty pleased. He grabs a few more boards from the back of his truck, sliding them across the bed before hoisting them onto his shoulder.

"Although," I muse, "somebody would be even luckier if you were in chaps."

I watch in amusement as Sam goes stock still. He pans to me slowly, the boards on his shoulder turning with him and a rakish grin taking over his face.

"You want me in chaps, stud?" he asks, voice carefully quiet.

"I want you every which way," I admit, chest feeling light when I get another of Sam's beaming smiles. "But add in chaps? Shit, Sam. Show up for me like that, and you can have *me* any which way."

Sam's eyes widen in clear glee. "You're a flirt," he states.

I bark a laugh. "I think that's you," I reply, grabbing some boards myself.

"No, no," Sam says as we head toward the backyard again. "Well, yeah. I *am*. But so are you."

"You must bring it out in me."

It's a partial truth. Sam *does* make me feel light. It's easy to flirt with him. But the truth is yes, I did used to be a little more bold, like Sam. That version of Harrison got pushed to the back over the past decade. But with Sam? I feel a little more like my old self again.

"Well, I like it," Sam says, setting his boards down beside the oak. "Flirt with me anytime, stud."

"Oh, really?" I say, stepping close. "So if I told you all I can think about is ripping off every single piece of your clothing, apart from that hat and those boots, you'd be okay with it?"

"Mm," he responds, hands back on his hips. He damn near looks like he's posing. "Sure would. It'd let you, too. If we were alone, I'd let you cover me with your hands and your mouth and your *teeth* until I was bare for you."

Jesus Christ.

I have a moment to register the sound of the sliding door before my dad's voice rings across the backyard. "You boys planning on doing any building? Or are you going to talk the treehouse into existence?"

Sam shoots me an amused look. "Your dad is *sassy*," he says quietly.

I huff a laugh, giving my dad a wave. He heads back inside. "He sure is," I say, doing a quick sweep of the windows at the back of the house before I walk past Sam, giving his ass a slap as I go. "C'mon. That wood isn't going to grab itself."

Sam snorts, following me back to his truck. It's nearly noon by the time Sam and I get started on the actual construction of the treehouse. I already printed up a design months ago, based loosely on one I found online. I modified the instructions and template a bit for the shape of our tree, but it's mostly the same. The treehouse will anchor to the thick trunk of the oak and be built on a platform about five feet off the ground, surrounding the tree itself. But we're also adding in supporting beams at ground level. Sam and I start there, digging the holes and pouring cement around the thick four-by-four posts. By the time that task is done, my mom is calling out the kitchen window, letting us know sandwiches are ready when we are.

"Break?" I ask Sam.

He gives me a nod, lifting his hat and using the bottom of his shirt to wipe the sweat from his forehead. The V of his abdomen is revealed with the move, as well as the expanse of his toned abs, and I ogle him shamelessly, imagining myself tracing the grooves of those muscles with my fingers and my tongue. I have no doubt, by the grin on Sam's face, he knows exactly what I'm thinking.

When we get inside, Sam hangs his hat on the hook inside the door, and I do the same. I'd grabbed my own once we got started, not wanting my neck to burn. We kick off our boots, and as we round the corner into the kitchen, Winnie pounces.

"It doesn't look like a treehouse," my daughter states, pouting.

"No," I answer with a huff. "Not yet. But it will."

"It's taking *forever*," she whines.

Sam grins my way before grabbing a plated sandwich from the counter. "Good things take time, li'l miss," he says. Looking my parents' way, he adds, "Thanks for the sandwiches, Mr. and Mrs. Bailey."

"Oh, Sammy," my mom says, walking over and squeezing Sam's shoulder. "Aren't you just precious?"

Sam's nose wrinkles up with his smile, and I cover my laugh. My God, he is precious. Among many other things.

As everyone takes a seat around the big kitchen table, Sam and my dad chatting about the Houston Astros, of all things, I have a brief moment of suspended disbelief. The sun shines in from the southern-facing window, adding light to the white pine table. There's a bird chirping not far off outside, its cadence happy among the rustle of wind. And in front of me sits my family.

My family and Sam, who looks entirely at ease after spontaneously meeting my parents just this morning. Sam, who has a big smile on his face, and who, without skipping a beat, convinces my daughter to eat a carrot because *I bet I can get mine to crunch louder than yours, li'l miss*. Sam, this man I wasn't expecting, who looks like every wet dream of mine brought to life, but who *cares* in a way I haven't let myself dream about in a very long time.

I think I could fall for Sam.

"Gonna join us, Harrison?" the very man asks, head tilted, grin out in full force.

"Yeah," I say, grabbing the last sandwich and heading to the table. "I'm here."

★

"Good Lord," Sam says, leaning against the wood plank in his hands. "I haven't sweat this much in forever. Even the sheep weren't this exhaustin'."

I give Sam a once-over. "I didn't know you were capable of tiring out," I admit.

Sam huffs a laugh. "Perfectly capable. Why, were you thinkin' of testin' my stamina?"

He waggles his eyebrows, and I shake my head. Sam has been running his beautiful mouth all day.

Haven't minded it one bit.

"We should call it soon," I say from my spot on the ground before cutting the final wall board to size. We've been working on constructing the walls, getting them put together so once the base is built, we can assemble the rest quickly. The base has to wait until the cement is dry, so we'll be doing that another day.

"Yeah, we should," Sam agrees, looking toward the back of the house. "It's nearly suppertime. Your folks... They really don't mind helpin' out, do they?"

"No, they don't," I tell him, standing upright and wiping my hands on my jeans. "I feel guilty relying on them so much, but they do love being around, and they watch Winnie every day after school. They actually moved here just after Winnie was born. Wanted to be close."

"That's real nice," Sam says softly. "I'm glad Winnie has 'em. Glad you do, too."

"Yeah," I agree, watching Sam closely. His eyes look a little hazy, and I wonder what he's thinking about. "Did you...have anyone you were close to growing up?"

Sam's lips twitch into a sad smile. "Not really. I had foster carers, like I told you, all over the state."

"Including in Plum Valley when you were nine," I recall.

"Mhm." Sam nods, seemingly pleased I remembered. "But none of my placements lasted very long. There were foster siblings, too, but it was the same thing. No one stuck."

"I'm sorry, Sam," I say gently.

"I appreciate that, Harrison, but it's been a long time since I was in the system. I'm not hangin' onto those memories in a bad way. It was what it was, and there were positives. Learned a lotta neat tricks."

"Like rodeo?" I ask.

"And how to wield a hammer," he adds with a grin before sobering. "Besides, I've got Tilda and Carl now. They stuck, and I think that's what counts, don't you? Family isn't given. It's earned."

I nod, swallowing down the tightness in my throat. Sam's sentiment hits closer to home than I'm sure he realizes.

"Yeah," I tell the softhearted man. "I think that's what counts. You, uh, wanna help me get this saw back into the shed?"

"You got it," Sam says, setting down the board in his hands. Together, we lift the portable saw and carry it inside. I'm about to head back out the door when Sam's touch stops me. "Harrison," he says, pulling me gently back his way.

I go willingly. "Yeah?"

He reaches up, removing my hat and then his own. "I just wanna kiss you. Is that all right?"

This man.

I nod, and Sam leans in, his lips hovering near the corner of my mouth for a long moment before he finally kisses me there. It's a small touch, just a press, and then he's moving to the other side. He places a kiss there, too, before his hand settles at my jaw. I just about melt into the floor when his lips whisper over mine in earnest, a brush stroke at most.

"Sammy," I breathe, liking the way that word sounds more and more these days.

I think Sam likes it, too, based on the way his mouth shifts into a smile against my lips. When he kisses me for real, it's hungry. Startlingly so. I react in an instant, grabbing Sam's shirt tight as my lower back hits the tool bench behind me. Sam makes an apologetic sound, tugging me back against his body, but I couldn't care less about the ache as his hands roam over my ass. He rumbles from deep in his chest, and I shiver.

"If I could," he says, dropping his lips to my neck, kissing me there between words, "I'd spin you 'round and eat you out right here."

"Jesus, Sammy," I groan.

"I'd tug down your pants, spread you wide, and fuckin' devour you. I adore this ass." He punctuates his point by gripping my ass cheeks hard over the denim of my jeans.

"It adores you," I answer, my words mostly breath as Sam's stubble rakes across the skin of my neck.

Sam *mmms* as his lips come back up to mine, and his hands tangle in my hair. The strands are sweaty, as am I, but he doesn't seem to care.

"God, Sam," I manage between kisses. "You make me feel..."

"What?" he asks, pulling back enough to look me in the eyes. His are hooded, and his mouth is wet.

"Light," I answer. "You make me feel light."

Sam grins, eyes raking over my face and pausing near my cheek. He bites his lip some before rubbing his thumb over the spot. "Oops."

"What?"

"You had some dirt," he says, eyes dancing. "But I made it worse."

Snorting, I give Sam a little shove, and he takes a step back, a near boyish smile on his face. He *looks* light, too. Like literal goddamn sunshine.

"Definitely an angel," I mutter, swiping at my cheek. Not like it matters. I'm sure most of me is a dirty mess. Sam is, too. "You should shower here before you go," I find myself telling him.

"Is that so?" he asks, grabbing our hats from the nearby shelf. He replaces mine before tipping his own back onto his head. "I don't have clean clothes to change into."

It doesn't sound at all like an actual refusal. Not that I expected Sam to refuse my offer.

"You can wear mine," I say. "We're the same size."

There's that rumble again. "All right." After a moment, Sam adds, "Hey, Harrison?"

I huff a laugh. "Yeah, Sam?"

"Can you tell me somethin' I don't wanna hear? I needa get rid of this before we head back outside." He gestures down to where his jeans are tented, and I shake my head, smile wide.

"I could tell you about the time I found a two-foot-long tapeworm in a dog's stomach. The owner thought the dog was pregnant. She was not."

"Oh, God. Gross. Yeah, all right," Sam says. "Keep talkin'."

Sam makes the funniest faces as I tell him about that particular client, and even though his erection dies down quickly, we spend another ten minutes inside the shed before joining my family for dinner.

I can't stop smiling the entire time.

CHAPTER 16

★

Sammy

"I take it back," Harrison groans, leg wobbling slightly as I spear my tongue inside his ass. "Devil. You're most definitely the devil."

"You want me to stop?" I ask, slipping my finger inside his body instead.

He plants his forehead against his arms, which are flat against the shower wall. "Don't you"—a huffing breath as I rub against his prostate—"fucking dare."

I kiss Harrison's ass cheek as I fuck him with a single digit. I really do adore it, his ass. Well, all of him really. But his ass is something else.

He curses lightly, locking his knee. "Two."

"You sure?" Harrison doesn't have any lube in his shower—silly man—and I don't want to hurt him. No more than he wants, at least.

But he nods against his forearm. "Two."

I spit against my fingers before bringing them back to Harrison's asshole. He adjusts his stance, standing wider, and the steam from the shower curls around him like mist. It's quite a sight from my position on the tile floor.

Harrison pushes against me as I slip two fingers inside his body, and I damn near combust on the spot. He takes me so well.

I nuzzle my face against his pert cheek, skimming my lips over the downy hairs there. Fucking sexy. He smells like melon, too. His soap, as I found out. I want to eat him up.

"Sammy," Harrison croaks.

"Yeah, stud. What d'you need?"

"To come," he manages. "I need to come."

Grabbing a hold of his hip, I spin Harrison until his back is against the tile wall. The stream of water buffets my side as I edge closer, reaching between Harrison's legs to rub against his hole. As I slip back into his body, I take his cock between my lips.

"God, Sammy," Harrison chokes, shielding his eyes with his arm for a moment before he looks back down at me, as if he can't decide whether or not he *wants* to look. "I can't... You..."

His lashes flutter closed, and he groans, legs shaking as I work the underside of his crown with my tongue. His hair is plastered against his forehead, cheeks flushed, and it might be the most beautiful sight I've ever seen.

"I'm gonna come," he says, opening his eyes at last.

I hollow my cheeks, sucking as I aim my fingers at his prostate, and Harrison starts to unload down my throat with a muttered curse. His hand lands on my head, locking me in place, and my own cock throbs, threatening to send my release down the drain. I hold it back by a hair as Harrison's blunt fingernails rake over my buzzed head, a sigh escaping him as his cock finally calms.

"Sammy," he states, expression soft as he looks down at me.

I let his dick go and carefully pull my fingers from his body. "Can I come on your ass?" I ask, giving myself a slow stroke.

Harrison's expression turns almost smug as he spins back around, shoving his ass out right in front of my face. I stand quickly, boxing him in against the wall and dropping my forehead to his shoulder as I rut against his crack.

"Fuck," I mutter, my entire body shivering, despite the humid air inside the shower.

He feels perfect. Hard. Muscular. Soft in all the right places. Warm everywhere. I anchor my hand against his abdomen as his ass cradles my dick, and Harrison twines his fingers with my own. It doesn't take long at all to follow him into orgasm. My balls draw up tight, heat flows through my veins, and my release paints Harrison's lower back and ass cheeks like a dirty fucking canvas.

"Ah," I sum up with a grunt.

Harrison shakes with barely subdued laughter. "Good?" he asks cheekily.

I answer honestly. "Always good with you."

As I let the man go, I keep my eyes on his ass for a moment, enjoying the sight of my cum on his skin. With a sigh, I aim the showerhead back our way.

Harrison grabs the soap, lathering up again quickly before rinsing himself under the spray.

"Why melon?" I ask, accepting the bottle he hands over.

His lips twitch. "It was a birthday gift from Winnie. She bought it herself with money she saved in her piggy bank because she knows I like melon. To eat," he clarifies with a little laugh. "Didn't have the heart to tell her it's not really my scent."

"I dunno about that," I say, tucking my face against Harrison's neck and inhaling the man. "I think you and melon are a perfect match."

"That so?" he asks, hands gliding up my wet back.

"Mm. You smell good enough to eat," I say, nipping his skin gently.

"Like you just did?"

"Mhm," I hum, memories still fresh.

Harrison chuckles. "Let's get out of here before we prune."

I nod, and Harrison and I step out of the shower. We towel off, and once inside Harrison's bedroom, the man picks out a set of clothes for me. I raise my eyebrow at the sweatpants he chose—sans underwear, mind you—but Harrison simply gives me a grin.

"All right," I mutter, tugging them on, followed by the soft blue t-shirt.

Harrison and I settle downstairs on the big couch in his living room. Winnie, of course, is asleep in her bedroom, and Harrison's parents left over an hour ago, after supper finished. Tigger, who slipped out of Winnie's room to follow us downstairs, jumps atop our laps on the couch. Her backside ends up on me, and Harrison gets her happy, tongue-lolling face in his lap.

From what Harrison told me, the dog doesn't usually leave Winnie's room at night except to go to the bathroom, but the little girl must be resting comfortably if Tigger decided to join us instead. She's a smart dog, particularly in tune to Winnie. I think she knows exactly when her tiny human needs her and when she doesn't.

"Can I ask you a question?" Harrison says once Tigger settles. He pets along her head and neck, a rhythmic, almost unconscious motion.

"'Course," I tell him.

"What was your longest relationship?"

"A guy named Mitchell," I answer, giving Tigger's leg a rub. "We were together nine months before he called it off. You?"

Harrison swallows before answering me. "Wyatt."

"The guy from Plum Valley," I say, remembering that tidbit of info.

He nods.

"What happened?" I ask gently.

Harrison takes a beat before answering. "We were together for two years. He moved in with me during the second one. And then I found out he was in love with someone else. His best friend. The one he was raising a kid with."

I wince, and Harrison catches it.

"Yeah," he says, shaking his head. "I should've seen it coming. The signs were there."

"Hey, somethin' like that is not your fault," I say.

Harrison keeps going, like he didn't even hear me. "You know the funny thing? He wasn't even a bad boyfriend. I know he cared for me. That he tried to be what I needed."

"But it wasn't enough," I fill in.

Harrison laughs a little harshly. "No, it wasn't. I think that's why it hurt so much, you know? I thought we had something good. But I was his second choice. I was *always* his second choice."

"Harrison," I say quietly.

He shakes his head again. "I'm afraid..." He cuts off, looking at me sharply, his blue eyes swimming. "I'm afraid you're going to feel like that, Sam. Like my second choice because of Winnie."

"Hey," I say, grabbing his hand and squeezing it tightly. "It's not the same thing."

"It is," he says.

"It's *not*. I'm not tryin' to compete with your daughter, Harrison. We're not even in the same race. I will never be mad at you for puttin' her first. Never. All I ask—"

"Is that I don't push you away," he answers. "And that I'm honest."

I nod.

"I'm scared," he says. "That's the truth. Days like today? They seem too perfect to be real. It's too *easy*, and as soon as I stop to think about it, I can't help but wonder when it's all going to fall apart. Did you even want kids, Sam? Was that in your plan? Because I'm guessing you sure didn't expect that when you asked me out for beers. You didn't expect all of...this."

"Stud," I say lightly, tugging his hand up to my mouth and kissing his knuckles. I'm starting to get an idea of where Winnie gets her rambling from. "No, I wasn't expectin' all this. But I am so fuckin' glad we didn't hook up that first night like I *was* expectin'. 'Cause if we had, I never would've gotten to hear you tell me about your dog and the fact that you were a stripper."

He croaks out a little laugh.

"I never would've heard your voice get all sleepy and soft," I go on. "I wouldn't have found out you're a person I wanted to learn more about. I might not have stalked you down and found all of...this." I wave my hand around, encompassing him, his house, and everything in it. "I like this, Harrison. I *did* want kids. Do want 'em."

"You do," he says, sounding relieved.

I huff a laugh. "Yeah, I do. And I want a partner to come home to. A family of my own. Someday," I add softly, not wanting to scare the man off. There's a difference between talking about hypotheticals and permanently implanting myself into his life a couple weeks in. But I do want him to know... "Honestly, Harrison, you're pretty much the perfect package from where I'm standin'."

"God, Sam." He shakes his head. "No one but you would describe me and my baggage that way."

Because you're mine. You're perfect for me and no other.

I don't say it. It's too much. One step too far for tonight. But I think it might be true.

"Well, I like you and your baggage," I tell him.

Harrison is quiet for a moment, playing with my fingers with one hand, the other resting idly on Tigger's head. "The last guy," he says slowly, eyes pinging to me, "wasn't a dog person."

I wrinkle my nose. "Your most recent ex? From, what...four years ago?"

He nods. "Yeah. He, uh, never really took to Tigger. Or Winnie, for that matter."

"What a dipshit."

Harrison huffs a laugh, but I shake my head.

"Seriously. The guy clearly wasn't for you," I point out. "You're a damn vet, Harrison. And a father. How was that gonna work?"

"He was good on paper," he answers, eyes swinging to me before landing back on my hand. He continues to play with my fingers, and the gentle ministrations send a shiver up my arm. "But that's why...why Winnie was watching you oddly the last time you were here. When you were down on the floor with Tigger. Hank was never like that."

"Oh," I say, understanding now why that moment seemed like something of importance. "Well, I *am* an animal person."

"Yeah," Harrison says with a little smile.

"I like dogs. And kids."

"Yeah," he says again.

The acknowledgement that Harrison and I are in tune on those matters hangs between us for a silent moment. Honestly, I think we're in tune in just about every matter. But I do wonder if he realizes he compared me to Hank, a prior boyfriend, in his daughter's eyes.

"I don't know when I'll be ready to tell Winnie," he says, as if answering my unspoken thoughts.

"That's all right," I tell him.

He shakes his head a little. "I don't want to be dishonest. I mean, it's not dishonesty exactly, what I told her. The fact that we're friends. But we're more than that. She's going to see it."

I give him a slow nod.

"What I mean to say," he goes on, "is that when I tell her you're my exclusive dating partner—"

"Harrison." I cut him off with a chuckle. "Can we call it like it is?"

He puffs out a breath. "When I tell her you're my boyfriend, do you want to be there? Do you have any opinions on what I say? Should I wait for a specific milestone or..."

He peters out, and I give his hand a squeeze. "I'm ready whenever you are," I tell him seriously. "And I trust you with the rest. If you want me there, I'll be there. If you wanna tell her on your own, I support that."

Harrison nods once before abandoning my hand to grab the back of my neck. He holds there for a moment, eyes pinging between my own, and then he tugs me forward, closing the gap between us. His lips meet mine in a hard press. A thank you, maybe, or something else. It feels like a promise. Or, perhaps, I desperately wish for that to be true. That this man is promising me a solid go at a future.

I can see it, if I close my eyes and look up at the stars. I can see what we could be.

When Harrison draws back, he doesn't go far. He leaves his hand on the back of my neck, toying with the short hairs there. I have to fight not to close my eyes and sink into the sensation.

"I want to see you again soon," Harrison says.

My heart leaps. "Yes."

He chuckles a little, his blue eyes bright. "Lunch this week? I'll come to you this time."

I nod in his grasp.

"And maybe another dinner, too?" he adds.

I nod again, wanting any and every chance to get closer to this man and all he has to offer. I'd be here every night with him, Winnie, and Tigger if it was an option. If Harrison was ready.

"Name the days and I'm all yours," I tell him.

He smiles, letting out a soft sigh. I know it's getting late, and I'll need to leave soon so Harrison can get his rest. But I'm not quite ready.

"Tell me somethin'," I say.

His smile widens. "One time, I found a rattlesnake in my boot."

"In your boot?" I repeat, horrified at the prospect of stepping into *that* disaster, quite literally.

Harrison nods. "This one's a long story," he says, settling more fully against the couch. His elbow is resting along the top, hand still clasped gently around the back of my neck. And as Harrison regales me with his tale of why it's never a good idea to leave your boots outside during a rainstorm, I let my fingers drift along the material above my hip, right over my tattoo.

Unable to help myself, I make another wish.

CHAPTER 17

Harrison

"How's your new toy?" my coworker asks.

I look at Deborah in confusion. "Pardon?"

She cocks her head, a sassy grin on her face. "That boy of yours," she says, nodding down to the phone in my hand, where a picture of Sam is onscreen.

I snort, shutting off the device before sticking it into my pocket. "He's not a boy. *Or* a toy."

"Really?" she asks. "'Cause it sure seems like he'd come with batteries."

A chuckle breaks free because she's not exactly wrong. Sam is full of energy.

"How would you even know?" I throw back. "You met him for half a minute."

She shrugs, pulling out a seat next to me in our small break room at the practice. We're the only two people in here at the moment. Deborah has her lunch with her, but I'm just waiting for my final patient of the morning to arrive so I can get through their appointment and go meet Sam. I probably could have been catching up on some paperwork instead of sitting in here ogling the man, but he sent me a picture of himself in his uniformed glory, cowboy hat in place, and I couldn't quite resist taking a moment to drink him in properly.

Deborah opens her container of chicken salad before answering me. "I didn't need longer than half a minute to figure out the man's got a vibrate settin' built in. I mean, damn, Harrison. I'd say it's cute the way he looked at you. But cute doesn't cover it."

She digs into her salad as my face heats. If only she knew how filthy the man truly is.

Sam *is* cute, all boyish charm, almost, and, yes, a literal bounce to his step. But he's also sexy, attentive, endlessly patient, and the things that come out of his mouth...

"I'm meeting him for lunch," I tell Deborah, who, after all these years, is my closest friend. I never really bothered making friends outside of work after I moved to this town with an infant Winnie. I was too focused on surviving. On figuring out how to juggle the sudden influx of responsibilities in my life. Friends weren't a priority. Neither were boyfriends.

But there's Deborah. We've worked together for nearly a decade now, and she knows me better than most.

She bounces her eyebrows. "Right. You're meetin' him for *lunch*. I'm sure that'll be the only thing goin' in your mouth."

"Jesus, Deb," I groan, glancing at the door. "Don't let Abbott hear you say things like that. The man would have a coronary."

She waves her fork in the air. "You and I both know he's too stubborn to let somethin' like a little heart trouble take him down. He'll outlast us all."

I shudder at the thought, but I wouldn't put it past him.

"Does he like your kid?" Deborah asks seriously, redirecting the conversation back to Sam.

"And how do you know he already met her?" I retort.

She raises a brow. "Because of the way *you* looked at him. You like that man, Harrison."

Yeah, I do.

"He's good with her," I answer, a little smile tugging at my lips.

"Good," Deborah says with a firm nod.

Tessa, one of our vet techs, sticks her head inside the door. "Doctor Bailey?"

"Yeah?" I answer.

"Your eleven o'clock isn't showin'. They just called to cancel."

"Thanks, Tessa."

She nods before backing out the door, and I hop to my feet. "Looks like I'm out of here," I tell Deborah.

She chuckles, waving her fork at me in a goodbye. "Have fun," she singsongs.

I grab the lunch I prepared for Sam and me and hoof it out the door, shooting Sam a quick text on the way to my truck to let him know I'll be early. I glance at the picture he sent one more time as his responding message comes through.

Sammy: See you soon, stud.

Smile on my face, I get into my truck and reverse out of my spot.

It takes just over twenty-five minutes to arrive at the Animal Control facility where Sam works. I park in front of the building, and I can hear the barking of dogs even before I've turned off the vehicle. It's a warm, sunny day in the seventies, and I grab my hat just in case we'll be outside. I keep one in my truck at all times, and it comes in handy often, especially on the days I visit large animal farms.

Admittedly, I could easily use a baseball cap instead, but one of my first purchases when I arrived in Texas for vet school sixteen years ago was a black leather cowboy hat. That thing went with me everywhere, and not only was it useful, but it made me feel more at home in a new place that was so far from my family.

I'm not a born Texan, but I sure am one by choice. And I think that's what matters most, like Sam said. Our choices.

When I push inside the building, Tilda is the first person I see. She's seated behind a check-in counter next to a large glass wall that offers a peek at the inside of a cat room. Dozens of felines are inside, as well as a few people, and the sight of a little girl waving a feathered wand in the air to get the attention of a nearby kitten has a smile on my face in no time.

"Well, hey there, Doctor Bailey," Tilda says. "What a surprise."

Judging by her tone and beaming smile, I don't think it's a surprise at all. Regardless, I smile and step forward. "Hi, Tilda. It's good to see you again. How've you been?"

"Oh, just fine," she says. "Glad to be back home, though. You here to see our Sammy?"

I give her a nod, holding up the bag in my hand. "I brought lunch."

Tilda sighs dreamily—actually *sighs*—before standing up and pointing toward a nearby door. "Through there."

I follow Tilda's direction, and she meets me on the other side of the door. A couple hallways branch off in either direction as we walk, and the sound of dogs becomes louder once more.

"Sammy is prob'ly out back," she says as we walk. "Whenever he has a spare moment, that's where he goes—to play with the dogs. You've got a dog, isn't that right, Doctor Bailey?"

"I sure do," I say with a chuckle.

Tilda hums. "That's good. Ah," she says, stopping in front of a windowed door and looking outside. "There he is."

I follow her gaze, and through the slightly dusty glass, I can make out Sam, running along a fence with a ball in his hand. Several dogs are chasing after him, and I bite my lip so hard it hurts. *My God.* This man.

"Is it okay if I head out there?" I ask Tilda.

She gives me a nod before turning around and patting my shoulder. "You bet. And Doctor Bailey?"

"Harrison, please," I tell her.

She nods again, her face soft, even as her eyes are sharp and on my person. "Harrison. Sammy's one of the good ones, y'know?"

I nod. I do know.

"He's not afraid to get hurt," she goes on. "And that's a rare thing. A rare and dangerous thing."

I nod again, feeling very much like I'm being dressed down by Sam's honorary mother. Frankly, I don't mind. I'm glad Sam has this. That he has his people.

"I don't want to hurt him," I tell her honestly.

Tilda appraises me for a second longer before squeezing my shoulder again and walking away. Blowing out a breath, I push the door open and step through.

The barking intensifies once I'm outside, and I take a quick look around. There are several large, fenced-in yards for the dogs to play in, as well as individual run-style cages underneath the shade of a metal roof. A family and another employee, based on their outfit, are in one of the smaller yards with a dog, likely feeling out a potential adoption.

But Sam... Sam is in a fenced area of his own with at least a dozen dogs, a wide smile on his face as he stops running and throws the ball as hard as he can in the opposite direction.

Most of the dogs pivot, chasing the ball, but a couple stop near Sam's feet, tongues out, doggy smiles on their faces.

When Sam turns his head and catches sight of me approaching, his smile goes crooked and bright. He jogs over, stopping on the other side of the wire fence.

"Hey," he breathes out, sounding winded.

"Hi," I return, my insides swooping. "Are you ready for lunch, or should I wait?"

"I'm ready," he says. "Just needa get these kids settled first."

"Okay," I say with a chuckle.

Sam gives me a wink before turning around and jogging off. He whistles, and most of the dogs follow him over to a gate near the covered section of cages. He opens it up, letting the dogs through, and then he starts dividing them up, putting one or two at a time inside the empty runs. Most of the dogs immediately go for the water bowls, and none complain about the shift of location, not even the final straggler, a fuzzy white dog that's last to go through the gate.

Once all of the dogs are secure, some already lying down with their stomachs against the cool concrete, Sam makes his way over to me. He looks so sure, as he always does, his strides purposeful. His navy-blue uniform fits him well, and that little silver badge on his chest gleams in the sun. He grabs his hat as he comes through the final gate, setting it back on his head, and then he's in front of me, brown eyes bright and so obviously glad to see me.

Transparent, like glass.

"C'mon," he says, canting his head. "There's a table out this way."

I follow Sam through another round of two gates and over to the side of the building. Much like at my practice, there's a picnic table here, but this one is covered by a large shade umbrella. Sam drops his hat onto one of the bench seats, but before I can sit down, he tugs me close.

"C'mere," he says gently, taking first the bag from my hand and setting it down, and then removing my own hat. As soon as it hits the wooden table, Sam lifts his arms and threads his fingers through my hair.

My eyes slip closed, and I'm pretty sure a little moan escapes, but the next instant, Sam's lips are pressed ever so softly against my own, and all other thoughts flee. I grab his arms, anchoring, tethering, and Sam nudges my mouth open. My breath stutters at the simple touch of his tongue against my top lip. Just a caress. A tiny thing.

And so very big.

How this man can reduce me to mindlessness with a single touch, I don't think I'll ever understand. It's his superpower, this pull he has over me. The way he makes me forget about grocery lists and upcoming school events and housework and every other tiny thing jostling for position in my mind. The way he tugs every ounce of my focus to him. The way he makes me *feel*.

He makes me feel so many bright, beautiful, terrifying things.

Sam's fingers rake through my hair once more as he pulls back from the relatively chaste kiss. When my eyes finally open, there's a soft, curious smile on his face.

"All right?" he asks.

"Mm," I answer.

He runs his thumb beside my ear before giving the lobe a little tug. "C'mon, then. Feed me before I wither."

Huffing a laugh, I follow Sam onto the bench seat, my thigh touching his. "That close to expiring, were you?"

Sam opens up the bag I brought, pulling out its contents. He makes a happy sound when he discovers the pasta salad. "It was definitely a close call," he jokes, making an even happier sound when he uncaps the thermos of lemonade. He grabs the two cups I packed and pours us each a drink. Sam moans around his first sip of the sweet liquid, and I watch his Adam's apple bob, remembering a very different thing he had in his mouth the last time I heard that noise.

Clearing my throat, I pull out forks and remove the lid of Sam's pasta salad for him. It's a recipe my mom used to make when I was a kid, and I love it to this day. It has grilled chicken, cucumbers, tomatoes, feta, and a hint of lemon. It's good cold, which means it's perfect for a day like this.

Sam thanks me when he finishes making love to his lemonade, and then he sets in on his pasta salad. I have to look away, focusing on my own lunch lest I pop a boner.

What is it with me and Sam behind our workplaces? And inside sheds?

Sam gives me a little nudge after a moment. "So, how was your mornin'?"

"Good," I answer. "Typical. Winnie reminded me at least four times during breakfast that she prefers waffles to eggs."

Sam groans a little. "Sorry. Did I make more trouble for you?"

"No," I say, bumping his knee with my own. "We both loved the waffles. Well worth it."

He smiles at that. "Is Winnie in any school clubs or anythin'?"

I shake my head, chewing my food before answering. "No. There will be more options once she gets to middle school, but she doesn't seem interested in any of them at the moment. She's loud and rambunctious at home, but Winnie is a little more reserved everywhere else. She has a couple friends she plays with outside of school, but most of the time, she would rather be at home exploring the backyard or reading."

Sam hums, nodding. "An introverted soul."

"Guess so," I agree. I don't even have to ask to know Sam is the opposite. I fall somewhere in the middle. I don't need to be around people to be happy and energized, but I also don't mind it.

"D'you think she'd like campin'?" Sam asks. "If she likes bein' outside, maybe that's somethin' we could try on a weekend. Even campin' in the backyard if you think goin' somewhere would be too much."

My heart beats staccato in my chest, and Sam falls silent, eyes darting my way like maybe he's worried he said too much. *Implied* too much.

I lick my lips. "I think she might like that," I say. "I don't have a tent, though."

"I do," Sam says, closing his container slowly now that his pasta salad is gone. "It's big, too. We could all easily fit if you...if that's somethin' you..."

"I'd really like that, Sam," I tell him, giving his arm a squeeze.

He smiles tentatively, shoulders dropping their tension. "Yeah?"

I nod, throat a little tight. Sam's the first guy I've dated who's *wanted* to hang out with Winnie. Who's suggested it outright instead of trying to find ways to work around my child.

"Yeah," I answer. "I've been meaning to buy a fire pit for out back. We could make s'mores."

Sam's grin is like the sun. I could get addicted to making Sam smile like that. I think I already am.

"She said she likes lookin' at the stars, right?" Sam says, on a roll again. "I could bring my book on constellations. Maybe we could find some if the sky is clear. And my tent is pet-friendly, so Tigger's nails won't be a problem. I even have some—"

Sam's ramblings cut off when I drag him in for a kiss. He tastes bright from the lemonade and a little smoky from the chicken, and I devour him greedily, my heart pitter-pattering away.

"Don't stop," I say, pulling back from Sam's lips.

"Kissin' you?" he says, trying to tug me back in. "Wasn't plannin' on it."

I give a quick shake of my head, holding him tight. "No. Don't stop being you. If I fuck up or say something wrong or *do* something wrong or—I don't know..." I swallow roughly. "Just don't stop."

Sam smiles. "I've never known how not to be me," he says simply. "I don't plan on changin' now."

I nod, voice gone, and his hands smooth along the sides of my neck.

"Now, are you gonna let me kiss you again, or do I gotta beg?" he asks.

I don't stop Sam this time when he leans in, and as his lips meet mine, that little seed inside my chest unfurls.

CHAPTER 18

Sammy

"You sure I'm doin' this right, li'l miss? My volcano isn't as tall as yours," I note with some concern.

Winnie nods confidently. "It's right. It doesn't have to be tall, Sam. It just has to be yours."

My eyes shoot wide as I look over at this little girl with her strangely powerful words of wisdom. "Well, dang. Okay, then."

"You two have fifteen minutes before dinner is ready," Harrison cuts in.

I turn to Winnie. "We gotta hurry."

She nods furiously, shaping her impressively tall volcano. She's wearing a pink dress today, and her hair is up in a messy ponytail that's failing its one job. There's clay smeared along her cheek, transferred from the lumpy volcano in front of her, and another gray streak rests along the bottom of her dress.

She is, quite possibly, the most charming creature I've ever set eyes on.

"C'mon, Sam!" Winnie says. "You're not building."

"Right," I say, lips twitching as I go back to finishing my own rather stout volcano. Mine, just like Winnie's, is sitting on a sheet pan from below the oven. Apparently, when we set the things off, it's going to make a monumental mess.

I can't wait.

Harrison makes a ding sound. "Time to clean up."

"All right, where're we puttin' these?" I ask, hefting my sheet pan.

Harrison points to the counter, and I bring the volcano over, setting it in a clear space. Winnie's volcano is next, and the little girl follows to make sure I don't botch the job. After that, Winnie starts cleaning up in the kitchen sink, and I head to the half bath.

There's a smile on my face as I wash the clay off my hands, and when I look up, I realize I have a splotch on my own cheek. I rub it off, stomach skipping all over the place.

I take a moment before I rejoin the Baileys, needing to breathe and process. Moments like this...they feel like a lost memory. Like something that maybe could have been for me long ago, back when I was still a kid. They feel like a missed opportunity come to pass.

I didn't have a terrible childhood by any means. I was fed, clothed, never abused. But I didn't have stability or folks in my life that cared who I became. My fondest memories are all scattered snapshots: adventures I had on my own. There was no family to share my life with.

There was no assurance I was loved.

Maybe it's silly to attach such sentiment to the process of building a volcano, but there's no doubt in my mind that Winnie's memories will be full of her dad when she's older. I can't help but wonder if I'll be there, too.

When I get back to the kitchen, Harrison is putting food on the table. I join the crew, giving Tigger a quick scratch as I pass her by. The dog loves me, I know it. But at meal times, her loyalties lie with the little girl with a propensity for disposing of vegetables. I get it.

"So, li'l miss, what's new in school?" I ask, dishing some green beans onto my plate. I add some to Winnie's, too.

Winnie shrugs, avoiding her veggies but eating her pasta.

"All right," I say slowly. "So, Harrison, what's new at work?"

The man chuckles. "Have I told you about my coworkers yet?"

"A bit about Deb, but that's it," I reply.

He nods, chewing his food before speaking. "Right. So there's this older guy that's worked at the practice for a long time. His name's Abbott Fry. We've all been waiting for him to retire, but... I don't know. The more I think about it, the more I wonder if his job is all he has."

I hum, pushing a bean closer to Winnie's fork. "No family?"

"Not really," Harrison replies. "No kids, at least. No spouse."

"Pets?" I ask, grinning at Winnie when she reluctantly eats a green bean. "By the way, this pasta is great, Harrison."

"Thanks, Sam," he says with a warm smile. "And he did have a couple Irish Wolfhounds, believe it or not"—I whistle at that; they're impressive dogs—"but they both passed of old age a few years back."

"You think he's lonely," I surmise.

Harrison nods, blue eyes creased. "Yeah, I do. Some of my coworkers gripe about his attitude, but I think we're all he has left. And, I guess, if the only people you have left are just waiting for you to go, wouldn't you be a little grumpy, too?"

"Dang," I mutter, pushing a piece of pasta around on my plate before shoving it in my mouth. I can understand exactly how Abbott must feel.

"Why doesn't he have kids, Daddy?" Winnie asks.

Harrison gives his daughter a wan smile. "Not everybody wants to have children, Pumpkin. Or is ready for it."

The end of his statement is said with weight, but I don't have time to ponder it before Winnie is turning big blue eyes my way. *Good grief,* with the way she's looking at me like a sad cartoon character come to life, I can tell exactly what's on her mind.

"Winifred," I say carefully. "Remember when I told you I hated kids?"

She nods, looking down at her plate.

"Well, that wasn't the truth," I tell her. "I was just teasin'."

"I know that, Sam," she says seriously, although she looks relieved to hear the words. "Does that mean..."

"What is it, li'l miss?"

"Does that mean you want kids?" she asks.

I give her a smile, my chest warmed with something scary and wonderful. "I do," I tell her. "I'd love to be a dad someday."

I don't say more than that. Don't dare push it. But Winnie nods, and when I chance a glance Harrison's way, there's a thoughtful expression on his face.

"Can we set our volcanoes off now?" Winnie asks, breaking the silence.

"All full?" he asks, looking at Winnie's plate. Much to my, and seemingly Harrison's, surprise, her beans are gone.

"Yep," she says, scooting off her chair. "C'mon, Sam."

With an amused huff, I pick up my plate and stand. Harrison and I clear the dishes before I carry the volcanoes back to the table. Winnie bounces the entire time, her enthusiasm infectious.

"Okay," I say, rubbing my hands together. "So how do we do this?"

"Baking soda first," Winnie says, grabbing the box Harrison already pulled out for us.

Winnie shows me how to pour some into the plastic cups built into the center of our volcanoes. I dump a little too much, but Winnie tells me it's fine.

"Soap," she says, making grabby hands Harrison's way.

With a chuckle, Harrison hands over the dish soap, and Winnie squeezes a dab into her cup.

"What does that do?" I ask.

"Makes more bubbles," Winnie informs me.

I squirt some soap into my own.

"Now we gotta do the vinegar," Winnie says. "But be careful, Sam, 'cause as soon as you pour it, it's gonna explode. You gotta be fast."

I huff a laugh. "All right. Show me how it's done?"

Winnie nods, and Harrison helps pour some vinegar into a measuring cup. Ever so carefully, Winnie kneels atop her chair, vinegar in hand. As soon as she pours it into the volcano, it starts spitting foam, and Winnie squeals, a huge smile on her face. I laugh along with her, understanding now why the sheet pans were a necessity.

"Your turn, Sam," Winnie says excitedly.

With a smile, Harrison hands me a cup of vinegar.

"Here we go," I say, holding it above my volcano. Taking Winnie's words about being quick to heart, I dump the vinegar all at once. The reaction is instantaneous. Fake lava comes shooting out of the top of my volcano, the vinegar having sloshed and rebounded upwards due to my hearty pour, and bubbles are quick to follow, cascading more gently down the sides of the clay creation. Winnie claps, and I laugh. I laugh and smile so hard my cheeks hurt with it.

"Holy cow," I say.

"That was a good one, Sam!" Winnie replies.

I turn my gaze Harrison's way. He's watching me with something soft in his eyes.

"Did you see that?" I ask him.

He chuckles a little, licking his lips. "Yeah, Sam. I saw it."

I turn back to Winnie. "That was so cool, li'l miss. Thanks for showin' me how to make a volcano."

"Next time, we can paint 'em," she says, already plotting. "And Daddy can buy more food coloring so it looks like *real* lava."

"Sure can," Harrison puts in.

"And if you come over early enough, we can make dinosaurs," Winnie says.

"Yeah?" I ask, hopeful little bubbles filling my chest.

"Uh-huh," she says. "Volcanoes are way more awesome with dinosaurs, Sam."

Harrison looks my way, a barely suppressed grin on his face.

"Sounds like a plan," I tell the little girl.

"Ready to clean up?" Harrison asks. "It's getting close to bedtime."

"Fine," Winnie mutters.

Harrison grabs a trash bag, and my eyes pop wide.

"We just throw 'em away?" I ask in alarm. Seems like a lot of work to dump the end product.

"It's okay, Sam," Winnie says, giving my arm a pat. Kneeling on the chair beside me, she can look me right in the eyes. "It's part of it. Sometimes you gotta just...let things go."

My heart does a complicated dance inside my chest, and based on Harrison's expression, he's feeling something similar.

"Is that so?" I ask the wise little girl.

She nods, helping hold the trash bag open as Harrison tilts her volcano inside. With a little push on his part, it topples into the bag, a mess of clay and soapy liquid.

"Besides," she says, wiping her hand on her dress, "Daddy needs the pans back to make cookies."

I bark a laugh, looking at Harrison, who's smiling to himself. "And what kind of cookies are your dad's favorite?" I ask.

"Sugar," she answers immediately, helping her dad dispose of the second volcano. I say a quick goodbye to my creation. "With sprinkles."

Harrison is blushing a little now. Sugar cookies with sprinkles. Noted.

"I'll go toss this outside," Harrison says, knotting the top of the trash bag. "Winnie, why don't you take a quick bath?"

"Okay, Daddy," she says around a sigh, sliding off her chair.

I grab the sheet pans to clean up.

"Can Sam listen to story time?" Winnie asks before Harrison can clear the room.

He stops, eyebrows popping up a bit. "If Sam wants to, sure."

There goes that little bubbling volcano inside my chest again. "I'd love to," I answer.

Winnie nods, like it's all settled, and Harrison continues outside to dump the trash. As Winnie heads upstairs for her bath, I clean up our mess, my eyes stinging a bit.

A minute later, Harrison reenters the room. "Sam," he says gently, grabbing hold of my shoulders from behind and resting his cheek beside mine. "You okay?"

I nod. I'm not surprised Harrison picked up on my emotions today. This whole evening has been...well, something special.

He kisses my cheek. "Come on up when you're ready. I'm going to help Winnie dry her hair."

I give him another nod, and Harrison's touch feathers away. I listen to him walk upstairs and finish in the kitchen before I follow. When I stop outside Winnie's bedroom, the pair isn't there yet. I take a seat on the floor near her bookshelf, flipping through her books as the blow dryer starts up down the hall.

When the pair come into the bedroom, Winnie hops onto her bed, pajamas already on. Harrison follows at a more subdued pace, sitting beside her, legs stretched out in front of him.

There they are again. One big. One small. A matching set.

"What are we reading tonight?" Harrison asks Winnie.

"Sam's choice," she replies.

"Really?" I ask.

Winnie nods, looking a little shy, so I turn my attention back to her bookshelf, plucking a book that caught my eye earlier. "How 'bout this one?" I say, passing it off to Winnie.

She nods, giving it to her dad. "Good choice. Daddy does *all* the voices, even the dragon. Just wait. You're gonna love it."

Harrison groans a little, but there's a smile on his face as he opens the book. "Just remember what you thought of me before this moment, Sam."

I huff a laugh, knowing there's no way my opinion of Harrison would worsen in the least. In fact, as he starts to read the story—silly voices included—my respect for the man only grows. I listen along with Winnie, transported, for a brief time, to a world of dragons and wonder. And I know—I'm certain of it—that this is different. What I'm building with Harrison, what I'm feeling right this moment, is unlike anything I've experienced before. It's new and exciting and quite possibly the most magnificent thing I've ever had the potential to lose.

When Harrison finishes the story, he gives me a little nod. "I'll be down soon, okay?"

I take my cue, standing up. "Night, li'l miss. Thanks for invitin' me to story time. I'll see you soon, all right?"

"Night, Sam," she says quietly, fidgeting with her blankets.

When I step outside the room, I pull the door closed all but a few inches and make my way downstairs. Tigger is on the couch, not yet having made her way into Winnie's room, and with a deep sigh, I sit down beside the dog. She climbs halfway onto my lap, even though she's certainly not a lapdog, and I dutifully rub her ears. Harrison has the best girls in his life.

"I'm fallin', Tigger," I tell the dog, looking down at her rusty orange eyes. "I'm fallin' harder than I ever have before."

Tigger doesn't answer me, but she does give my arm a big lick. And even though I know it's selfish, I wish I could stay in this house tonight. Stay right here with Tigger and Winnie and Harrison.

I wish, I wish, I wish.

CHAPTER 19

★

Harrison

"Can I put chocolate on these?" Winnie asks.

My lips twitch, but I shoot her a look as I grab the milk from the fridge. "Not this time."

She sighs, cutting into her French toast. "I bet Sam would let me," she mumbles, her casual suggestion nearly knocking me on my ass.

"Think so?" I ask, sitting down at the table and filling up her milk glass.

She shrugs, and my mind tumbles over the idea of discussing Sam in a more official manner. Winnie is getting close to him; that's clear. And at this point, I'm more than certain Sam isn't flitting out of my life anytime soon. I don't want him to, either. And yeah, I don't want Winnie getting hurt. But trust needs to start somewhere.

And I think—possibly—I was using her as an excuse. As a reason for *me* not to get attached too soon.

Too late for that.

"Hey, Pumpkin," I start.

But Winnie's head perks like a meerkat's, and she hustles onto her knees atop her chair. "Is that Sam?" she asks, looking out the window.

My head whips that way, and my mouth falls open in shock when I spot Sam in the backyard, a tool belt around his waist.

"What's he doing here?" Winnie asks, her breakfast completely forgotten. She perks up even more as it dawns on her. "Is he finishing my tree fort?"

"Looks like it," I say slowly, watching Sam check the sturdiness of the posts we put in last weekend.

Winnie slides off her chair, but I hold out a hand.

"Hold on," I say. "Breakfast first."

She pouts. "But I wanna see."

"After breakfast," I repeat, pointing toward the chair.

Winnie reluctantly scoots back into her seat and shoves a big forkful of French toast into her mouth.

"Besides," I say, tearing my own gaze away from the man outside, "there's something I wanted to talk to you about."

Winnie looks at me, her mouth stuffed full while she chews, and I nearly roll my eyes, knowing the lack of table manners is her tiny act of rebellion at having her fun squashed.

"You know that Sam has been coming over a lot," I say, the very evidence of that standing outside.

She doesn't answer, just keeps chewing. Okay, then.

Blowing out a breath, I go on. "Well, we decided we'd like to be more than friends."

It's only a beat before she says, "He's your boyfriend now?"

"Yes," I answer. "How do you feel about that?"

She shrugs. "He's nice, I guess. Nicer than Hank."

My chest squeezes tight. Hank is the only past boyfriend of mine that Winnie remembers. I'm not sure exactly how many details she can recall of the man himself, but clearly, he made enough of an impression.

Guilt hits all over again that I dated him in the first place. He wasn't good for us. I don't want to make that sort of mistake again.

"Sam *is* nice," I agree. "But that doesn't really answer my question."

"It's fine," she says flippantly. "Can I be excused now?"

I let out a sigh. Whenever Winnie says so little, it means there's a lot on her mind. I don't want to push her, though. She knows this means change. I just hope it's one she—and I—can handle.

"Sure," I tell her. "You're excused. Just don't get too close to Sam while he's working."

Winnie pushes away from the table and brings her plate to the side of the sink. She calls for Tigger as she heads toward the back door, and the dog follows not a moment later, short nails tapping down the hall.

I watch out the window as Sam's head turns when he catches sight of Winnie coming into the backyard in her big pink muck boots. He grins before bending down to greet Tigger, whose stub tail wiggles so hard her back legs do a little dance.

I shake my head, covering my mouth as my insides fizz. He fits. How does he fit?

After finishing my own breakfast, I clean up our dishes and head outside. Winnie is on one side of the yard with Tigger, the both of them investigating something under a bush. She's not wearing a jacket, but at least it's warming up quickly. Sam is over by the oak tree, nailing up the first of the supports for the floor of the treehouse. He sees me coming but finishes with the board in his hand before turning my way.

"Hey," he says warmly. He's wearing jeans today, like he usually does when he's off work, and a black t-shirt that hugs his body tight. His hat is on his head—no surprise there—and the morning sun hits him from the east in a way that highlights the definition of his abdomen while simultaneously lighting his face. The entire effect is stunning, and my tongue gets stuck to the roof of my mouth.

When I don't say anything, too caught up in taking in this man before me, Sam's expression falters.

"Should I have called first?" he asks. "I figured I'd surprise you, since you told me to keep bein' myself, and this is totally somethin' I would do. But now you're starin' at me, not sayin' a word, and I can't tell what that look means."

"Sam," I breathe out.

"Yeah, Harrison?" he asks tentatively.

"I like the things you do."

He exhales, tension dropping and smile snapping back into place. "Yeah?"

"Yeah. I'd like to kiss you if that's okay."

His eyes ping to Winnie across the yard. "You told her?"

And *fuck*, that hope in his voice.

I tug Sam in, and his lips meet mine, hat brushing my forehead before it's knocked away. He grips my side tight, and he's solid and warm and all the things I've been thirsting for. He lights me up inside in a way that's been absent from my life for entirely too long.

I pull back before the kiss can get heated—there are some things this parent doesn't need to do in front of their child—and Sam grins.

"Does this mean I'm definitely, officially your boyfriend now?" he asks.

I huff a laugh, grabbing Sam's hat from where it fell on the ground. "Yeah, Sam. So why doesn't my boyfriend get his cute butt back to work while I start some laundry? I'll be out to help soon, okay?"

Sam's grin never falters, even as I plop his hat back on his head. "You think my butt is cute?"

Of course that's the part he focuses on.

"What do you think?"

"I dunno, Harrison," he says with a playful smirk. "Maybe you oughta repeat yourself. I might've heard you wrong."

I step closer, putting us nearly toe to toe. I know Sam isn't fishing because he's remotely self-conscious about his body. He just likes the tease.

And damn if I don't like it, too.

"Your ass isn't cute," I amend, voice quiet. "It's practically illegal."

He hums, all satisfied and smug, and I have to step back, lest I start mauling him in front of my daughter.

"Make sure Winnie and Tigger stay away from the tools while you work," I say, walking backwards toward the house.

Sam tips his hat, giving me a wink. "You got it, stud."

Glancing at Winnie one last time—I don't need to know why her and Tigger are on their stomachs—I turn and head back inside. I toe off my boots before diverting into the laundry room. As the washing machine fills with water, I head upstairs and call my mom.

"Hi, dear," she answers quickly.

I pull Winnie's drape to the side, peeking into the backyard. "Hey, Mom. I have something I wanted to tell you and Dad. Before Winnie beats me to it."

"Okay, hold on," she says. A minute later, her voice is louder but farther away. "You're on speakerphone. Your dad and I are both here."

I don't bother wasting time with formalities. "Winnie knows about Sam."

"That you're dating?" my mom asks.

I nod, phone tucked between my ear and shoulder as I grab Winnie's laundry basket from her closet. "Yeah. She's still processing, I think."

"She'll be okay," my mom says.

"And she probably already knew, son," my dad adds. "It's not like you bring a lot of *friends* around the way you have Sam."

I groan a little, heading back down the stairs. "Thanks, Dad. So helpful." But he's likely right. Winnie, on some level, probably already knew.

My dad tsks at me.

"I like him," Mom says, not for the first time. She's been asking after him all week. "He's such a sweetheart."

A sweetheart. Yeah, that's Sam. That and so much more.

"I'm glad you're giving it a go again," my dad says.

I stop in front of the washing machine, opening the lid to pause the cycle before putting my parents on speakerphone. I set my phone down while I load the washer. "It has been a while," I admit.

"I was worried that..." My dad trails off.

"What?" I ask.

My mom fills in the silence. "We were worried you might be depressed, Harrison."

I exhale, hands at the edge of the washing machine as my pulse starts to thrum. "What?"

"You've been going through the motions for a long time," my dad says. "Now, don't get me wrong. You're a wonderful parent, and you always make time for Winnie. You give her your all."

"But?" I prod.

"But you don't leave anything for yourself, dear," my mom says gently. "And that can burn a person out. Believe me, I know."

I can't even deny their words.

"You haven't been smiling much lately," my dad goes on, voice a little sad. "It's been hard to see. But you wouldn't take our suggestions to get away for a bit—"

"I did," I remind him. "Remember? I went away to Plum Valley for a few days, and Winnie struggled the entire time through."

"And now she's okay," he says firmly. "She bounced back. But, Harrison, if you never leave her, she's not going to learn it's okay to let you go. You have to give her the chance in small doses."

I shake my head, even though I know what he's saying is true. "It's hard," I tell him. "I can't stand her suffering."

"We know," my dad shoots back, deadpan. "Believe me. We understand how you feel. We've been watching our son suffer for years now."

It hits me in the gut, those words.

"You can't use your daughter as a reason to pause your own life," my mom says softly. "You need to find a balance. Give Sammy your time, too. It'll be good for you."

"I...I am. I do," I tell her, realizing it's the truth. I have been making time for Sam, even when, before, that felt impossible. But we've already had more dates in the past few weeks than Hank and I did in our entire first few months together. It hasn't been hard, finding that time with Sam. Prioritizing it.

"Good," my mom says. "We just want you to be happy, dear. Sammy seems like the ticket."

I bark a strained laugh, walking into the hallway and looking out the back door. Sam is hard at work, the entire bottom frame of the treehouse now in place. He's looking over the design I printed out, nodding occasionally at Winnie, who's sitting about ten feet away, gabbing incessantly. Tigger is at her side, one paw swiping at a butterfly beside her in the grass. The butterfly flits away, and I head back into the laundry room.

"I need to go," I tell them. "Sam's here to finish the tree-house."

My dad makes an approving sound at that.

"Tell that boy we said hello," my mom says.

With a little huff, I toss the rest of Winnie's clothes into the wash and shut the lid. "Will do. See you guys on Monday. Love you."

"Love you, too, dear," my mom says before my dad chimes his own goodbye.

When I hang up, I stand in the laundry room for a moment, my head reeling.

Have I been using my responsibilities as an excuse? Have I been hiding away, putting my love life on hold because I was—what, afraid of trying again?

I don't even know that I can refute it. I had a similar thought earlier, didn't I? When I was thinking about why I was waiting to tell Winnie about Sam.

And then there's the other thing they said. Was I—*am* I—depressed? That I'm unsure of. I have felt hopeless a lot these past few years. I felt stuck, in a way. And yes, a little joyless at times.

But I don't... I don't feel like that right now. Sam has made everything a little brighter, even inside my own head.

Shaking it off for now—I have other things to do—I step back into my boots, grab my hat, and head outside. As I approach the oak tree, I can make out Winnie's ongoing ramblings.

"...but I don't think that's fair, do you, Sam? Why should Penny be able to have a snack during quiet time if nobody else can? It's totally fudged."

"Well, Winifred," Sam returns seriously, even as he lays another board onto the developing floor of the treehouse. He doesn't comment on Winnie's pseudo-swear, the one she *knows* she's not supposed to be saying. "If Penny is diabetic, that means her body needs a li'l extra help. You can prob'ly go from lunch to the end of school without hurtin', right?"

I stop a good ways away, not wanting to interrupt the conversation.

Winnie is quiet for a moment as Sam hammers in a board. "Sometimes I get a little hungry," she finally answers. "But it's just an ache."

"Right," Sam says, notching his hammer in his belt and climbing down the ladder he was on. "But for Penny, she might get really sick if she doesn't eat somethin'. She could end up in the hospital. That's more serious, don'tcha think? Mrs. Turner just wants to make sure Penny stays healthy. It's not meant to be unfair to the rest of you." He pauses, catching sight of me. "Oh. Hey, Harrison."

My heart patters away as Sam gives me a grin.

"Daddy says you're his boyfriend now," Winnie interjects.

My eyes shoot to her before landing back on Sam. He never stops smiling.

"That's right," Sam says, grabbing another board. "That okay with you, li'l miss?"

Winnie picks at a few blades of grass before answering. Sam doesn't seem perturbed by the silence. He just climbs back up the ladder and continues working.

"Guess so," Winnie says before hopping to her feet. "I like that you make him smile more."

With that, she's off, leaving my head swimming. I grab my knees, my breath coming short as spots dance suddenly in my vision.

"Hey, hey," Sam says gently, right in front of me now. His hands are on my shoulders, and he's bent down, eyes wide as he looks at me.

"I..." *Shit.*

"Here. C'mon," he says, leading me over to the wrought-iron bench that sits on the small patio square beside the back door. There are potted plants to either side of it, and my hand brushes the leaves of one as Sam guides me into the seat. He squats down in front of me, rubbing my thighs. "What just happened?"

I suck in an aching breath.

"I thought I was doing what was best for her," I get out, rubbing my clammy hands on my pants. "I thought..." I shake my head, the motion making me dizzy. "But even my own daughter can tell I've been sad, Sam. I had no clue she saw that, and I..."

I can't even finish my sentence, my thoughts as jumbled as they are. Even my own daughter could see I've been smiling more these past few weeks than I was before. Have I been a bad model of what I want for her? Have I been transferring my own unhappiness onto my kid?

Sam's eyes are creased at the corners as he watches me, his gaze solid. "You've been sad?"

"I..." I swallow roughly, the sound loud to my own ears. "I think so. I haven't been *happy*. Not really."

He lifts his hands, thumbs flitting under my eyes. "I wanna make you happy, Harrison."

"You do," I answer a little wetly. That, at least, I'm sure of.

It's everything else I'm suddenly very *unsure* about.

"What is it?" he asks gently, squeezing my thighs.

My heart thumps, the beat heavy and erratic.

"God, Sam," I choke out. "Am I a terrible dad?"

CHAPTER 20

Sammy

"Am I a terrible dad?" Harrison asks.

My breath catches. "Of course not," I say vehemently.

Harrison bends over again, shaking his head. He looks a little pale, and I glance over my shoulder, finding Winnie and Tigger digging around inside an empty grow frame for early season seedlings. Winnie's knees are dirty, but the little girl doesn't seem to care, and I know Harrison won't either.

"C'mon," I say, giving him a little tug. "Let's get you somethin' to drink." As Harrison stands, I call out to Winnie. "Winifred, your dad and I are gonna be inside for a minute, all right?"

"Okay," she calls back, not bothering to look our way.

Harrison is quiet as I lead him into the house, but he kicks off his boots inside the door. I do the same before guiding him into the kitchen. He lets me plop him into his customary chair, and I divert to the fridge to find something cool. I grab a pitcher of lemonade and pour a glass, figuring the sugar might help.

"Here," I say, passing the drink Harrison's way before taking a seat next to him where I can keep an eye out the window.

Dutifully, he drinks a sip. "Harrison, you're not a terrible dad. Why would you say that?"

He swallows roughly before looking at me, his pale eyes a little glassy. I wish it didn't make him more beautiful, whatever this pain is, but I feel honored to see it. Honored Harrison is choosing to share it with me.

His vulnerability is stunning.

"What kind of role model am I if my own daughter can tell I've been struggling?" he finally says.

"A human one," I answer.

That gives Harrison pause.

"Stud, it's okay to be sad sometimes. It's human nature. And I think it's okay for kids to see that. To know it's all right to show their own emotions. But if..." I think of how to word what I want to say, knowing it may not be my place. "But if it's overwhelmin', what you're feelin', it might not be a bad idea to talk to somebody about it."

Harrison nods idly, but he doesn't respond to my comment, so I switch gears.

"But just 'cause you've been strugglin', that doesn't make you a bad father," I say. "Pretty sure all parents struggle."

He grabs my hand, a slow movement, and squeezes, not letting up the gentle pressure.

"I didn't think I'd have kids," he says quietly.

"All right," I reply, giving him the option to go on. It's something I've wondered about, of course—how Winnie came to be.

"You know I wouldn't give up Winnie," Harrison says, looking down at our joined hands.

"I do," I say. I know that wholeheartedly.

"But sometimes," he goes on, "all I can think about is getting away for a little while. Just having a minute, an hour, a day to myself. I'm pretty sure that makes me a bad parent, Sam."

"It doesn't," I say, certain of it. It makes him an overworked one.

"The messed-up thing," he continues, as if he didn't hear me at all, "is that when I *am* alone, all I want is to be back with the person I love more than anything. It's a guilty fucking cycle, wanting my own life when I know my life is my child." He pauses, swallowing. "My parents said I'm using her as an excuse."

"What d'you mean?"

He looks up at me finally. "Their implication was that I'd been wallowing in my self-pity. That I *can* live my own life, but I haven't been trying."

"And what d'you think?" I ask, twisting my fingers with his.

"I think..." he says, looking out the window. I follow his gaze, catching sight of Winnie spinning in the early morning sun. Tigger is dancing around her feet, bouncing ever so slightly. "I think you don't get let down if you don't try."

I digest that for a moment, watching Harrison's little family enjoy a quiet morning outside these walls.

"I'm not a parent," I say softly. "So, I don't know that I can understand what it feels like for you to love somebody so damn much that you changed your entire life for them. 'Cause that's what you did, isn't it?"

He nods, a small thing.

"But we both know what it's like to care for the animals that are put in front of us," I say. "To want the best for them. To want to keep 'em healthy and safe. If that's even a fraction of what you feel for your daughter, I can only imagine how big that feelin' is. And I respect the hell outta you for holdin' it."

Harrison swallows again, eyes on where our hands are clasped.

"But you're not alone," I add.

He looks up at me, inhaling through his nose.

"You're not. And I think that's what your parents want you to know. Maybe you did have to sacrifice a lot when Winnie was a baby. Late at night, when it was just you and her, and you didn't get to sleep 'cause it was more important that she did. You prob'ly felt alone. You prob'ly felt that a lot. But you *do* have a support system, Harrison. Your parents moved here to help. You have them. And..." I give his hand a squeeze. "You have me. It's okay to take care of yourself now without the guilt."

"I don't know how to let go of that," he says, voice hoarse.

"One step at a time," I suggest, shrugging a little. "Start with somethin' small."

Harrison looks back at our clasped hands, fingers running idly over my own. "Like what?"

I glance out the window again, a smile on my face. "Take the mornin' off."

"What?" he asks, stilling.

"Take the mornin' off," I repeat. "The next four hours. I'll watch Winnie."

"Sam, I can't ask—"

"Number one, you didn't ask," I point out. "I offered. Number two, you can and you will. Go take a bath or a nap or do absolutely nothin' at all. Don't touch the laundry or whatever else you have on your list. We'll catch up on it after lunch. For now, just go take some time for yourself."

"I..." He peters out, seemingly at a loss. And *God*, the fact that he can't even accept something as simple as this tells me a lot. When's the last time he's done anything for himself and himself alone?

Well, time for that to change.

Giving Harrison a tug, I pull him upright and shove him gently toward the stairs. "Go on. Go rest or do whatever it is you wanna do. And don't you dare feel guilty about it. There's nothin' to worry about. If she needs you, I'll come get you."

"Sam, I..." He shakes his head a little, standing near the bottom step.

"Go," I say again, shooing him.

He takes a single step before halting. I can see the fight in him plain as day.

"Don't make me redden your ass," I tell him with a growl.

That earns me a sharp inhale and wide eyes, followed by a slowly blossoming smile. *Finally.*

"Fuck, Sam," Harrison says, shaking his head slightly. "That mouth of yours."

"Mhm. And if you're good, you'll get full use of it later. Now get."

Harrison gives me a brief nod, lips turned up at the corner. "Thank you."

"You got it. And Harrison?"

"Yeah, Sam?" he says with a chuckle.

"You're not a bad father," I tell him again, taking a step closer and resting my hand on the banister at the bottom of the stairs. "When I was a kid, all I wished for was somebody who cared the way you do. Winnie knows she's loved, all right? She has a great dad. She just wants you to be happy. So, maybe, it's okay to let yourself be."

He lets out a breath, lips trembling slightly. "Yeah, okay."

"Okay. Now get outta here," I say playfully, swatting Harrison's ass. "I don't wanna see your gorgeous face 'til lunch time."

Harrison shakes his head, but he finally ascends the stairs. I turn toward the back door, my chest so very tight.

When I get outside, Winnie is sitting on the patio bench, swinging her legs. Tigger is beside her on the cement, looking out over the yard. Both heads swivel my way as I approach.

"Heya," I say, stopping beside the pair. "Your dad is takin' a break, which means I could prob'ly use a hand gettin' this treehouse built. What'cha say? Know of anybody who can help?"

Winnie squints at me. "Daddy said I can't use the tools yet."

I figured as much and wasn't about to let Winnie do anything that could inflict any damage, but I still tell her, "Thanks for bein' honest about that, Winifred. I appreciate it. Think you could hold a board for me instead?"

She watches me for a moment longer, waiting for a catch. Apparently not finding one, she springs into action, jumping up and racing over to the oak tree. With a smile, I follow.

———★———

It's one o'clock when Winnie and I head inside for a late lunch. With the little girl's assistance, I finished the floor of the treehouse and attached the sides we already made that fit around the limbs of the sprawling oak. Now, it just needs a roof and a ladder. Although I have an idea for the roof I want to run by Harrison. Something that would let Winnie look up at the stars like she wanted.

Winnie is a right mess when we step inside the house, and I briefly debate having her clean up first. But, in the end, I figure a little dirt never hurt anybody. I still tell her to wash her hands in the sink, though.

While she's scrubbing the dirt from her nails and I'm putting together sandwiches, Harrison joins us in the kitchen. I don't notice him at first, not until he's wrapping his arms around me from behind and placing a kiss against my neck. I rumble happily, settling my clean hand over his arm.

"Thank you," he says quietly, his stubble rasping across my skin. He breathes deeply, and I know I probably smell like sawdust and sweat, but he doesn't seem to mind.

"Of course," I say, twisting my head toward him. He kisses my cheek. "How're you feelin'?"

"Mm." He nips my ear lightly, and lightning shoots down my spine. "Horny," he whispers.

I nearly choke on my spit. Definitely feeling better, then.

"I volunteer," I whisper back.

Harrison shakes against me. He places one more kiss beside my ear before stepping back. I blow out a deep breath, attempting to rein in my excited dick. *Sandwiches*, I remind myself. *We're making sandwiches.*

"Have a good morning, Pumpkin?" Harrison asks his daughter.

"Sam let me use the saw," she says, and there goes that choking again.

I spin around, and Harrison's eyes are wide.

"I did *not*," I defend, and Winnie starts giggling. *Giggling.*

Harrison relaxes immediately, failing to hide his smirk as Winnie comes over and steals a plate of food.

"Sam did let me help, though," she says, walking over to the table and taking a seat. "I got to bring him boards, and he nailed them up. And then I got to stand on the ladder so I could see, but we were *careful*, Daddy, and Sam held me the whole time. It looks like a real fort now, did you see? And Sam said he could build me a bookcase for inside, which is good, because *everyone* knows it's not a fort if you don't got books."

Winnie shoves her sandwich in her mouth as soon as she's done talking, and Harrison looks over at me. *Thank you*, he mouths. I smile, chest feeling oh so tight again.

"That's great, Pumpkin," Harrison says, sitting down. "I'm glad you two got so much done."

Winnie stops eating long enough to tell her dad about the bird that kept landing on the edge of the treehouse and how *we really do need to get that roof up quick, though, or the birds might poop inside, and how gross would that be?* She has a point, and I nod along, swinging by the fridge on my way to the table to grab a bag of baby carrots. I put four on my plate, four on Harrison's, and then four on Winnie's.

Winnie gifts me with a scowl. "I don't want carrots, Sam."

"Then you can give 'em to Tigger," I tell her, taking my seat.

Winnie stares at me silently as I go about eating my own lunch. Harrison is quiet, but his foot touches mine beneath the table. I shoot him a little smile, appreciative of the fact that Harrison never seems to mind letting me try to work these things out with Winnie on my own.

After a minute, the little girl leans down. The next second, I can hear Tigger chomping up the carrot Winnie gave her. She keeps watching me after that.

Finally, she breaks her silence. "You really don't care if I don't eat them?" she asks, sounding frustrated.

"I never said that. I do care," I tell her, wiping my hand and giving her my full attention. "I care because I want you to be healthy, and eatin' a rounded diet is part of that. I know you like sandwiches and cake better, but balance is important." Harrison's foot shifts against mine again. "But, honey, I'm not gonna force you. And hey, the carrots are good for Tigger, too."

Winnie's light blue eyes appraise me for a long moment. Finally, she picks up a carrot and nibbles off a bite, and I go back to my lunch, not wanting her to feel watched as she graciously eats her veggie. Inside, though, I'm pumping my fist.

When Winnie's plate is clear, she turns to her dad. "Can I be excused?"

Harrison nods, and Winnie hustles off her chair, bringing her plate to the counter. She washes up quickly before skipping out of the room, Tigger on her heels, and then the back door crashes shut.

"I don't know how you do that, Sam," Harrison says, shaking his head a little. "I always have to play Bad Cop to get her to eat her vegetables."

I reach over, giving his arm a squeeze. "You're not Bad Cop. Just a parent, enforcin' appropriate rules for his daughter. I can't make those rules, so I'm just doin' the best I can with what I've got."

Harrison's smile is warm. "You're doing pretty darn good, Sammy."

I beam, glad he thinks so. Standing up, I grab our empty plates. His words ring in my head, though, so before I pass Harrison, I stop and lean down to whisper in his ear.

"If you wanna play Bad Cop later, though," I say slowly, "I'm all yours."

Harrison sucks in a breath and then smacks my ass as I pass him, and I laugh, loading our dishes into the dishwasher.

"Sam," Harrison says seriously, standing up and following me.

"Yeah, stud?" I turn as he steps close, and his arms circle around my back, front pressed to mine.

"Thank you. For today," he says. "I feel like I've been nothing but a mess in front of you. Scattered and emotional. But you're still here."

"'Course I am," I tell him, wrapping my thumbs in the belt loops at the sides of his hips. "And maybe it's not such a bad thing, y'know?"

"What's not?" he asks.

"You bein' emotional. Maybe that just means you're processin' some stuff that's been buried for a li'l too long."

Harrison is quiet as he mulls that over. "I don't want you to leave."

"I'm not goin' anywhere," I fire back.

But Harrison chuckles a bit at my affronted expression and shakes his head. He leans close, his cheek against mine as he hugs me. "I want you to stay tonight."

My heart lifts and swells. Bursts, nearly. "Then I'll stay."

"Okay," he says.

"Okay."

He takes a step back. "Hope you're ready, though."

"Ready for what?" I ask, curious about that twinkle in his eye.

He heads toward the hall. "Bad cops are known for roughin' folks up."

I stare as Harrison disappears from sight, my mouth open and my cock swelling against the front of my now too-tight jeans.

"You promise?" I call out.

Harrison chuckles, the sound throaty and amused, before the back door shuts and cuts off the sound.

"Good grief," I mutter, pressing down on my cock. "I think I might've met my match."

CHAPTER 21

Harrison

"What if Grandpa fell?" Winnie asks, her voice small as she worries her lightweight comforter between her fingertips. "What if he needed to go to the hospital?"

"Grandma would bring him," I answer, tucking her sheets more firmly around her body. Her bedroom is already dark, the star-shaped night-light adding a soft glow to the room.

"But what if she couldn't? What if you had to?" she presses.

"Then I'd wake you up and bring you with me," I say gently, used to this game of Winnie running through hypotheticals at night when she's particularly stressed.

"What if there was an emergency at your work?" she counters.

"At this time of night?"

"What if?"

"Then I would wake you up and bring you with me," I say again. "Winnie, there is nothing on this earth that would cause me to leave you here alone when you're still so young. Or before you're ready to be left alone. I'm not going anywhere. I'll be right down the hall all night."

She nods, even as her throat works.

I'm well accustomed to this. The nighttime struggle. But it doesn't make it any easier.

"Pumpkin," I say gently, brushing her blonde hair back.

"I'm scared to be alone," she cuts in, and my heart breaks right down the center.

"I know," I reply softly. "But you're not alone."

"She left me, though."

Fuck. *Fuck*.

I tuck Winnie's hair behind her ear, giving my fingers something to do while I get my emotions under control.

"I'm not your mom," I say at last. "I won't ever leave you. Not like that. Not for any reason, you hear?"

Winnie nods, but her bottom lip is trembling, and it's all I can do not to curse Danielle's name. It's for the best she didn't stay. I know that—I do. Lord knows what would have happened if she'd kept Winnie, but it still angers me to no end when I'm put in this position. A position where I have to lie to my daughter.

When do I tell Winnie the truth? Do I? Danielle didn't want her to know.

"Try to close your eyes and rest, Pumpkin," I say, running my fingers soothingly through Winnie's hair.

She does as I ask, turning slightly and wrapping one arm over Tigger, but the tension doesn't leave her face for a long time. It's not until a good twenty minutes later that Winnie's breaths are even and her expression is smoothed in sleep.

I exit her room carefully and stop to listen outside the door, letting out a deep breath when all stays quiet. Heading down the hall, I find Sam in my bedroom, shirtless and sitting against my headboard. The light in the en suite is on, and the mirror is still a little fogged from Sam's shower.

I lock the door before approaching, and Sam tilts his head. "What's wrong?"

"Rough one," I answer, sitting on the edge of the bed. I'm not surprised he could read it on my face.

"I'm sorry," he says gently. "Do you wanna talk about it?"

"Maybe later," I say, rubbing my eyes before squeezing Sam's leg over the sheet. He looks a little sheepish suddenly, and I notice the bottoms of his arms are hidden away under the white linens, same as his legs. "Why do you look like that? Are you hiding something?"

Sam gives me an almost apologetic smile before he lifts his hands out from under the sheet. His wrists are bound together with a tie.

I slap my hand over my mouth, barking a laugh. "Sammy, what did you do?"

"Well, I thought you might wanna play," he says slowly. "And don't worry. I coulda gotten out. But, uh, now you seem like you might need a hug instead."

He twists his hands, reaching one toward the tie like he's going to free himself, but I grab the fabric between his wrists, halting his movement. His eyes ping to me, watching, waiting.

"You really wanna play Bad Cop?" I ask, pulse firing.

He licks his lips. "Well, I'm already tied up for ya."

"Oh, Sam," I say, rolling to my knees and crawling up over his body. He tilts his head back, eyes moving with me as I settle on his lap, his bound hands between us. "You're good for me, you know that?"

I get one of those grins that make my knees a little weak.

"Are you naked under here?" I ask, slipping my hand beneath the sheet and encountering bare skin. I flit my fingers along Sam's hip, right where his constellation should be.

"I've already been debriefed," he says, deadpan.

I laugh again, my insides feeling so damn light. "Fuck, Sammy." Grabbing his wrists in one hand, I bring them up above his head. My body is thrumming in anticipation, and after the day I've had, I *do* want to play. I want to lose myself for a little while in this man. I want to thank him for everything he's done. For who he's becoming to me. "Looks like you're mine tonight. You okay with that?"

"Yeah, Officer," he answers, voice taking on a hoarse edge. "Do your worst."

My cock bucks, and Sam stays still, watching me patiently despite the hunger I can see in his eyes. He's wearing that glass heart of his right on his sleeve, transparent as ever, and I want to protect it. I want to place it beside my own. A perfect pair.

Maybe he can protect mine, too.

Leaning forward, I bring my lips to Sam's. He meets me eagerly, tongue tangling with my own and hips moving restlessly, seeking friction. When I lean back, he chases. Chases my tongue, my touch, my very essence, it seems. He asks for more.

I want to give him everything.

"Hands behind your head, Sam," I tell the man, giving the tie binding him a squeeze before letting go.

Sam rumbles—*purrs*—as he lowers his wrists, settling them comfortably behind his neck. I ease back, raking my fingers down his torso as I take the man in. His reddened lips. The flexed arms. His broad chest and defined abdominals, and the trail that leads down below the sheet. The way he's fixed on me, trust and something that feels a lot like familiarity in his gaze.

"You said I could use your mouth," I say, flitting my fingers over Sam's crotch and the outline of his cock.

Sam nods, cheeks flushed. "Yes."

I rub him more firmly. "What else?"

"Anythin'," he answers on a breath.

"Mm." I give his dick a squeeze. It looks almost obscene cloaked in white linens, the tease of it more tantalizing than if he were bared before me. "Your ass?" I ask.

"Yes," he answers immediately, chest rising and falling.

"Because you like it?" I check, shifting down his body. "Or because I asked?"

"I like it, stud," he answers, those warm brown eyes intent on mine as I step off the bed and back up a little. "And I'll like it even more because it's you."

This man.

Taking a breath, I toy with the button on my shirt. "I don't want to be rough with you, Sam. Not tonight."

He nods, accepting that easily.

"But you're going to stay just like that," I say, tracing a finger down the midline of my chest. "And you're going to watch."

He swallows roughly, throat bobbing. "Are you..."

His question trails off as I flip the top button of my shirt open slowly. I haven't done this in a long damn time, but some things you don't forget.

Sam groans as I start to sway my hips, moving my body to a silent beat. His breath is harsh in the otherwise quiet room, and I listen to each hitch as I ping my buttons free, one at a time.

"Stud," he rumbles. "Look at you."

"That's the point," I retort, turning as I slowly drop my shirt off the back of my shoulders. Sam makes a tortured noise as I shake my ass, and I look back at him, easing the shirt down my arms before dropping it to the floor.

"I'm startin' to regret this," he says, wiggling the fingers of one hand.

"You'll survive," I tell him, giving him a prime view of my ass as I drop my upper body low and then roll upwards.

He curses, and I can't help but smile. This is a lot more fun with Sam.

"Besides, I'm Bad Cop, aren't I?" I say. "I can't let you go that easy."

Sam hums in what might be disagreement, but he doesn't move an inch as I start unbuckling my belt. He simply watches me, gaze heavy on my backside as I slide the belt free and drop it to the floor.

"So why..." Sam clears his throat as I start shimmying my jeans down my hips, never breaking stride. "Why didn't the stripper thing work out? You're clearly good at it."

I huff a little laugh, taking the praise for what it is. "Didn't like grinding on women," I tell him, turning back his way, my jeans low enough he can see my tented briefs.

He makes a curious sound, gaze on my crotch. "Not that it matters to me one way or another, but I assumed you were bi," he says, and it's not hard to guess why. I have a daughter.

"Gay," I tell him, slipping my pants off.

Sam makes another noise, watching intently as I roll my body, my hands sliding down my stomach and hips. He blows out a breath. "*Stud.*"

Smile on my face, I slip my thumbs under my waistband and ever so slowly lower the material, stopping when my briefs are halfway down my cock. "You want me to take these off?"

"Yes, I goddamn do," he says, his biceps bunching like he's having trouble keeping still.

"Since you asked so nicely," I say, slipping the material down my legs.

Sam blows out another breath, his eyes darkening as I walk closer. Abandoning my dance, I jump onto the bed and straddle his body, hands going to the sheet sitting low on his hips.

"Keep those hands behind your head," I tell him, easing the sheet down. Sam's cock is fully upright, hard and leaking precum, and I hum at the sight before meeting the man's gaze. "You took care of me today. Now, I'm going to take care of you."

Sam's nostrils flare as I bend low, and the last thing I see before my lips meet his crown is the look on his face, open and raw and pure. He groans as I suck the head of his cock into my mouth, and his salty flavor bursts onto my tongue. I lave it up, squeezing him at the base as my own dick throbs.

I love Sam's taste. The way he's velvety smooth against my tongue. I love the sounds he makes and how he rumbles deep in his chest as I suck him down my throat. It's addicting, hearing those purrs, and I think I know exactly how to get more of them.

Easing back, I release Sam's cock with a soft plop. His chest heaves as I shift to reach the nightstand, and he watches me curiously as I bring back lube and something else. Something I keep hidden in my hand.

"You trust me to make you feel good?" I ask.

Sam's brows cinch together, but he nods immediately. "I trust you."

My heart kicks.

"Good," I say, pulling the sheet entirely off of him and giving his leg a slap. "Spread 'em."

Sam huffs a laugh, but he does as I ask, bringing his knees up and spreading his legs. I nudge him a little further until he's right where I want him, opened up and on display for me.

It's a breathtaking sight.

"You're gorgeous," I tell him because I don't think I ever have. I think there's a lot I've left unsaid when it comes to Sam, too afraid to speak plainly. Too afraid to let myself *hope*.

"Should I be jealous you're sayin' that to my asshole and not my face?" he asks.

I give his knee a kiss before opening the lube. "All of you, Sammy," I say seriously, meeting his gaze as I wet my fingers. "I'm saying it to all of you."

Sam rumbles at that, the sound turning into a moan as I focus my attention lower and press against his ass. I rub over his hole, then along his perineum. His arms bunch again, and his cock flexes.

"You do like this," I say, smiling.

"Mm."

Going slow, I ease a finger inside his body. "I'm not going to fuck you today."

"No?" he asks, voice all breath.

"Not this time. There's something else I want."

He licks his lips.

"I *am* going to torture you a bit, though," I say, grabbing the object I left hidden behind me.

Sam's eyes widen when he sees the anal vibe in my hand. It's not a large toy, just a couple inches long in total and an inch wide at the base of the tapered shaft, but damn does it feel good.

"Well, aren't you full of surprises?" Sam mutters.

I give him a swift grin, stretching him with two fingers as I roll the toy in my palm. His dick leaks a drop of precum onto his stomach.

"Ready?" I ask.

Sam nods, and I remove my fingers, easing the toy in instead. It glides in effortlessly, and Sam's rim holds it tight as the shaft disappears and the flared base settles against his ass. I give it a little wiggle, and Sam moans.

"Mkay," he says. "Yep. Not gonna survive."

"Oh, angel," I tease. "You just wait."

When I press the vibrating toy on, Sam's hips buck, and the man himself lets out a garbled moan. Grin on my lips, I grab his cock, angling it my way and licking the head. Sam closes his eyes tight, his hips moving up off the bed, chasing my mouth or pressure against the vibrator or maybe both. I'm not sure he himself knows. And with his eyes shut as they are—surely in an attempt to keep himself in check—he doesn't see as I start stretching myself.

"Stud, I..." he says, lashes fluttering. "I'm gonna come if you keep doin' that."

That's kind of the point, but I do ease back, letting Sam's cock go and turning off the toy. He opens his eyes, and I get up on my knees, reaching for Sam's wrists where they're resting behind his neck. I pull them up and over his head, giving him a little tug.

"I need you flat on your back," I tell him.

Sam doesn't question me. He simply scoots down the bed, moaning about the vibe *doin' such good things* as he goes. The moment he's flat atop the mattress, I climb up over his body and press his hands above his head. His eyes widen when I roll a condom down his shaft and then hold the base of his cock, positioning myself over him. He opens his mouth, but as his crown slips inside my body, his eyes roll back, and his voice is lost. I drop down quickly, too goddamn eager for this man, and with one hand wrapped around the tie between Sam's wrists, I reach back and turn the vibrator on.

Sam jolts, his muscles bunching, hands tensing into fists as I start to ride him. For once, he doesn't say a single word, only stares at me with unfailing focus and dark eyes as I bounce on his cock, rolling my hips the same way I was doing during my striptease. The tie around his wrists keeps him bound, but I know Sam could move if he really wanted to. He told me as much, that he could untie himself easily. This isn't about giving up control for him, the way I think something like this would be for me. This is about giving me *himself*, just like he's been doing ever since he walked into my life.

He's been giving me pieces of himself every single day.

"You, Sam. You make me feel…"

"What?" he asks, chest flushed. It rises and falls rapidly as I fuck myself down on his cock.

"So much," I answer, moving my hand from his wrists down to his chest. Reaching back, I kick the toy up a notch, knowing the settings by feel at this point, and Sam shuts his eyes tight, his jaw tensed and his abs contracted.

I'm not sure how much longer he can last.

"Sam," I croak. He opens his eyes in an instant, and I get stuck there. Trapped in that transparent gaze. I feel like I'm on the edge of some precipice, teetering, waiting to jump. "I need…"

"Anythin'," he says.

"I need you to touch me."

Sam doesn't hesitate. He twists his wrists, tugging at his binding with one hand and quickly unfurling the tie. It drops, loose, to the bed, and Sam reaches for me. Hands on my ass, fingers digging into my flesh, he tugs me down as his hips punch upwards, and I'm lost. I'm lost and in freefall as Sam's cock and touch and deep, rumbled groans light me up from the inside out. It won't take but a touch to splinter apart, and as Sam's hand wraps around my cock, I'm there, coming across his chest as my release courses through my body like I'm a live wire and Sam my power source. It's unstoppable, and I wouldn't stop it even if I could. But I know, as Sam stutters out a moan, hips grinding against me as he comes, that whatever this is—whatever we're building day by day, step by step—is something I'm going to see through to the end.

Maybe we will crash. Maybe we'll fizzle out, no spark left between us in the end. But I'm going to try. I'm damn well going to try.

And that—that feels like a revelation.

As Sam's fingers loosen their grip on my ass, the man himself groans. "Harrison, you gotta turn it off."

I bark a laugh, reaching behind me to stop the vibrator, and Sam's body falls lax.

"Fuck," he sums up.

"Fuck," I agree.

Sam gives me a grin, big and lopsided, and I lean down, cupping his chin as I bring my lips to his. So sweet. So earnest.

"I think," he says when I sit upright, "I like your methods of torture, Officer."

I chuckle as I hold Sam's condom in place, easing myself off his body. He rubs my thigh, turning toward me as I crash, spent, down to the mattress.

"So, *good* Bad Cop?" I ask.

"Best Bad Cop," he says, watching me for a moment. Neither of us seems to be in a hurry to clean up, and the vibe is still in Sam's ass, but I don't think he minds now that it's off. "D'you think..."

"What?" I ask, running my fingers over Sam's shorn hair. He hums.

"D'you think you'd like bein' tied up sometime?"

I swallow, the idea more than appealing. "Yeah," I tell him. "I think I'd like that."

He smiles a little wickedly, and I swear I can already see the gears turning.

"Let's get cleaned up," I tell him, running my finger through the cum on his chest. "Before we fall asleep like the debauched mess we are."

"I like bein' a debauched mess with you," he says, although he does sit up, a little gingerly, mind you, because of the toy. "I mean, fuck, stud. D'you realize how goddamn sexy that was, you ridin' me like that? I don't know how I didn't come the moment you sank down on my cock."

"And there's that mouth I love so much," I tease.

Sam laughs, eyes twinkling as he follows me off the bed and into the en suite bathroom. "You like my mouth, do you?"

"You know I do," I say, starting the shower. "You know what else I'm going to like?"

"What's that?" he asks, leaning against the side of the glass stall. I don't know how the man looks so utterly relaxed when there's still a toy lodged up his ass, but he manages it.

"I'm going to like falling asleep with you," I tell him, my cheeks heating as soon as I realize how vulnerable that statement makes me feel.

But Sam's eyes soften, and he tugs me close, fingers flitting along my jaw. "I'm gonna like fallin' asleep with you, too."

"Yeah?"

"Yeah. So, c'mon. Get this thing outta my ass so we can shower and get back to that big bed of yours."

I crack a smile. "Deal."

CHAPTER 22

Sammy

"Oh hell, is that the alarm?" I ask, reaching blindly.

Harrison grunts, and I open my eyes, finding my boyfriend rubbing his nose.

"Shit, stud, I'm sorry."

He waves me off before letting his arm fall back over my chest. "It's not the alarm. It's Winnie. The TV is on, which means we have approximately five minutes before she's up here, demanding breakfast."

"Better get a move on, then," I say over my yawn, not really *wanting* to move. In fact, I want to stay right here, curled up beside Harrison's warm body for as long as I possibly can.

But I suppose hungry ten-year-olds wait for no man, even on a Saturday.

"Daddy?" a voice calls.

Harrison huffs out a laugh, and I smile with him, feeling damn giddy for reasons I suspect have to do with this man and waking in his bed. I give his pec a kiss before rolling away.

"I'll get food started," I say, grabbing my jeans off the floor and stepping into them. I pull a t-shirt over my head before ambling for the door.

"Sam," Harrison says. He's standing near the en suite now.

"Yeah?"

"You really don't mind?" he asks, face doing something complicated.

I cock my head. "Of course I don't. I'm happy to help out." He still seems unsure, so I tack on, "Consider it one of the many perks of havin' your boyfriend stay over." When I waggle my eyebrows, Harrison chuckles.

"Yeah, okay. Thanks, Sam."

"You bet," I tell him, chest heating at the little smile I receive in return.

As Harrison closes the bathroom door, I head into the hall to face the tiny human's wrath.

"Mornin', Winifred," I call out, jogging down the stairs.

The little blonde pops into view, looking at me from over the back of the couch. "Sam," she says evenly. If she has opinions on my being here first thing in the morning, she doesn't let them show. "Are you making breakfast?"

"Sure am," I tell her, although I'll need to empty my bladder before I get started. "What're you in the mood for?"

"Waffles," she replies instantly.

I crack a smile, not surprised. "How 'bout waffles and eggs, all right?"

"Fine," she mutters, going back to her show.

I swing by the downstairs bathroom and relieve my bladder before heading into the kitchen. Luckily, I left my waffle-maker here, so I get it plugged in before setting to work on the batter. Harrison joins me before long, looking all sleep-rumpled and adorable in his sweats and a soft blue t-shirt. My gut swoops and rolls at the sight.

"What?" Harrison asks, rubbing at his eye as he grabs eggs from the fridge.

"Nothin'," I reply. "You're cute, is all."

He huffs a laugh, squinting at me. "I think you need your eyes checked."

I scoff, setting down my whisk and stepping up behind the man. He leans back against my chest with a sigh, and I wrap my arms around him tight. "Stud, you're a damn fine sight *all* the time, but right now? First thing in the mornin' when you haven't had your caffeine yet and there's a pillow line across your cheek? I consider myself lucky to be able to see you like this."

He hums, and I nuzzle behind his ear. He smells fresh, soft, and warm, like biscuits right out of the oven.

"Plus," I say, kissing his neck swiftly. "Knowin' that yawnin' mouth of yours was wrapped around my dick just eight hours ago?" I rumble my appreciation as I recall that very thing. Harrison's mouth. His body clamped around me tight as he rode me. That damn toy he stuck up my ass that nearly drove me out of my mind. *Christ.*

"Sam," Harrison rasps, likely remembering the same thing.

I give him a squeeze. "Don't ever doubt how much I want you, all right?"

That earns me a soft smile, and satisfied, I head back over to the waffle batter.

"So, what's the plan for today?" I ask, pouring out the first waffle.

"Well," Harrison says, clearing his throat. "I thought, maybe, we could go camping in the backyard."

My head whips around so fast, I nearly get whiplash. "Really?"

Harrison chuckles. "Yeah, really."

"All right," I say excitedly, mind whirring. "So, I'll needa run home and get the tent. And then did you wanna pick up that fire pit you were lookin' at? We'll need stuff for s'mores, too, and prob'ly a sleepin' bag for Winnie, unless she already has one? I have a couple adult sizes, but she'll need somethin' warm, don'tcha think?"

"Sam," Harrison says, smile on his face. "We'll get everything squared away. We have plenty of time. Take a breath."

"Right," I say, nodding along. "D'you think Winnie would like makin' popcorn over the fire?"

Harrison laughs, cracking eggs into a bowl, and I wonder if this is what it feels like to make plans for more than myself.

I like it. I like it a lot.

———————— ★ ————————

"There we go," I say, snapping the final tent post into place. "Voila."

Winnie claps slowly, two times, the little sass-monster. Apparently, pitching the tent is *not* the exciting part of camping.

"Can we make s'mores now?" she asks.

That's the exciting part.

"Soon," Harrison replies from beside the new fire pit. A small orange flame is flickering in the metal bowl, and he prods the wood pile with a stick, getting a better burn going.

"Wanna help me get the inside ready while we wait, li'l miss?" I ask.

Winnie grumbles, but she picks herself up off the grass and comes over to where I'm standing. I toss her a sleeping bag before grabbing the rest of the supplies, and we crawl inside the tent. It's a fairly decent size. Not tall enough for *me* to stand up, but Winnie can just manage it. She sets down her sleeping bag, looking bored until I pull out a strand of battery-powered fairy lights.

"What're those?" she asks.

"They're our stars," I reply, using a few pieces of tape to string the lights along the top of the tent. Winnie waits patiently, and once in place, I flick the power on.

"*Oh*," she says, and *there* it is. The magic of camping.

"We'll look at the real ones, too," I tell her. "But this way, we'll keep 'em with us when we go to bed."

"It's kinda like my night-light," she says softly.

Exactly.

I give her a smile. "Should we see if your dad is ready for us now?"

Winnie nods exuberantly before skipping from the tent, and I follow. Tigger is sitting next to Harrison, nose suspiciously close to the bag of marshmallows in his lap. When Winnie walks up, Harrison hands her a roasting stick, already loaded with a mallow on the end.

"Want some help?" Harrison asks her.

Winnie shakes her head, taking a seat in the camping chair beside Harrison. Her tongue sticks out as she carefully positions her marshmallow over the fire. Tigger, I notice, has shifted her attention to Winnie, possibly hedging her bets.

I chuckle, taking the chair on Harrison's other side. Squeezing his knee, I ask quietly, "Gonna offer to help hold my stick?"

He bites his lip, a smile twisting the corner of his mouth. "You're fully capable."

"Sure," I agree. "But it's more fun when you do it."

Harrison shoves the bag of marshmallows at my face, and I barely dodge the soft attack in time. Snatching it from him, I blow him a kiss and stick two marshmallows on my roasting stick. He shakes his head, opening a packet of graham crackers.

Harrison gets crackers and chocolate ready for Winnie, and when she finally pulls her marshmallow away from the fire, he helps her maneuver the entirely too-white mallow onto the sandwich. In no time at all, the plate is in her lap, and marshmallow and chocolate are smeared across her cheek.

"Here," Harrison says, handing me a prepped plate, as well.

"Thanks, stud."

Harrison grabs the bag of marshmallows, setting to work on his own s'more, and once my mallows are fully browned—*not* charred—I slip them between my graham crackers. Harrison, I note, put *two* rows of chocolate in my s'more instead of one. I like his style.

I hum as I take my first bite, the treat feeling nostalgic in the best way. I went camping a lot when I aged out of the foster system, having picked up the basics of it from one of my carers who ran a summer camp. Once I turned eighteen and was officially on my own, I found solace in packing up my tent and camping under the stars.

All my life, I'd never had a place where I belonged. But there, underneath the starlit sky, I felt at home. I think it's because I knew, somewhere out there, my family was under the same roof.

All I had to do was find them.

Harrison knocks my boot with his own, drawing me to the present. "Okay?" he asks.

"Yeah," I say, giving him a smile. "I like this."

His lips turn up. "I like this, too."

I finish my s'more as Harrison eats his own, followed by another three. Winnie only manages two and a half.

The sky is turning dark by the time we're done with our treats, and as the fire dies down, Harrison heads inside with Winnie to get ready for bed. I enjoy the last vestiges of warmth with Tigger, who's pressed against my leg, soaking up the scratches I'm giving her.

"This is the life, huh, Tigger?"

She doesn't respond, but she does look up at me, rusty orange eyes flickering slightly in the glow of the fire. She seems content here, Winnie's little sidekick. I don't blame her. I think anyone would be lucky to belong to the Baileys.

When Harrison and Winnie get back outside, Winnie is dressed in warm pajamas, and her hair is down and brushed. She makes a beeline for her treehouse, clearly not quite ready to settle in for the night. Halfway up the ladder, she calls out, "Come *on*, Sam. You said we could look at stars."

I huff a laugh. That I did.

"You go ahead," Harrison says, starting to collect our trash. "I'm just going to clean up first."

"You sure?" I check. "I can help."

He shakes his head. "Go on. You can show her the book you brought."

"All right," I say, but I can't quite resist stepping up to him first. As I loop my arms around his body, Harrison pauses, graham cracker box held in one hand, his other finding my hip. His blue eyes are soft, the strain that was there when we first met absent. I like seeing him so relaxed. So at ease.

I fit our mouths together gently, and Harrison swipes at me with his tongue. He tastes like sugar and chocolate. Like sweetness and sin. I'd devour him if I could, but I know this isn't the time for that.

And truthfully, I like this night a whole lot just as it is. I like these moments with this family. With him.

"*Sam*," Winnie calls.

Huffing a laugh, I let Harrison's lips go and step back. He shakes his head, cheeks a little flushed as he goes back to cleaning up our mess. I stop by the tent to grab my book about constellations, and then I make my way up into the treehouse.

Winnie is waiting inside, lying down on the old blankets Harrison said she could keep up here. She points at the roof when I crawl inside her *tree fort*, as she likes to call it, and I take my cue, turning the latch to open it up. In reality, the moonroof is just a swinging door built into the top of her treehouse, but its sole purpose is for this. Stargazing.

I settle beside Winnie on the blankets, my knees bent so I can fit. "Wanna see if we can find the Big Dipper?" I ask, holding up my book.

Winnie nods, and I flip it open to the right page. It shows a star map of the constellation, and as Winnie tries to match the shape to the stars above, I read her the mythology behind the greater bear, Ursa Major. The Big Dipper only comprises seven of the stars in Ursa Major, but they're the easiest to spot. It's a constellation that's visible year-round in Texas, and after some help on my part, Winnie and I find it riding low in the northern sky.

"I like stars. They're neat," Winnie says, relaxing back against her blankets.

I nod, setting my book aside before laying my head in my palms. "They are. You've got good taste, li'l miss."

She's quiet for a moment. "Sometimes, I don't like the night, though."

"No?" I ask, turning my head to look at her.

She doesn't answer, just looks up through the hole in the roof. I don't push her on it, but I wonder if it's because she feels most alone at night, when it's dark.

"I like the starlight," I tell her.

"Why?" she asks.

I hum, turning my gaze to the dotted sky. "It's like...hope. It's full of wishes. Those stars come out at night, and I look up at 'em and see my future. I see all the things I want my life to be. And maybe it's a dream, but I think... I think hope and wishes are what make our dreams come true."

Winnie is quiet for a long while. "Will you make a wish with me, Sam?"

My chest squeezes tight. "I'd love to," I reply, voice a little hoarse. "First, you gotta pick a star. Got one?"

She gives a nod in my peripheral vision.

"Good," I say. "Now you hold onto that star, and you make a wish, right inside your heart, all right? You gotta feel it."

"Okay," she says softly.

"Okay. Here we go." Taking a deep breath, I pick out a star in the blinking night sky. "I wish..." I prompt.

Winnie mimics me, her voice quiet. "I wish..."

Neither of us finishes our wish aloud. We keep them in our hearts, just like I told Winnie to do. But of all the wishes I've made in my life—of which there have been a great many—this one is the biggest. I *can* feel it, deep inside, where all my dreams lie. I can feel it, and I want it so damn badly I ache. I want it more than I've wanted anything in my entire life.

"Sam?"

A smile curves my lips. "Yeah, Winifred?"

"I think we're friends now, don't you?" the little girl asks.

Ah, God.

Blinking rapidly, I clear my throat. "Yeah, li'l miss. I do."

"Okay, good," she says. "Can you tell me about another constellation?"

"Of course," I reply, grabbing my book. I open it up, reading to Winnie about Orion's Belt, and she listens raptly, eyelids seeming to get heavy as we lie there inside her treehouse learning about the stars. It's so perfect I could cry.

A few minutes later, footsteps ascend the ladder.

"Hey," Harrison says softly, peeking his head inside. "Time for bed."

"Aw, man," I groan. "Really?"

Winnie snickers, getting up and climbing over my body, nearly kneeing me in the gut as she goes. Harrison gives me a smirk before disappearing down the ladder, and Winnie follows him. I look up at the Big Dipper one more time before closing the top of the treehouse.

When I get to the tent, the other two are already inside. The fairy lights flicker above us as we settle in for the night, Harrison and I on either side of Winnie because that's how she insisted we be. Tigger lies near my feet, and Harrison reads Winnie a bedtime story. Her eyes are shut before he's even finished, and he looks over at me in awe, closing the book quietly.

"That's a first," he whispers.

"Magic of campin'," I reply.

He gives me a soft smile, laying his head down on his pillow. I do the same, easing out a breath. It's not lost on me, the fact that I'm staying here for the second night in a row. I wonder what that means.

I wonder if, someday, I could spend *all* of my nights here.

"Sam," Harrison says gently, careful not to wake Winnie. The little girl seems out, though.

"Yeah?"

"Tell me something."

I nearly bark a laugh, and Harrison grins like he can tell. I ease onto my side, too, settling my head in my hand, and I start to talk, telling Harrison about the first time I went camping on my own. How amazed I was at the quiet, still air and the sight of so many twinkling stars above, like a blanket of light. I tell him about what that day meant to me and how I got my tattoo shortly after.

I don't tell him about my wish that night. How I dreamed of a family to share the magic with.

But as I look at Harrison's gentle, sleepy smile and see Winnie and Tigger lying close, I recall the words my heart whispered earlier. The ones that have changed, I realize—morphed from the vague form they once were into something specific and concrete. And I let myself hope that maybe, just maybe, they could come true.

I wish...

They were mine to keep.

CHAPTER 23

✦

Harrison

"Shit," I mutter, looking at the small cut on my finger. Setting the knife aside, I wash my hand in the sink, cleaning the cut. "Winnie," I call out. "We need to get moving."

"Coming," she yells down the stairs.

I glance at the clock again, realizing we're going to be late if we don't get out the door in the next three minutes. After wrapping a Band-Aid around my finger, I finish Winnie's sandwich and load it into her lunchbox.

"Ready," Winnie says, coming to a halt inside the entryway to the kitchen. Her hair is up in two lopsided pigtails, and I bite my lip against my laughter.

"Sam do your hair?" I ask.

She gives me a nod and a beaming smile. "Yep. Isn't it awesome? He said he's gonna try a braid next."

"That's great, Pumpkin," I say, stuffing her lunchbox into her backpack. "Get your shoes and jacket on, please."

Winnie heads toward the door, and I curse.

"Winnie," I call out. "Where's your art book?"

"Here," Sam says, skidding into the room. He shoots a grin my way as he tosses the booklet. I catch it as Sam proceeds to hop on one foot so he can tug his sock into place. His shirt is riding halfway up his stomach, and his belt is unbuckled.

The man looks like a beautiful, rumpled mess.

"Christ, we're runnin' late today," he says, righting his shirt.

"And whose fault is that?" I ask, zipping Winnie's backpack up.

Sam looks unrepentant. "You're just so warm in the mornin', stud. I like puttin' my mouth on you. Tastin' all that delicious skin."

"Sounds like something a zombie would say," I mutter, even as said skin flushes hot at the memory. I do so love Sam's mouth.

He barks a laugh as Winnie reappears in the wide doorway.

"Y'all coming?" she asks, hands on her hips. "We're gonna be late."

Sam and I share an amused look.

"Let's go," I say, heading for the front door.

Winnie runs ahead, getting seated in my truck, and I toss her backpack in the back of the cab with her. Before I can get into the front, Sam is there, tugging me around gently. Hand on my cheek, he gives me a kiss.

"See ya later, stud," he says.

"Yeah," I mutter a little breathily.

Sam shoots me a wink before rounding his own truck and getting in. He drives off first, but I'm quick to follow, my head still reeling and my heart pounding like a drum.

Has it really been three weeks of this? Three weeks of Sam staying over most nights? Three weeks of sleepy cuddles and mornings together and kisses before he goes?

I'm already accustomed to the change. Accustomed to having Sam here, cooking breakfast or doing Winnie's hair. Playing out back with Tigger and sharing my bed at night. Feeling like, for the first time in a long time, I have someone of my own. Someone who's mine, but who's also here for my family. Someone who makes me feel lighter than I have in a long time.

What am I going to do if he goes?

I swat the thought away. Sam hasn't given me a single reason to think he isn't in this for the long haul. I have to trust in that. And I do.

Luckily, I get Winnie to school just in time for her not to be late. She hustles out the door after a quick, "Bye, Daddy," and I wait until she's being ushered inside by a teacher before pulling away. Not so luckily, the minute I get to work, I realize I left my own lunch at home on the counter. *Damn it*. I'll have to grab something later.

Except later doesn't end up looking so hot. My first client of the day—a little shih tzu—pisses on my boot. I knock my head on an open cabinet door an hour after that. And then I bump into Abbott on my way around a corner, knocking his papers to the ground.

"Watch where you're goin'," the older man grouses.

"Sorry, Abbott. Let me grab those," I say apologetically, crouching down to pick up the loose sheets.

"I should hope so," he says. "Considerin' you made the mess."

I don't bother responding, instead handing him the papers once I'm upright. He grumbles something else before walking off, a slight hitch in his step that didn't used to be there a year or so ago.

I watch him go, a little frown on my face.

"That was somethin'," a voice in my ear whispers.

Whirling around, I give Deborah a look. "Stop creeping."

She laughs, following me down the hall. "I wasn't creepin'. Just happened to catch the crash. You doin' all right? You've got a whole...face goin' today."

"Thanks," I mutter.

She bumps me with her elbow. "C'mon, now. It's a good face."

I huff a laugh. "Just can't catch a break," I answer, pulling out my phone when it pings. There's a new text from Sam.

Sammy: Want to do tacos tonight? I bet I can get Winnie to try avocado.

There's a picture below the text of a smiling Sam because the man likes to tempt me. Or maybe he simply wants to make me happy. I'm not sure if there's even a difference.

"Yum," Deborah says, looking over my shoulder.

I hum my agreement.

"Doctor Bailey?" Tessa says, sticking her head around the corner. "Your eleven o'clock has been waitin' for ten minutes."

"Shit," I mutter, pocketing my phone. "Thanks, Tessa."

She nods, and Deborah laughs, slapping me on the shoulder as I hustle away. The rest of my morning passes before I've blinked, and as I'm putting the finishing touches on my patient files, my phone starts to ring.

The school.

I answer quickly. "Hello?"

"Hello. Is this Harrison Bailey?"

"Yes," I say, stomach sinking.

"Good day, Mr. Bailey. I'm callin' because Winifred is in the nurse's office. She's all right, but she and another student bumped into each other pretty hard on the playground. We've got an ice pack on her elbow, and the nurse assured us it's only a bruise, but we wanted to let you know."

My pulse comes down. That's not so bad. "Thank you for the call."

"Of course. We'll let you know if anythin' else comes up."

We say our goodbyes, and I tuck my phone back in my pocket, bracing my hands on the counter. *It's okay*, I tell myself. *This day has been a fucking disaster, but it's okay.*

"Harrison, comin' to lunch?" Deborah asks from down the hall.

I shake my head. "I need to grab something to eat. I left my lunch at home." Except... *Shit*. Checking my calendar, I realize I'm off-site this afternoon. Which means, "I have to go, Deb. See you later."

Deborah's face is creased in concern when I head around the corner, but I don't stop. I grab my supplies and make my way directly to my truck. The Hortons' farm is a good forty-minute drive from here, so I'll have to skip my meal after all.

"Seriously, can't catch a break," I mutter, pulling out of the clinic parking lot.

My phone dings on the drive over, but I don't check it. My mind is distracted enough as it is, and with the way today is going, it'd be just my luck to add a texting-while-driving collision to the list.

When I get to the Hortons', I park my truck and grab my hat, settling it on my head just as the elder Mr. Horton comes out of his house.

"Roy," I call out, lifting a hand in greeting.

"Doc," he calls back, hustling my way, his usually ruddy cheeks even redder than normal. "I'm glad you're here. We've got a situation."

"Uh-oh," I say, grabbing my med bag. "What's going on?"

I walk with Roy as he leads me toward the barn. The Hortons run a small dairy cow operation, but they also have a handful of family animals: a couple "pet" cows, a donkey, a few pigs, and a pony. I was supposed to be doing a checkup on the old pony to evaluate whether or not she's ready for arthritis meds, but it sounds like that's about to change.

"One of our dairy girls went into labor last night," Roy explains. "She's been at it for a while, and the calf's feet are visible, but it's not comin' out."

"How long have you been able to see the feet?" I ask.

"Gerald's been with 'er," he says. "Said it's been two and a half hours."

Crap. "All right, lead the way."

When Roy and I reach his family barn, he drives a 4-wheeler out from inside. We take the vehicle over the bumpy land to his dairy operation about five minutes away, where the cow in question is in a straw-lined stall. Gerald, Roy's oldest son, is inside with her.

"Heya, Doc," Gerald greets, rubbing his forehead with the sleeve of his shirt.

"Hi, Gerald," I return, setting my bag down and stepping into the stall. "I hear we're having an issue with delivery?"

The younger man nods. "Seems so. She keeps pushin', but nothin' much has been happenin'."

He gestures toward the cow, who's lying down in the straw, and I step closer. The calf's hooves are clearly visible, but if they've been that way for over two hours without progress, the cow might need assistance.

"Okay, let me get cleaned up real quick, and I'll take a look," I tell him, heading back out of the stall.

Roy is waiting outside. "Thanks, Doc. Glad you're here today. Life has a funny way of workin' out like that, don'tcha think?"

I hum. "Where can I wash up?"

Roy leads me over to a bathroom, and I wash my hands and arms before pulling on gloves that nearly reach my shoulders. Back in the stall, I kneel near the cow's rear end and check her progress.

It's been a while since I've had my arm up a cow's vagina.

"Well," I say, removing my hands and peeling off the gloves. "The calf's breech, but the mama's cervix isn't fully dilated yet. So, at this point, we need to give her some time. Is this her first calving?"

Gerald shakes his head. "No, her second."

"Okay, that's good," I say. Although it doesn't explain the lengthy delivery. "I'll keep checking her progress. Once her cervix is open, I can assist the calf out. But until then, we wait."

And wait we do. I keep checking the cow's progress, but another two hours in, we're no closer to a birth. And, at this point, I'm starting to get worried for the mama. She's been pushing steadily for hours now, and the exertion is starting to show.

"I'll be right back," I tell the two men, exiting the stall and grabbing my water. I guzzle some down, and when my phone pings from inside my bag, I fish it out. Cringing, I see three missed texts and a missed call. Two of the texts and the call are from Sam, and the other text is from my mom.

Sammy: Everything all right, stud?

Sammy: Seriously, Harrison, are you okay? It's not like you not to respond.

And...

Mom: Hey, dear. Just a reminder that your dad and I have tickets to a show tonight. We'll need to leave by 5.

Shit. *Shit.*

I check the time. I would need to leave here within the next thirty minutes to make it to my parents' in time to pick up Winnie before they have to go.

"Doc?" Gerald calls out. "Somethin's happenin'."

I drop my phone and water and head back into the stall. More of the calf's legs are now visible, so I pull on my gloves and check the cow's progress.

"She's fully dilated," I say, to which Roy breathes out in relief. "I'll give her a little time to see if she can pass the calf herself, but if not, I'll help it out."

Gerald nods, wiping his forehead again. The poor guy looks sweatier than the cow.

When my phone starts to ring, I excuse myself, stripping off my gloves once more and stepping out of the stall.

"Yeah?" I say, answering the call.

"Harrison?" Sam asks in concern.

"Hey," I breathe out. "I'm sorry I didn't get back to you, but today has been a shitshow, and I haven't had a moment to slow down."

I step in front of the stall door, watching as the mama pushes the calf out another few inches. Sam is saying something, and I realize I missed the first part of it.

"...if you think tacos would be all right. I can take care of it."

"I... Shit, Sam. Sorry, I don't know if..."

The cow pushes again, and my focus is waylaid. She's getting tired; I can see it in her frame. I may need to help pull the calf the rest of the way out. There's no way I'm getting out of here in the next half hour. Goddamn it, I'm going to have to call my parents. *Fuck.* They'll miss their show.

"Harrison?"

I shake my head. "Sam, I have to go. There's too much going on, and I need to make arrangements for Winnie, and I just can't think about dinner right now, okay?"

My tone is terse, but I can barely focus, one eye on the cow, my thoughts on my child and this fucked-up day, and yet again, I miss part of what Sam is saying.

"...do to help?"

"Doc?" Roy calls, turning my way.

"Sam, I'm sorry," I say into the phone. "I have to go."

"Wait, I—"

"I can't do this right now," I say hotly, my frustration bleeding into my tone. I feel bad for yelling, but I haven't eaten, nothing has gone right today, I have a cow very nearly in distress, and I'm going to have to let my parents know I'll be late. On the one night they have plans. It's too much. Too overwhelming. I can't deal with Sam on top of it.

I don't wait for Sam's response before hanging up the phone. I drop it on my bag, step into the mouth of the stall, and freeze. My gut clenches, anxiety ratcheting tenfold, as I realize what I just did.

Sam asks hardly anything of me except not to push him away. He *told* me. He doesn't deal with abandonment well, and in a split second of annoyance over my own issues, I tossed him aside as if he isn't the best damn thing to happen to me in who knows how long.

Shit, shit, mother-fudging shit.

"Doc?" Roy calls.

"I'm sorry, Roy," I say, hopping to and pulling on a glove to check the cow. The calf's position is good, despite being breech, but the cow's strength may have waned too much at this point to get him or her out. "I need two minutes to fix a mistake, and then I'll get this calf out, okay?"

He gives me a knowing nod. "Problem with the missus?"

"Mister," I correct, tugging off my glove and standing. He doesn't even blink. "Excuse me."

Out in the hall, I grab my phone and hit redial. My heart races as I wait for Sam to pick up, and blessedly, he doesn't make me wait long. He answers on the third ring.

"Harrison," he says, his hurt evident in the one word.

"*I'm sorry*," I breathe out. "I'm so sorry, Sam. This day has been shit, but it's no excuse for how I just spoke to you."

"You hung up on me," he says, voice smaller than I've ever heard before, but also laced with steel. Sam has his guard up, and I'm the reason. He's never sounded like that with me before, and I hate it. I hate that I made him hurt. I hate that I was that careless.

"I shouldn't have done that."

"I'm on your side, y'know?" he says.

"I do." I do know that. Sam always makes things easier, except when I'm being too pigheaded to let him. "Sammy, I need your help."

He blows out a breath, and his voice sounds much more like the Sam I know when he answers me. "'Bout time. What can I do?"

The pressure in my stomach eases as I finish my phone call with Sam, and when I hang up, I'm feeling lighter. I head back into the stall and pull on my gloves, and twenty minutes later, a new calf is born at the Hortons' farm.

Maybe this day was an unmitigated mess. But it made me realize some important truths. And now, I just have to decide if I'm brave enough to face them head-on.

CHAPTER 24

✡

Sammy

"All right, li'l miss. You see if you can find Cassiopeia. I'm gonna finish cleanin' up the kitchen."

Winnie nods, tugging her tablet closer and scrolling through the interactive star map I downloaded for her. My constellation book is opened up next to her on the floor, and the little girl looks back and forth between the two, trying to match up Cassiopeia's shape on the app.

With a smile, I leave her to it, climbing out of the living room fort. Tigger follows, padding along beside me as I make my way into the kitchen.

"Your dad'll be home soon," I reassure the both of us. Tigger merely sits down in front of me, her tongue-lolling face making it impossible not to give her a good dozen or so scratches. "Stop bein' so cute," I tell her with no real venom. "I gotta clean up."

Tigger gives me a lick, and I drag myself away, putting the last of the supper dishes into the dishwasher while my nerves tumble over. Winnie and I already ate supper, and it's getting close now to her bedtime. Harrison texted a half hour ago to let me know he was finally on his way home, and considering the day he had, I want to make sure everything is cleaned up before he arrives.

My chest goes through a complicated roll of sensations—tightness, worry, relief—as I think about my own day.

I'm not sure I've ever been more freaked out than I was this afternoon when Harrison wasn't returning my texts. It wasn't like the man. And then that phone call? *Hell*. He'd never spoken to me that way before, like *I* was part of his burden. It made me feel equal parts small and terrified.

I've dated plenty. And as I told Harrison the day we met, I've been broken up with plenty, too. I can always tell when it's about to happen—when my partner's voice turns from one of fondness to irritation. I heard that, ever so briefly, in Harrison's tone, and for the handful of minutes before he called me back to apologize, I thought that might be it. The beginning of the end.

I've been alone, in one way or another, for most of my life. But I don't want to end up that way. I don't want to leave this life the same way I came into it. It's why I always tried so hard to make my past relationships work. Why I always kept digging, hoping to find that *something* that would make me and my partner last. It's why it always hurt so much when I was left, once again, on my own.

It's different with Harrison. It has been from the get-go. I didn't have to dig deep to feel that spark. It was there from the beginning, and it's grown steadily over the past couple months. And now, for the first time in my life, being alone isn't what I fear most.

I'm afraid of being without *him*.

I don't know exactly when that changed, but somewhere along the way, I fell for Harrison in a way I've never fallen for anybody. I can feel the difference, plain as day. I *love* that man. I love his life, his daughter, and his dog. I love the rushed mornings and the treehouse in the backyard. I love his blue eyes and his talented tongue, and even the goddamn vibrator he keeps in his nightstand drawer. I love the quiet moments. The ones where he looks me in the eye and says, "*Tell me something.*" I love all the messy pieces that make up his beautiful existence and the way he opened up the door for me to step into it.

I love his fragile heart, and I don't want to ever let go.

But I don't know if Harrison is there yet. The blip we had today showed me his automatic response is still assuming he has to do everything on his own. He trusts me with Winnie; I know that much. The evidence is in this evening. He asked me to pick her up from his parents' and take care of her until he was home.

But trust isn't the same as knowing, deep down, that he can rely on me. It's not the same as love.

And with Carl's words about being careful ringing in my head, I wonder... Do I tell Harrison that I love him? Or do I just keep showing him and hope that, one day, he'll feel the same?

When the door from the garage opens, Tigger hops up, scrambling out of the kitchen. I ease out a breath, following her. Harrison is inside the laundry room pass-through, kicking off his boots when Tigger wiggles up to him. He gives her a tired smile, pausing with one boot still in place as he rubs along her neck and down her sides. When he catches sight of me, he straightens and finishes the task of removing his boots.

"Hi, Sam," he says tentatively, worry etched in the line of his brow.

Enough of that. I step close, scooting around Tigger to pull Harrison into my arms. He practically falls against my chest, holding onto me tight as his breath stutters against my neck. He smells like a barnyard—like straw and animals and sweat—and he trembles slightly in my arms.

"Sam," he says again, voice as shaky as his body.

"Hush now, stud," I reply, squeezing him tight. "We'll talk about it later, after you've had some food."

He blows out a breath, nodding against me, and then tiny arms wrap around us from the side. I look over, and there's Winnie, giving me and her dad a hug.

"Hey, Pumpkin," Harrison says, shifting one of his arms around his daughter. "How's your elbow?"

"Fine," she replies. "Sam and I already ate dinner, but there are tacos left for you. And Sam let me have a cookie, but just one. Then we made a fort, and I found the Big Dipper all by myself. I'm gonna be an astrologer one day."

"Astronomer," I correct.

"Astronomer," Winnie says, wrinkling her nose before stepping back. "Daddy, why do you smell?"

Harrison laughs a little wetly, blinking fast. "I helped a cow give birth."

"Oh. You should probably take a bath," she says matter-of-factly before running off. Most likely back to her fort.

Harrison's gaze swings to me, eyes wide as he shakes his head.

"C'mon," I say, giving him a little tug. "Food."

Harrison follows me silently into the kitchen, his steps slow and heavy, and when he sits down at the table, I plop a small plate in front of him.

"What's this?" he asks, brow drawn.

"Dessert first," I tell him with a wink. "I'll grab your tacos."

"Sam." He picks up the cookie. Sugar with sprinkles. "Did you get these for me?"

I hum, setting to work on assembling his meal. "Figured you could use a li'l pick-me-up."

Harrison scoots out of his chair, swinging me around to face him. He kisses me then, all fire and pluck and desperation, and I didn't quite realize how much I needed that, but it settles something in me, that kiss. It reaches deep and tugs. Soothes. Lights a fire.

Harrison's hands bracket my face as he pulls back. "Sorry I'm so gross."

I huff a laugh. "I don't mind, but you can wash me later if it'll make you feel better."

His lips lift at the corner before his face falls slightly. "I'm sorry about today, too."

I lead Harrison back to the table, shoving him gently into his seat. At my insistent look, he picks up his cookie and takes a bite.

"It's all right," I tell him, going back to his tacos. "What all was goin' on?"

Harrison sighs, brushing crumbs off his fingers before leaning back in his chair. "It was just...everything. I got peed on. I was a mess at work. Winnie's school called because she hurt her elbow. I forgot my lunch at home and never had a chance to eat. And then I had my hands up a cow, and suddenly, it was nearly time to pick up Winnie, and I just... I just lost it, and you were the one I was talking to at the time."

I nod, taking a seat next to Harrison and passing him his food. "It hurt," I tell him honestly, "that you didn't want my help."

"It wasn't that I didn't want it," he says, leaning forward and squeezing my arm, his thumb near my wrist. "I'm just so used to doing everything by myself. I'm not used to having a...*you*. I forgot, for a minute, that I didn't have to figure it all out on my own. Sometimes..." He breaks off, looking down at his plate. I give him a moment to compose his thoughts. "Sometimes I feel like you give me so much. Maybe too much. I don't have as much to give you in return."

"You give me plenty, stud," I say softly.

Harrison's eyes raise to mine. "Do I?"

I nod. "Yeah, you do."

You give me everything I've ever wanted.

He blows out a little breath, and I nudge his plate closer to him. Letting go of my arm, Harrison eats his late supper and then the rest of his cookie, and I watch on, satisfied to no end when he moans happily around the treat.

"Everything go okay here?" he asks once he's done.

"Yep," I tell him. "Winnie wouldn't eat the avocado after all, but I got a couple cucumber slices into her. And your parents were really nice when I picked her up. Pretty sure your dad might even love me. He asked how that *takin' it slow* thing was goin' in that sassy voice of his."

Harrison barks a laugh. "Sounds like him." He smiles a little before adding, "I think we're going just the right speed for us, though. Don't you? Even if it is a little fast?"

I don't tell him that, for me, *too fast* doesn't exist where he's concerned. I just link my fingers with his. "Yeah, stud. I like our speed."

He nods, giving my hand a squeeze.

"Now, what was this about you gettin' peed on?" I ask.

Harrison lets out another laugh.

Fifteen minutes later, he and Winnie are upstairs, getting ready for bedtime, and Tigger and I are out in the backyard. I throw the ball for her a few times, but the dog sits beside my foot before long, not as energetic as some Brittany Spaniels I've met.

"Ready to head in?" I ask her.

She looks up at me before trotting toward the door. Smart dog.

We get inside around the same time Harrison is coming down the stairs. He runs his hand through his hair, looking tired. "Shower?" he asks.

I nod, following Harrison down the hall as Tigger slips through the crack into Winnie's room. In his en suite, Harrison turns on the shower and strips out of his clothes. It lacks any finesse, and something about that hits me. The fact that Harrison isn't concerned about looking sexy or needing to put on a show when he's so dog-tired. It's that natural vulnerability he possesses. The way he lets me see his true self.

It makes it easier to be vulnerable with him, too.

"Harrison," I say gently, stepping naked into the shower after him.

"Yeah, Sam?" he asks, turning my way. His hair is wet, pushed back from his face, and the shower spray hits him along his shoulders. Harrison tugs me close, positioning me with him under the water. It heats me quickly.

"I wanna be real clear about somethin'," I say.

He swallows, nodding for me to go on.

"I know I joke around a lot, but I'm serious about this. About us. The way I see it, we're partners. So when things are bad, just know you can lean on me, all right?"

"Yeah, Sam," he says softly, fingers drifting over my back. His hips press against mine, the pressure of his body making my cock plump despite the more solemn nature of our conversation. "I'm here for you, too, okay? I'm sorry I didn't show that today—"

"But you had a bad day," I interject. "It happens."

"Still," he says, fingers drifting down to my ass cheeks. They stroke there, almost absentmindedly. "I *am* sorry. I don't want to fuck this up with you. The idea of losing you…"

My pulse kicks up. "You can't get rid of me that easily," I assure him. "If you fuck up, or if I fuck up, we talk about it, and we move forward, yeah?"

"Yeah," he breathes out, laying his forehead on my shoulder. Despite the almost tender nature of the embrace, one of Harrison's hands drifts between our bodies, circling my cock. He strokes me slowly with a wet grip, propelling me quickly to full hardness.

"Harrison," I rasp, my mind starting to haze over.

His lips skim my neck. "You smell like sunshine," he says. "How do you smell like sunshine?"

I hang my head back as Harrison's mouth sucks at my skin. "Stud, if this is an apology…"

Harrison draws back, blue eyes meeting mine. He doesn't let go of my dick. "It's not an apology," he says, giving me another stroke. "I won't use sex like that. I heard you loud and clear, Sammy. And now I want my partner's cock in my mouth. Is that okay with you?"

"*Fuck*," I mutter, nodding quickly. "Yep. Yes. Fine."

Harrison chuckles, his gaze turning whip-sharp right before he drops to his knees. My hands find his hair, and I hold on tight as Harrison swallows me down.

Partners.

Yeah, that sounds just about perfect to me.

CHAPTER 25

───────── ✦ ─────────

Harrison

"You have everything packed?" I ask Winnie.

"Yep." She bounces on her toes.

"Your toothbrush?" I check.

She rolls her eyes. "Yes, Daddy."

"And Sam grabbed your sleeping bag from the garage?"

"Yesss," she says, sounding like a teenager, not the ten-year-old she is. "Can I go wait downstairs now?"

"Yeah, okay," I agree, watching my daughter fly down to the first floor.

Sam steps lightly from my bedroom. "All right?"

I nod my head, but it becomes a shake. "What if we forgot to pack something?"

"She'll survive," Sam says, stepping close and wrapping his arms around me. "It's just one night."

"What if she doesn't like it?" I ask. "What if she has to come home?"

"Then your parents will bring her home," he answers calmly.

"What if..." I cut myself off. *God*, I sound just like Winnie.

"Stud, it'll be all right," Sam says, his drawl soothing me somewhat. "She's been excited about this for a week. She'll prob'ly have so much fun with all the other kids, she won't even have time to think about worryin'. And if she can't sleep or gets sad, your parents will be there to help."

I blow out a breath, nodding. Winnie *has* been excited about *star night at the museum* ever since Sam floated the idea. The local museum does overnights for kids once a month, and this month, the theme is constellations. It seemed too good to be true, and Winnie jumped at the chance to go.

This is supposed to be a night for just Sam and me. A night that's ours, and ours alone. My parents were all too happy to sign up as chaperones for the event, so they'll be going with Winnie. Realistically, I know my daughter will be fine. Sam is right; she'll probably have too much fun to even think about missing home. And me.

But the anxious side of me can't stop worrying. I need to put it aside; I know that. I can't let my concern cloud my date night with Sam. But after the way Winnie reacted to my being in Plum Valley, there's a knot in my stomach, like I'm just waiting for tonight to go wrong.

Sam's lips press along my jaw, startling me somewhat. "D'you need me to distract you?"

My shoulders lose some of their tension. "Might not be a bad idea," I admit.

Sam rumbles, his lips drifting down to my neck. I ease my head further to the side. "I can do that."

"Tell me where we're going?" I ask. Sam refused to let me have a part in planning our night. He said he had it handled.

He chuckles. "Not yet. You're gonna have to be patient."

"We could just stay here," I suggest, thoughts running wild as Sam nips my earlobe.

He rumbles again, the vibration of it traveling from his chest to mine. "Nah. I think I'd rather tease you all night. And only once you can't stand it anymore will I bring you back here—to an *empty* house—and have my wicked way with you." He licks my earlobe. "Maybe I can get you screamin' my name again."

I puff out a breath. "That mouth."

"Mm."

"Daddy!" Winnie yells. "Grandma and Grandpa are here."

Sam pulls back slightly, warm brown gaze raking over me. "Better?"

"Huh?" I ask, my mind still floating.

Sam chuckles, linking his hand with mine and giving me a tug toward the stairs. My parents are inside when we get down to the foyer, my mom helping Winnie into her light jacket and my dad rubbing Tigger's head.

My mom gives us a big smile. "You boys look handsome."

I huff a laugh—we're not dressed that much differently than normal—but Sam beams.

"Thanks, Mrs. Bailey," he says, straightening his shirt somewhat. My heart squeezes tight as I realize Sam probably never had this. A parental figure to fuss over him.

I squeeze his hand.

"Sammy, call me Cordelia," my mom says. "Mrs. Bailey is much too formal for family."

Sam squeezes my hand back. Hard.

"Got everything you need?" my dad asks Winnie.

She nods rapidly, her backpack already over her shoulder and sleeping bag tucked under her arm. "I'm ready," she says. And *Christ*, she sounds it.

Am I making a bigger deal out of this than I need to?

"Hugs first," I remind her.

Winnie doesn't set down her sleeping bag; she just steps into me and hugs me with one arm, letting go much too soon before she moves to Sam. He looks surprised when she hugs him, too, but he hugs her back, eyes closed for a second.

When Winnie steps back, I tell her, "Make sure to listen to Grandma and Grandpa tonight, okay?"

She nods. "I will."

"Okay. Have a great night, Pumpkin."

"You, too, Daddy," she says before turning toward the front door, bouncing anxiously on her toes. Tigger steps up beside her, the pair looking out over the neighborhood.

"You'll call if you need to?" I ask my mom quietly.

"Only if we need to," she says. "Enjoy your night out, dear."

My dad slaps me on the shoulder before opening the front door for Winnie. "Let's go see these stars, kiddo."

My daughter rushes for my parents' car, my dad follows, and my mom gives me a kiss on the cheek before she, too, heads out the door. Then it's just Sam, me, and Tigger, watching them drive out of sight.

"C'mon, stud," Sam says gently. "Lemme show you a good time."

My heart does a slow roll in my chest, and I give Sam a nod.

After letting Tigger outside one last time, Sam and I get into his truck. He doesn't ask me to close my eyes or anything as we drive, and before long, Sam is pulling into the parking lot of...a bar?

"Sam," I say a little shakily, looking his way.

"I know," he says with a small shrug. "It's simple for a date night."

"But perfect," I add quickly, and I mean it. *God*, this man hears me, doesn't he? He's always listening. Always surprising me in the best possible way.

He shoots me a relieved smile as he puts the truck in park. "Then c'mon. Let's go get a beer."

Inside the bar, Sam finds us a small booth in the corner of the room. The place is busy, and, as far as I can tell from a visual sweep, queer-friendly.

Sam doesn't take a seat with me. He stays standing, one hand on the back of the booth and the other on the table as he leans close. His scent washes over me, and the muscles in his arms bunch. "What d'you want?" he asks.

What I *want* is Sam, but I know he's talking about beer choices.

My lips quirk as my mind flashes back to the day we met. "How about a stout?"

Sam gives me a blinding smile and a wink before turning and heading toward the bar. My eyes slide down to his ass and stay glued there the entire time he's walking away because *damn*, why the hell not? When he reaches the bar, he leans over the top, putting that denim-clad ass even further on display, and I must sigh or make a sound of some sort because the guy in the booth next to ours looks over at me.

"The one in the red shirt yours?" he asks.

I huff a laugh. "Yeah, he sure is."

He gives me a smile. "The one in the black is mine. I'm Evan."

Evan reaches over the back of the booth, and I shake his hand.

"Harrison," I reply.

Evan nods, his light blonde hair flopping. "Nice to meet you, Harrison." When he settles back in his seat, his gaze returns to the bar. "We're on our third date. You?"

"Oh, well. I kind of lost count," I admit.

"Ah," Evan says knowingly. "You're already there. Gotcha."

"Already where?" I ask.

He waves a hand through the air. "The serious phase. Y'know, like you're *together* together. I was there once. Before it fell apart."

"Sorry," I say because even though this guy is a total stranger, I know exactly how that goes.

He shoots me a small smile. "Aren't you sweet? Oh, mine's comin' back. Have a good night, Harrison."

"You, too," I say, chuckling a little as Evan faces his table again. The guy in the black shirt takes a seat across from him just as Sam looks over his shoulder. When our eyes catch, he grins, and my pulse jumps.

Together together. We are, though, aren't we? Sam *is* mine. I know it on an instinctual level. I can feel it down to my toes. This man is mine for good if only I wish it. He's been hinting for a while now, or saying outright, how much he likes my baggage. How he wants me, a home, a family.

Winnie, Tigger, and I... We could be that for him.

My breath catches as I roll those words back through my head.

We could be that for him. He could be *ours*.

Sam returns a minute later, setting two pint glasses onto our table before sliding into the booth next to me. "Here we go," he says, thigh resting against my own. He lifts his glass, sipping his beer and then humming. "That's the stuff."

"Sam," I say, tugging his chin toward me.

"Mm?"

I kiss him, a short but sincere thing. "Thank you for tonight. This is just...perfect."

"You're welcome, stud," he rumbles, looking at me a little curiously before the expression shifts into his usual smile. "But the night's only startin'. And you haven't even taken a sip of that beer. Better hop to before it grows legs and walks off."

I chuckle, doing as he says. My eyes slip closed as I swallow down a mouthful of the stout, all fresh and cold and frothy against my lip. For tonight, I don't have to worry about being *Dad*. Winnie is still on my mind, sure, but I refuse to let myself get hung up on worst-case scenarios. Unless I find out otherwise, I'm going to assume she's having a wonderful time at the museum with my parents.

And me? I'm damn well going to enjoy being *just Harrison* for the night.

And Harrison really wants Sam.

"There it is," Sam says, sounding pleased.

"What?" I ask, opening my eyes.

"You look like you just shed twenty pounds."

I huff a laugh. "I feel like it."

"Good," he damn near purrs, shifting until his lips are ghosting over my ear. "'Cause I want you to enjoy yourself tonight." His fingers slide up my inner thigh, and heat coils in my stomach. "I don't want you to feel a thing other than happy"—his knuckles glide over my half-hard cock—"and horny"—teeth whisper along my earlobe—"and *satisfied*."

"Shit, Sam," I mutter, looking around the room. Luckily, we're in the corner where it's darker and less people are around, but still. It wouldn't be impossible for someone to see where Sam is touching me underneath the table.

"Mm," he says, sliding his hand down my thigh and holding tight as he shifts back against his seat. He picks up his beer and takes a sip.

Clearing my throat, I grab my own pint glass. "You really *are* going to tease me tonight, aren't you?"

"Yes, I am," he says, grinning and looking so boyish I can't help but laugh.

"You're something, Sammy," I tell the man.

"Somethin' good, I hope," he says, a tiny bit of vulnerability leaching into his tone.

"The best," I tell him honestly, shifting enough that I can lean my elbow on the back of the booth. I run my hand up the back of Sam's neck before teasing my fingers beneath the collar of his shirt.

If he's going to torture me, I might as well give it back just as good.

Sam leans into the touch. He does love it when I stroke him like a cat.

"How's Tilda doing?" I ask.

Sam lets out a laugh at the serious question, and his fingers tighten on my leg. "She's good. Has a new grandbaby she's been fussin' over. She's sent me a million pics. Wanna see?"

I nod, and Sam pulls his phone from his pocket. He shows me pictures of the baby, and then he tells me about Carl's new neighbor, who was scared of Rosie before she realized how much of a sweetheart the bully mix is. I fill him in on work and how Deborah installed a new fence to keep the deer out of her garden. And for the next hour and a half, Sam and I talk about benign topics, pretending we aren't edging each other under the table. Pretending our hands aren't wandering and that we aren't both getting progressively more desperate to be alone.

By the time we finish our second round of beers, I'm ready to crack. I need this man in me or on me or *under* me.

But Sam lifts his hand from my leg right before I can beg him to get me out of here already. "Be right back," he says. "I'm gonna hit the head."

I make a split-second decision and grab his arm, my pulse firing. "Do you...want company?"

Heat and understanding flare in Sam's eyes, but he shakes his head slowly. "Not this time, stud. I've got plans for you."

"Oh, you do, do you?" I ask, liking the sound of that way too much.

Sam nods, leaning close. "Mhm. And believe me—you're really gonna like what I have in store."

I don't doubt it.

Sam gives me a wicked grin, and then he's scooting out of the booth. I watch him go, cock stiff, chest warm.

I think, quite possibly, I want to know all of Sam's plans for the two of us, both near and far. I think I'm going to like them a lot.

CHAPTER 26

✦

Sammy

I have to wait a good couple minutes for my dick to calm down enough to pee, but once I manage it, I wash my hands quickly and head back out to the bar. There's a massive grin on my face, anticipation simmering heavy in my gut as I think about all the dirty, wonderful things I'm going to do to Harrison tonight. But the moment I catch sight of my boyfriend being boxed into our booth by a cute little twink, that grin falls right off my face.

Harrison is laughing, and the slender blonde is smiling much too wide, his hand on the arm Harrison has thrown along the top of the booth.

Oh, nuh-uh. Nope. Nope, nope, nope.

I'm striding over without a single hesitation, not slowing until I'm directly beside the blonde. I've never been one to throw my size around, and I don't do it now. But I do stand my ground, staring down the man as his head turns my way, eyes wide. "Sorry, sweetheart, but you're gonna have to move along. This one's *mine*."

I don't clarify if I mean the booth or the man inside of it, but I don't think I need to.

The guy blinks at me, a smile, of all things, spreading across his face. He looks back at Harrison. "Oh, he *growls*."

I'm about to growl again when the blonde removes his hand from Harrison's arm. He steps back and gestures me in.

"All yours," he says.

I slip into the booth, retaking my seat next to Harrison, who's looking at me with big, blinking blue eyes. I give the blonde another glance—okay, *glare*—and he chuckles before stepping away.

"Bye, Harrison. Have a good night," he practically sings.

"See you, Evan," Harrison returns.

The silence is heavy once *Evan* is gone, and I run my finger along the condensation left on the tabletop from my beer.

"Sam," Harrison says lightly.

"You know him?" I ask, throat tight.

"Just met him tonight. He was here on a date."

I nod, swallowing, a little relieved to hear that.

"Sam," Harrison says again. "You growled for me."

"I didn't *growl*," I grumble.

"You growled."

I bite my lip until Harrison tips my face his way. "Sammy."

"I'm sorry," I get out, chest aching. "I know that was rude. I just... I get a little..."

I don't know how to finish that sentence because any which way I do, it makes me sound like a caveman. *I get possessive over what's mine? I get jealous at the thought of other men coveting you?*

I get scared someone or something is going to take you away from me?

Luckily, Harrison doesn't ask me to finish my thought. He simply hums, stroking over my jaw. He doesn't seem upset. In fact, he looks quite the opposite.

"I've never had anyone fight for me, Sam," he says quietly.

I give a start, his words about his ex floating into my mind. How Harrison was his second choice. I never—*ever*—want Harrison to feel that way with me, whether or not the truth of it makes me sound like a possessive ass.

"I will *always* fight for you," I tell him truthfully.

He stutters a little breath, his eyes on my mouth. "Because I'm yours?"

"Yes," I answer, the one word resolute. I wait to see what Harrison will say. Wait to see if it's too much.

He strokes along my jaw again, eyes meeting mine. "Then take me home and show me, Sammy."

Relief hits hard, and I nod, holding out my hand. Harrison grabs on, letting me lead him from the bar.

The trip home is made in silence, but Harrison's palm rests above my knee the entire way there, a steady, warm presence. He doesn't say a word when I park in front of his house, and when I drag him up the stairs, he follows willingly. I shut and lock his bedroom door once we're inside, more out of habit than anything else, and Harrison watches me steadily.

"I have a surprise for you," I say, backing him slowly toward the bed. His legs hit the mattress, and he sits down. I slide between his knees.

"Are you going to tell me what it is?" he asks, hands holding tight to my hips.

I shake my head slowly. "No, I'm gonna show you."

Harrison licks his lips, swallowing, as I start to unbutton his shirt. He lets me maneuver the material off his arms, and then he leans back on his elbows as I set to work on his pants. I pull his jeans down one leg at a time, dragging them off his body. His cock is already tenting his briefs, and it springs free when I tug the material down.

He's a fucking sight.

"God, Sam," Harrison says softly.

"What?" I ask, standing upright.

"That look in your eye."

"What do you see?" I ask him, stepping close again, slotting myself between his legs as I brace my hands near his.

He takes a beat to answer, the quiet extending a long moment. "So much."

My heart skips fast, and I step away.

Harrison makes an affronted sound. "Where are you going?"

"To grab your surprise," I tell him with a wink, walking backwards toward the bathroom. "Stay there, all right?"

He looks confused, but he nods, and when I reach the en suite, I shut the door. I blow out a breath before finding the bag I stuck in here earlier. My change of clothes is inside.

When I come out of the bathroom, Harrison is mostly where I left him, just moved up a bit, lounging against the headboard. His eyes shoot wide the moment he sees me, and he sits forward, chest heaving with his sharp inhale.

"*Sammy*," he gasps. "Ho-ly shit."

Trying—and probably failing—to hide my amusement, I walk forward a few paces, keeping the second part of Harrison's surprise hidden away behind my back. I let him have a good look at the rest of it, though. The cowboy hat. My mostly naked body. The *chaps* buckled around my hips, a brown leather that feels buttery smooth against my legs. It doesn't cover my crotch, though. Or my ass.

"Oh. My God," Harrison mutters, his cock bucking as I reach the foot of the bed.

"You once said if I showed up in chaps, I could have you any which way," I remind him.

Harrison nods, swallowing, his eyes pinging all over my body.

"You trust me?" I ask.

Another nod.

I run the rope I'm holding along my palm behind my back. It's soft and smooth, meant for humans, not livestock. "You say stop, I stop," I tell him, making sure he hears each word.

He nods a third time, eyes finding mine and holding. "Okay."

"Okay," I repeat.

Tossing my hat aside, I hop up onto the bed. In five seconds flat, I have Harrison on his back, his wrists bound together, and the tail end of the rope secured to the headboard. I give it a firm tug, inching Harrison's arms higher, and he sucks in a lungful of air, his eyes wide and pupils blown.

"*Sam*," he rasps, gaze dropping to my crotch as I hover above him.

I scoot down Harrison's body, grabbing his legs and tugging his bottom half up into the air. He gasps out again, and without wasting a second, I wrap his legs behind my head and bring my face to his ass.

"*Sam*."

It's a shout this time, and I can't stop my grin as I run my tongue over Harrison's asshole. He squirms, body shifting, a litany of curses leaving his lips, but I hold on tight, not willing for a second to let this man go.

"Oh my God," he groans, voice hoarse. He bucks against me. "Sam, I'm gonna come."

I huff a laugh, circling his cock and squeezing. "You are not."

"I *am*," he insists, breathing heavily. He groans as I push my tongue inside his body. "You...you've been edging me for two hours. Two *hours*, Sam. And you just emerged from my bathroom like...like the sexiest goddamn thing I've ever seen in my life. And now you've got your tongue up my ass, and *fuck*." He pants, whole body jolting. "And my hands are tied to the headboard. Definitely gonna come."

Well, we can't have that, can we? At least, not yet.

I give Harrison's ass cheek a kiss before lowering him back to the bed. His eyes zero in on my crotch, and he groans again, watching me as I reach into the nightstand.

"You own those chaps?" he asks breathlessly.

I flip open the lube. "I do. Why?"

He licks his lips. "I'm gonna need you wearing those at least once a week for...well, forever."

A smirk takes over my face. "I think that can be arranged," I tell him, slipping a finger inside his body.

"Sam, I need you to work fast."

"All right, stud," I say around a laugh. I stretch Harrison with two fingers, making sure he's plenty wet, and then I grab a condom because we haven't yet talked about going without. After adding more moisture to my cock, I line up, and Harrison gives me a nod.

I press forward, and it's bliss. Always is.

I bottom out in one deep thrust because I'm well aware Harrison prefers stretching on my cock. He doesn't mind the initial biting sting, not as long as I give him a moment to adjust. And that's what I do, stalling out against his ass, running my hands over his torso and along his sides. I worship him with my fingers, this beautiful man.

So perfect. So perfect for *me*.

When he starts shifting against my hips, I pull back and give him a firm thrust.

"*Yes*, Sam," he breathes, the exclamation muffled.

"Stud," I say, grinning wildly as I lean forward and fuck into him hard. His arms are resting up above his head, and his cock rubs over my stomach as my hips slap his ass. "You don't gotta be quiet tonight."

"You wanna"—his breath huffs out as he bounces on my cock—"make me scream?"

I groan. "That a challenge?"

He nods. "Mhm."

"All right," I say, getting up on my knees and holding his hips tight. "You might wanna hold onto somethin'."

Harrison bites his lip as I slam into him, and his hands fold around the rope stretched taut between him and the headboard. I don't take it easy. I fuck Harrison as hard as I've ever dared to, and he takes every thrust with relish, his sounds getting louder, his body becoming more and more slack.

The way he's laid out before me—legs around my hips and ass off the mattress, arms tied up, and hooded gaze pinned on my person—it's not something I'll ever forget. It's the single most intense moment of my life. Harrison is bound, but he's open. I can see it in his eyes. In the way he's surrendered. And knowing he trusts me with his body like this, that he trusts me to take care of him, makes me want to shout my joy.

Until a tear leaks out the corner of Harrison's eye.

I halt in an instant, my pulse skyrocketing. "Stud," I say in alarm.

He shakes his head rapidly.

"*Shit*. It's too much?" I ask, reaching for the rope.

"No," he says loudly, shaking his head again. "Don't. Don't untie me. Don't stop. Don't let go, Sam."

My breath stutters out as I realize what he's saying, and I ease myself down against Harrison's chest, cloaking him with my body. He holds eye contact, his gaze swimming.

"I'm not lettin' go," I say firmly. "Stud, you're not my second choice. You hear? There's no way I'm lettin' you go."

Another tear slips down the side of his face, and I curse, rubbing my thumb along the line. But Harrison turns his face, settling his cheek into my palm.

"I'm not on my own anymore," he says quietly. "Am I?"

"No," I croak out. "No, you're not."

And neither am I.

He hiccups, nearly a sob, before he looks up at me again. "I love you, Sam."

I freeze, my already still body tensing as I stare down into Harrison's eyes. I'm almost afraid I heard him wrong. Afraid my mind is spinning fantasies.

But Harrison repeats himself.

"I love you. And I know I probably shouldn't be telling you this while your cock is buried inside me, but it's been rolling around my head all night long, for days really, and it just...it's too big. Too much. I can't keep it inside any longer. I love you, Sammy. I love you so much."

My breath catches and releases, chest clenching tight as Harrison watches me, those blue eyes never wavering.

"You love me?" I ask, nearly in disbelief. No one has *ever*. Not like that.

He nods, a slow roll of his head against the pillow. "So damn much."

"I...I'm in chaps," I point out, hardly even aware of the words coming out of my mouth. "I'm wearin' chaps right now, and my dick is up your ass."

He huffs a laugh, the motion causing him to tighten around my cock. "Uh-huh. Fucking sexy. Hottest thing I've ever seen."

"And you're tied to the bed," I go on, not sure why these facts are what I'm stuck on.

"Sure am," he says, grinning a little as he grinds his ass against my hips.

I squeeze my eyes shut, trying to focus. "And you love me."

"Yeah, Sammy," he says, soft and gentle. "I love you."

I blow out a breath, leaning down to press my lips to Harrison's cheek. "We really gotta work on our romantic settin's."

Harrison laughs again, and I groan as his body wrings my cock.

"First the shed," I say, shaking my head. "And now this."

"It's perfect," Harrison says. "I like our idea of romance."

"God, stud." I ease back, and I'm pretty sure there might be a tear in my own eye, but Harrison doesn't comment on it. "I'm gonna finish fuckin' you," I say, rolling my hips slowly. Harrison moans, nodding his head. "And then you're gonna say that again."

"Anytime you want," he tells me, chest rising as I thrust into him a little harder. "Anytime."

God, he's beautiful. So handsome. Strong. Vulnerable. Perfect.

Mine.

Harrison urges me on with his heels, and I brace my palms against the mattress as I look down into his eyes, seeing that open emotion now for what it is. *Love*. It's love. For *me*.

I don't stop this time. I fuck Harrison deep and steady, letting him feel every one of my responding emotions loud and clear. I hold onto his hips, pulling him down on my cock, watching the bounce of his dick and the way his eyes keep rolling up, like it's all too much in the best way. I drive into him again and again, forcefully enough for the headboard to thud against the wall.

And when Harrison finally yells out "*Sammy*," I wrap my hand around his dick and tug. It's all over from there. Harrison groans louder than I've ever heard before, and he's coming over my fist before he can even warn me. His body grips me tight, and I grind against him, my whole being flushing hot, singing, crying out, as my release is dragged from me near violently. For a moment, I see stars, and I wonder if wishes really do come true.

Harrison is panting hard when I come down on top of him, and he kisses my cheek over and over until I turn my head. Then he's kissing me properly, his tongue sweeping into my mouth, warm and eager and feeling like home.

As soon as I slip from his body, Harrison breaks from my lips. "I love you," he says quickly. "I love you, Sam."

"God, Harrison." I ease up onto my elbows, my entire being pulled tight, like a rag wrung dry and hung in the sun. "I love you so much it hurts."

He smiles somewhat shakily. "The good kind of hurt, right?"

"The best kind," I say, kissing his lips slowly. A whisper. "I love you."

"Oh God," he says around a little chuckle. "Say it again."

"I love you," I repeat, nudging his nose.

"I love you, too." His laugh is breathy, full of wonder. "We're going to be saying that all the time now, aren't we?"

"I sure hope so," I tell him truthfully, dropping my face to Harrison's neck and breathing in his scent. Melon. My favorite.

When he moves a little, like he's stretching out his limbs, I pull myself upright and reach for the rope. I slip the knot free and bring Harrison's arms down, rubbing them gently for a moment before I set to untying his wrists.

"That was..." Harrison swallows, gaze tracking my movements. "That was so hot, Sam."

Laughing, and more than a little pleased, I set the rope aside. "Yeah?"

"You...you had me tied up before I could even blink. I didn't know how to react. I was stunned. And horny. Really damn horny."

I strip off my condom before settling down beside him. Harrison turns his head to look at me. "Told you I was calf-ropin' champion three years in a row," I remind him with a smirk.

He bites his lips. "Hot," he mutters again, eyes drifting lazily down my body.

I snicker. "I think I broke ya."

"Mhm. Break me anytime."

Chuckling, I rub my hand up Harrison's arm. "You should drink some water before bed. Don't want you to cramp."

He hums his assent just as a scratch sounds against the door. Harrison looks that way before huffing. "Tigger probably needs to go out."

"Poor girl," I say, hopping out of bed. "Left all alone while her daddies played."

Harrison's laugh sounds at my back as I toss a robe around my body and head out the door. Tigger, as expected, is waiting just on the other side, and she hops up, tail wagging furiously.

"Heya, girl. Let's get you sorted."

Tigger does her business quickly in the backyard, and then the two of us head back upstairs to the bedroom. Harrison is in the en suite when we arrive, washing the cum off his stomach—which makes *my* stomach somersault—and then he joins us on the bed. I guess with Winnie gone, Tigger is choosing to grace us with her presence. I give her a good pat.

Harrison doesn't hesitate to curl up against me, head on my shoulder. I wrap my arm around him as his hand traces patterns over my chest. "So..." he says.

"What is it?" I ask.

His eyebrow hitches. "We have all night?"

I bark a laugh, sliding my hand down to Harrison's ass. "Got plans, stud?"

"Yeah, Sammy," he breathes out. "I have a lot of plans where you're concerned."

Well, shit. I like the sound of that a lot.

CHAPTER 27

★

Harrison

Light is streaming through the window when I wake, and it's such an unusual occurrence, I snap to consciousness immediately. It only takes me a moment to remember last night and the fact that Winnie isn't home yet.

My body relaxes right away, but the disturbance must have been enough to wake Sam because he shifts against me, humming slightly as he wakes up. One eye blinks open, the other staying shut, and a slow smile spreads over his face.

"Mornin'."

My heart does a little flop. "Morning, Sam."

He rumbles as he stretches, his foot nudging Tigger, whose head perks. "Needa go out, girl?"

Tigger jumps down from the bed, doing a dance at the door, and Sam chuckles. He kisses my forehead before easing out from under the sheets. My eyes drop straight to his bare ass as he stops to pull on a pair of pants, and my sigh is more than a little wistful.

Sam shoots me a wink as he leaves the room, and I roll onto my back, staring up at the ceiling as my mind turns over everything that's happened in the past day. Week. Couple of months, even.

A smile spreads slowly across my face, and for the first time in a very long time, I feel...excited. Excited and hopeful and curious about what the future has in store.

When Sam returns, I'm just leaving the bathroom. His head swings from the empty bed to where I'm standing in the doorway, and his grin widens, even as his hands stay behind his back.

My cock kicks beneath my sweats because the last time Sam was hiding something behind his back, I got the dicking of a lifetime. In fact, I'm pretty sure I'll never look at rope—or calf roping—the same way again.

But Sam produces a small plastic clamshell bakery box from behind his body and holds it out my way.

"Is that...cake?" I ask in surprise.

Sam nods, meeting me at the bed. He motions for me to hop up, so I do, seating myself at the headboard as Sam settles next to me. Carefully, he flips the lid open and hands over the cake, followed by a fork.

"Last slice," he says with a somewhat shy smile.

Oh, God.

"Did you buy a single piece of cake just for me?"

"Yes?" he says, nose scrunching. *Jesus, he's cute.* "You said once that you never got the last slice anymore. That it's one of the simple things you miss from when your life was a li'l less...complicated."

I swallow hard. I did say that.

"Well, here you go," he says. "Last slice of cake. It's all yours."

"Sam," I breathe out, shaking my head. First, arranging a night alone and taking me out for beers. Now, this. I've never had someone listen to me so clearly. Never had someone try so hard to put me first. "I love you."

Sam's face breaks into a beaming smile, like simply hearing those words means the absolute world to him. "Love you, too, stud."

Damn. Yeah, not going to get over that any time soon.

"Thank you, Sammy," I add. "For the cake."

"You bet," he says, giving my fork-holding hand a little nudge. "Now eat up before Winnie gets home and you lose your chance."

I huff a laugh but get to it. At the first bite of strawberry goodness, I groan. Cake for breakfast should be a new rule.

Sam's eyes drop to my lips as I lick the crumbs away. "Good?"

I tug him in, sharing the flavor, and he hums happily against me. So easy to please, this man.

The thought gives me pause.

"Sam," I say slowly, plucking up another forkful of cake. "There's something I need to tell you." He looks concerned for all of a second before I add, "Nothing *bad.*"

"All right," he says, pressing his leg against mine. "Shoot."

I chew before speaking, using the time to collect my thoughts. So few people know about this, but I don't feel right not telling Sam. Not anymore.

"Biologically, Winnie is not my daughter," I finally say, the words like a heavy weight dripping off my tongue.

Sam's eyes widen. There's a brief pause before he says, "She looks so much like you, though."

I nod. "She's my niece."

"Oh. Oh wow," he says, moving his head up and down a little like he's getting his bearings. "All right. You have a brother, then? Sister?"

"Sister," I confirm, throat catching. "Danielle."

Sam places his hand on my thigh and squeezes. "God, Harrison. Thank you for sharin' that with me. Would you tell me what happened?"

"Yeah," I answer, setting the cake aside. My gut hollows a bit. I haven't said any of this aloud in so long. "Danielle... She's always been unstable, for lack of a better word. My parents tried really hard when she was younger to get her proper help and medication, but my sister found ways to avoid taking her meds. She was just...flighty in a way that caused issues with school and friends and her own health. And she didn't like being told what to do. As soon as she was old enough to leave, she did. She's not a bad person," I explain. "But she's not balanced, either, and she was in no way ready to take on the responsibilities of parenthood. She knew that much, at least, which is why she turned up on my doorstep when Winnie was two days old. We didn't even know she was pregnant."

"Oh, Harrison," Sam says, increasing the pressure on my leg.

I nod slowly as memories flit through my mind. They're so clear, as if it happened yesterday. "She couldn't take care of Winnie, but I couldn't... I couldn't *not*. She was this tiny thing, you know? Utterly defenseless, wrinkled, and gorgeous. Danielle left before the adoption paperwork was even finalized."

He squeezes again, but I can't seem to stop talking now that I've started.

"It was a couple months after I left Plum Valley. I was living a few hours away from here at the time, but the job I had picked up wasn't enough to take care of me and a newborn. So, I applied all around the state and lucked into the full-time vet position here near Houston. My parents moved at the same time to help out, but it was like my entire world got flipped upside-down in the blink of an eye. All of a sudden, I was a *dad.* I wasn't expecting it, and during some of those early days, I didn't even want it. But what was I supposed to do? Danielle couldn't raise a child. She knew it. So did we. If she wouldn't have come to me, who knows what would have happened to Winnie? I can't even stand to think of it, but *fuck*, Sam. Her choices completely changed the course of my life."

Sam is quiet for a moment, his palm rubbing softly up and down my leg. I take a moment to calm my racing pulse as all of those old resentments flare to life, followed by guilt for even feeling them in the first place. Always with the damn guilt.

"You chose to be a father," Sam says softly. "That was your decision."

"Yes," I admit because that much is true. I could have refused Danielle when she showed up with Winnie. My parents would have raised her, or Danielle could have given her up for adoption. But... "I did make that choice. You're right."

"Stud," Sam says softly, nudging me until I look his way. There's a soft smile on his face. "That wasn't a criticism. I'm not sayin' you're wrong for bein' upset about the way your life changed. I'm just...I'm a li'l in awe over here."

"What?" I ask in surprise.

"You chose to be a dad in what amounts to a moment," he says. "Most folks think about that for a long time. They plan for it, or at least have time to plan around it. And you...you didn't have that. But you *chose* Winnie. You put her first that day, and you became a dad. D'you realize how remarkable that is?" He shakes his head a little. "I spent my childhood with dozens of foster carers, and what they did for me was remarkable in its own right. But not one of them took up that mantle for me. You stepped up when Winnie needed you most, and *God*. I just...I respect the hell out of you for that, Harrison."

Christ.

"She doesn't know," I say because I can't come up with a single reply to Sam's heartfelt words. The way he sees me...it's too much sometimes. I'm far from perfect. "Winnie doesn't know Danielle is her mother. She's only met her twice when my sister was passing through, but for all intents and purposes, Danielle is Winnie's aunt. It's what my sister wanted, and we—me and my parents—agreed it was for the best. But sometimes... Sometimes I hate the fact that I have to keep something so big from my daughter. When do I tell her the truth? All she knows is that her mom couldn't stay because she wasn't prepared to be a parent. That it wouldn't have been healthy or safe for either of them. But Winnie is going to want to know more. At some point, that's not going to be enough. And then what? Will she hate me for lying to her? Will it change things when Winnie finds out I'm technically her uncle?"

"Never," Sam says, sounding sure. "You're her dad, end of story. You'll always be her dad. Biology doesn't change that. When—and if—it's the right time to tell her, you'll know. She won't hate you, Harrison. She could never."

"I feel like I'm not enough," I whisper. "Sometimes I feel like I'm not enough for her. Maybe that's why she's struggling at night. Maybe that's why—"

"You. Are. Enough," Sam says, cutting me off, his tone brokering no argument. "You are more than enough, stud. You're everythin' to that little girl. Her trouble sleepin' alone is not due to some perceived fault of yours as a parent. Some kids just have trouble fallin' asleep, while others don't. Some kids don't like bein' alone. Others have no problem with it. Heck, some kids run through the streets, fearless, and others are always gonna want a hand to hold. We're all different. Our fears, our worries, what we're good at, what we're not—I don't think those things are shaped entirely by the outside world. Part of it is just *us*. So stop takin' all those burdens on your shoulders like you're singlehandedly responsible for whether or not Winnie likes broccoli or can sleep with the light off. Your daughter is uniquely herself, and you're doin' your best to raise her to know that whoever that person is? She's okay *just* as she is."

"Goddamn it, Sam," I all but croak, swiping at my eyes. "How do you always know the exact right thing to say?"

"Do I?" he asks, running his thumb along my cheek before reaching over to grab my long-forgotten cake. He breaks off a piece with the fork, bringing it to my mouth. Dutifully, I eat the bite. He looks a little unsure as he says, "Even when I'm bein' a jealous ass? 'Cause I can't promise that's not gonna happen again."

"Oh, Sam," I huff, marveling at how open this man is with me. I've never felt so comfortable baring my soul with another human being before, and I think a big part of that is Sam himself. The way I can so clearly see to the heart of him. But that means I'm not the only one vulnerable in this relationship. Sam needs the reassurance just as much as I do. "That doesn't bother me."

"You really don't mind?" he asks, feeding me the last piece of cake.

I lick the frosting from my lips when I'm done and shake my head. "No, I don't mind. I told you that last night. But Sammy?"

He leans back as I swing my leg over his lap, settling myself there. His eyes, so big and brown, watch me carefully.

"Just to be clear," I say slowly. "I won't be looking anywhere but at you."

His lips twitch into a smile, and some of that usual *Sam fire* enters his eyes. "It's the chaps, isn't it?"

I bark a laugh. "They sure don't hurt."

Sam rumbles a hum, dragging me down against his crotch. I start to plump as my cock rubs against his through our clothes, but then Sam stops.

"Harrison, I really appreciate you tellin' me those things," he says. "I don't wanna make light of that."

"I didn't think you were," I assure him.

He nods, fingers stroking over my sweatpants. "I remember that first night we met. You told me you felt like you were livin' someone else's life." I cringe a little at that, but Sam goes on. "I understand that more now. But I also know you don't regret any of it."

"I don't," I say firmly. I think, sometimes, it's simply hard not to wonder *what if.* I was feeling so very alone that day back in Plum Valley when Sam and I met. Alone, tired, overworked, and overwhelmed. And I didn't even realize, until recently, how often I was stuck feeling that way. Feeling like my life was falling off the tracks.

"I just..." Sam goes on. "I just hope I'm helpin'. Not addin' to everythin' on your plate."

My breath whooshes from my lungs. "Sam," I say, framing his face in my hands. His bristle is sharp, and I stroke my thumbs along those hairs that fire like electricity. "You are my angel."

He huffs a laugh, looking down, but I give him a little shake.

"My angel of cock and cake, remember?"

He chuckles again, and I run my hand down his chest, just to convince myself he's real.

"My angel of veggies and filthy sweet words," I continue. "My angel of chaps and beer and backyard camping." My chest warms as I recall what I overheard of his conversation with Winnie that night we camped in the backyard. How sweet he was with her inside the treehouse. How absolutely stunning in his own childlike wonder. "You've made everything in my life better from the moment you showed up. The only thing you add to my plate"—I hold up the empty cake box—"is this."

Sam grins, but it's a sweet thing. Gentle and warm.

"In fact, you should probably change your name," I tease. "Cox just isn't enough."

"I dunno, stud," he drawls. "Sammy Cox-And-Every-thin'-Else just doesn't have the same ring to it."

His tone is joking, but I give a start. "Wait. Is your first name *actually* Sammy?"

He gives me a funny sort of smile. "Well, yeah."

"Oh my God," I say, a little horrified at my own assumption. "I just thought you were being cute."

"I mean, I'm that, too," he says with a wink. Because of course he does. "But no. Legally, my name is Sammy Cox. The guy who found me at the fire station named me that."

I shut my eyes, leaning my forehead against Sam's own as a million different thoughts race through my head. Including the fact that that could have been Winnie. Her story and Sam's, they don't start that differently. I'm just grateful Danielle came to me. That she had the presence of mind to do so. It makes me ache that Sam never had that as a child. He was truly alone.

"I'm sorry," I say, leaning back. My ass is still resting on Sam's lap, and I vaguely wonder whether or not it's comfortable for him—I'm not a slight guy, after all—but with the way Sam's hands are clamped around my hips, I don't dare move. "Would you prefer I call you Sammy? I didn't mean to be rude."

He huffs. "Please. Like you're ever actually rude. And no, stud. I quite like that you call me Sam. Feels like a nickname that's all yours. Well, yours and Winnie's, really. And, y'know, it makes those times you *do* call me Sammy somethin' special."

His eyes light a little at that, and I have no doubt what he's thinking. Because the times I call him Sammy are usually the times he's about to make me come.

I clear my throat. "If you're sure."

"I'm sure," he says, hands slipping around to my ass. He tugs me a little closer, mouth opening, as if he's about to speak. But then the sound of the front door thudding shut reaches our ears, and his expression changes from suggestive to almost serene.

"Daddy? Sam?" Winnie calls out.

Sam gives a happy little sigh. "What d'you think? Should we go welcome your daughter home?"

"Yeah, Sam," I say, slipping off his lap, my stomach doing all sorts of skips and hops. "Let's go."

CHAPTER 28

★

Sammy

"How'd the big date go?" Carl asks, wiping his forehead with his sleeve. I don't bother pointing out he just smudged a bunch of dirt across his brow.

"Good," I tell him, more than sure my face is sporting some sort of loopy smile.

Carl eyes me. "That's all you're gonna say?"

I shrug, trimming off the sharp ends of the wire fencing we used to patch a small hole out back behind Animal Control. I volunteered Carl and me for the repair job, figuring there was no use hiring outside help for such a small task. We were able to handle it just fine, even though Carl spent the last half hour grumbling about the extra work.

"All right, what the hell is goin' on?" my coworker asks, straightening up and sticking his hands on his hips. "You're bein' *quiet*, and I don't like it, Sammy. It's not like you. In fact, you've been quiet all day. Not a single word about that 'mighty fine' doctor of yours or his 'mighty fine *ass*-ets.'" His expression shifts to concern, arms dropping. "Is somethin' wrong?"

I huff a laugh, standing up, too, the wire clippers in my hand. "Nothin's wrong, Carl," I say seriously. "I, uh..." A dog barks nearby, which kicks off a few others, and for once, I don't even know what to tell my friend. "I love 'im."

Carl blinks at me. Once. Twice. "*Love* him, love him?"

"Yeah," I answer. "Big time."

"And, uh…" He swallows. "Does he know?"

My smile softens, and I clasp Carl on the shoulder, understanding his concern. He's afraid I might still get hurt. But I know that's not going to happen. Not this time. *Not ever again*, a little voice inside my head pipes up. I'm inclined to believe it.

"He knows," I tell him. "He said it first."

Carl's face breaks into a huge smile. "Sammy," he says simply.

"I *know*, Carl. I'm gonna get hitched, just you watch. I'm gonna marry that man and have his babies. Well," I amend, shrugging a little as I let Carl go, "not literally, but we sure can try. Often and hard."

"Aw, c'mon now," Carl groans, hiding his face behind his hands. I ignore his mumbled, "*Why?*"

"And then there's Winifred," I go on with a soft smile. "She's warmin' to me. It's slow goin', but I don't mind. We've got time."

"That's the daughter?" Carl asks, dropping his arms.

I give him a nod. "Yeah. She taught me how to make a volcano." I grab the extra wire fencing off the ground as I tell him, "We're gonna add dinosaurs next time."

Carl shakes his head a little, walking with me toward the building. "It's kinda wild to hear you talkin' about a kid, y'know? You've never dated anybody with a family before."

"I know," I say, having realized the same thing myself. It wasn't a conscious choice by any means. It just happened that way. I like the fact that Harrison comes with Winnie. I like the both of them a hell of a lot.

Carl holds the door open for me, and I bring our supplies inside. Our footsteps echo a little as we walk down the hall, until the sound of barking dogs takes over.

"I'm happy for you, Sammy," Carl says at last, stopping outside the storage room. He opens the door for me so I can stash the extra wire and clippers inside, as well as the little bag of metal connectors I had in my pocket. "There's no one who deserves it more than you."

"Dang, Carl," I say, huffing out a breath before I tug my friend in. He slaps my back, and I slap his. "I appreciate that. But, uh, what about you? Countin' yourself out?"

He rolls his eyes. "I'm doin' all right. Got Rosie, after all."

"Yeah," I say with a little smile. "Maybe Rosie could meet Tigger sometime. We could have a cookout."

"Won't say no to that," Carl says, stepping with me down the hall. "See ya tomorrow?"

"You bet," I tell him. "Have a good night, Carl."

Carl tips his head before pushing into the employee break room, and I divert toward the front of the building. I find Tilda inside one of the cat rooms and give the glass a little knock before circling around to the door that leads inside.

"Hey there, Sammy," she greets, an orange tabby in her arms.

"Tilly. Fence is all taken care of," I let her know, bending down to scratch the back of a kitten trying to claw up my leg.

"Thanks, hun." She gives my head a little pat.

I snort.

"So," Tilda says slowly. "How're things goin' with that doctor of yours?"

"You and Carl both seem awfully preoccupied with my love life," I note, not unhappily.

"Well, of course," she says. "We care."

My chest warms at that, and I look up from my crouched position. A couple of cats have come over to me now and are rubbing against my legs, and I run my hands along their backs as I catch Tilda's eye. This woman, who didn't know me until I was already an adult, but who pseudo-adopted me anyway.

"I love you, Tilly," I tell her, using, like always, the name she told me to call her upon our first meeting. Because *family calls me Tilly, Sammy boy*. "You know that, right?"

"Oh, Sammy," she says fondly, setting down the cat in her arms before opening them wide.

I stand up, meeting Tilda for a hug, my throat more than a little tight.

"I know you do," she answers, her presence surrounding me like a comfortable cloud. "I love you, too. And I'm so very happy for you."

"Why's that?" I ask, stepping back.

Tilda raises an eyebrow. "'Cause you found the one, of course."

I bark a laugh, can't help it. "And how d'you know that?" I only just told Carl about the whole *I love you* thing a handful of minutes ago.

She pats me on the cheek. "I can tell. Will you bring him and that little girl around? I'd love to meet her."

"Yeah," I say, my emotions doing their best to fill me to the brim. "I'll do that."

"Good," Tilda says, sighing a little. "C'mon now. Time to head home."

Home. Harrison's place. Same thing, isn't it?

Tilda and I separate in the parking lot, and I give her a little wave as she gets into her car. By the time I arrive at Harrison's familiar blue house, it's just after five-thirty. Tigger greets me at the front door, her little stumpy tail wagging, and I bend down, giving her a thorough petting and assuring her she's the sweetest thing in the whole wide world, *yes she is*. Then I toe off my boots and head into the kitchen. As I expected, Harrison is there, getting supper ready. He looks over his shoulder when I arrive, and a whole swarm of butterflies lets loose in my stomach.

"Hey," he says softly, giving me a smile before he goes back to stirring whatever is on the stove. It smells good, like tomatoes and herbs.

"Hey, stud," I reply, coming up behind him and wrapping my arms around his chest. He hums happily, and I nose at his neck, breathing in that sweet scent that makes me equal parts fond and horny.

Harrison chuckles when my cock kicks up its own greeting.

"I needa wash off real quick," I let him know. "But then I can set the table." He nods, and I add, "Winnie outside?"

He makes a noise of affirmation. "She's finishing up her homework in the treehouse."

Of course she is.

I give Harrison's cheek a quick kiss before stepping back and hurrying up the stairs. Inside his en suite, I use my own soap—because his gives me a boner—and then dry and dress in clean clothes. I have a few that migrated here after Harrison casually mentioned it would make sense to keep some extras on hand. I wasn't about to argue.

When I get back downstairs, Winnie is coming through the door. "Hey, li'l miss," I greet her.

"Hi, Sam," she says solemnly, trudging past me down the hall.

"Somethin' the matter?" I ask, following her into the living room. Her backpack is sitting on the couch, and she stuffs a binder inside. Her homework, presumably.

"Astronomers gotta be good at math," she states, flopping onto the couch. Tigger jumps up beside her, and Winnie pats the dog's head.

"And that's a problem?" I ask.

"I'm *not* good at math," she says, and now I understand.

"Well, that's all right."

She gives me a scowl, and I hasten to reassure her.

"It is," I say, sitting on the arm of the couch right next to her. "Just 'cause it doesn't come naturally to you, that doesn't mean you can't learn. You might just have to try a li'l harder, and there's nothin' wrong with that."

She doesn't look convinced, so I give her a nudge.

"Sometimes we gotta fight for our dreams," I say. "You can still be an astronomer, if that's really what you want. Your dad and I will help you."

She's quiet for a moment, hand running over Tigger's fur. "You really think I could do it?"

"Of course. Now, d'you needa clean up before supper? It's almost time to eat."

Winnie nods, sighing before hopping off the couch. She trots up the stairs, and hoping what I said helped even a little, I return to the kitchen. Harrison is pulling off an oven mitt, and I grab plates to set the table. This time of day has become one of my favorites: supper with Harrison and Winnie.

When we all sit down, I can't quite gauge Winnie's mood, but she goes right for the garlic bread, so she must not be too forlorn. Tigger takes up her customary spot beside her.

"I've been meanin' to ask," I say, dishing up some pasta when Harrison hands the bowl my way, "who picked the name Tigger?"

Harrison and Winnie exchange a look, and I nearly laugh.

"Joint effort, really," Harrison says. "We were reading a Winnie the Pooh story the night we adopted her. Tigger, still being a puppy, was bouncing around on top of the bed, and it just...fit."

Winnie nods sagely. "We're best friends, just like in the story."

My heart warms at that.

"I haven't read any of those books," I admit, and both Winnie and Harrison gasp.

"Why not?" Winnie asks, but then she waves her hand. "Never mind. It doesn't matter. We'll fix that."

"Oh, we will, will we?" I ask, hiding my smile as I take a sip of water.

Winnie nods over and over. "Mhm. Don't worry, Sam. I've got lots of Winnie the Pooh books upstairs. Daddy and I will read them to you."

I can't hide my smile this time. "Can't wait," I tell her. "So, which character would I be?"

Winnie puts some serious thought into the question, her brows drawn together as she munches on her second piece of garlic bread. I sneak a look at Harrison, and he gives me a smile, bumping his foot into mine.

"It's too bad you can't be Pooh Bear," Winnie finally says.

Because the name's taken, I guess.

"Yeah?" I ask, curious why she thinks I'm like the infamous bear. "Why would I make a good Pooh?"

"You're like a hug," she states, as if those words are simple. As if she didn't just irrevocably alter part of my being—the part of my heart that has been growing in size just for her.

Harrison squeezes my arm, and I'm grateful for the tether.

"That's okay, though," Winnie goes on. "You can be Roo since you have lots of energy."

"And what about me?" Harrison asks, giving me a much-needed moment to compose myself. "Who would I be?"

"Rabbit, of course," Winnie answers.

Harrison's face scrunches. "Oh great. I'm the stick in the mud."

"No," his daughter says, rolling her eyes. "You're the one who looks after the rest."

And there goes Harrison's hand again, squeezing my arm tightly. I know how he feels.

I place my hand over his, and the look in his eye when he meets my gaze is one I'm starting to recognize. Parental pride—I think that's what it is. I see it a lot on Harrison's face. The love there. The appreciation for what he has. The overwhelming feeling I'm only just starting to get a taste of.

It's what makes the hard parts worth it; isn't that what Harrison is always telling me? Because how could you ever regret love?

As the three of us are clearing up the table, Harrison's phone rings. He wipes his hand dry before fishing it out of his pocket and frowning at the screen.

"Hello?" he answers. "Deb?"

I can't hear what's being said on the other end of the line, but Harrison's face smooths from concern to understanding, and he nods.

"Of course," he says. "I can be over shortly. Uh-huh. See you soon."

"Problem?" I ask.

He pockets his phone. "Deborah locked herself out of her house, and I have her spare key. Do you, uh..."

"What is it?" I ask.

Harrison's gaze shifts to Winnie, who's parked in a chair near the window, one of her storybooks in her hands. Always reading or running, that one. Harrison lowers his voice a little. "Do you think you could watch Winnie? I could bring her with me, but..." He trails off, shrugging a little, but I hear the unspoken. He'd feel comfortable leaving her with me.

"I'd be happy to watch her," I say, hooking my hands around his hips and tugging him close. "Thank you," I add softly.

He doesn't respond verbally, just leans in and brings his lips to mine. It's brief, but even the smallest kiss from Harrison is one I hoard like gold.

"Winnie," he says, stepping back. Her head perks. "I'm going to run over to my coworker's house really quickly. Sam will be here while I'm gone."

"Okay, Daddy," she says, face back in her book.

"Okay, then," Harrison says to me. "Should only take me half an hour."

"Sounds good, stud. See you soon."

Harrison gives me a quick smile before stepping off into the laundry room. A minute later, the garage door opens, and Tigger is nudging me in the leg with her ball. I huff a laugh, opening my palm, and Tigger drops the ball happily, her stump wiggling.

"Winifred, wanna join me outside for a bit?" I ask.

"Sure," she says, closing her book and scooting off her chair. In a flash, she's put on her boots and is running out the door.

I follow as Tigger circles my legs. As soon as we're in the backyard, I toss the ball as far as I can toward the fence. Tigger races off after it. There's a bite in the air tonight, a gentle whisper of wind that has me shivering ever so slightly in my short-sleeve tee as I watch Tigger come to a quick halt in front of the ball.

"Winifred," I call out. "You need a jacket?"

"Nah," she yells back from the treehouse.

I'm pretty sure kids are impervious to the cold, at least when they're having fun. Still, I make a mental note to grab it if we're out here long.

Tigger drops the ball at my feet, and I throw it again. We're on the tenth or eleventh pitch when I hear the sound no parent or guardian wants to hear of the child in their care—a thump, followed by a scream. Not a happy scream or even a startled one. A scream of pain.

I'm racing toward the treehouse in a snap. "Winnie!" I call out. My stomach sinks when my eyes land on the little girl curled up on the ground beside the treehouse ladder.

"Sam," she cries.

Shit.

I drop down beside her, taking stock quickly. Winnie is reaching toward her foot, but the moment she touches it, she cries out again and falls flat.

"Fudge," she pseudo-swears.

"What hurts?" I ask, checking her eyes—pupils are even. I skim my hands through her hair. No blood.

"My ankle," she says, openly crying now. "Sam, it hurts."

Fuck. "Honey, how did you land?"

It's obvious, even though I didn't see it, that Winnie fell from either the top of the treehouse or from the ladder itself. I heard the thump. But if she landed on her back or—Heaven forbid—her head or neck, me moving her might make it worse.

But Winnie just closes her eyes and says, "I landed on my legs."

Good enough for me. Swooping her up, I head swiftly for the house, whistling for Tigger to keep up, even though the dog is already at my heel.

"Sam," Winnie says again, crying out. I do my best not to jostle her.

"I know, honey," I say, keeping my voice even. "I got you, all right? You're gonna be fine. Just hold tight."

Winnie nods, her cheeks wet, but even as my mind races ten steps ahead and I rush the little girl to my truck, my heart falls somewhere in the vicinity of my boots. Harrison trusted me to watch his daughter, and only ten minutes in, I failed. I failed him, and I failed her.

And I don't know what that means for *us*.

But I push it out of my head because right now, Winnie still needs me, and I refuse to let her down any more than I already have.

"You're gonna be just fine," I assure the both of us.

CHAPTER 29

★

Harrison

"Ugh, thanks, Harrison," Deborah says, giving me a chagrined look as I meet her in front of her house. "I can't believe I locked myself out."

"Happens to the best of us," I say, handing over her spare key.

She snorts at that, unlocking her door and beckoning me in. "Ever happen to you?"

"Well," I hedge.

"That's what I thought," she huffs. "C'mon. I've got some homemade snickerdoodles in the kitchen."

"I won't say no to that," I reply, following Deborah into her kitchen. She opens the container of cookies, and I practically salivate when the cinnamon smell smacks me in the face. The two of us take seats at her table, two plates and the cookies between us.

"So," she says, waiting until I've taken a bite to speak. "How're things goin' with that hunk of man you call a boyfriend?"

I shake my head, a smile on my face. "What, we're gossiping after hours now, too?"

"Give it up, Harrison," Deborah chides with a smirk. "Abbott and his delicate sensibilities aren't here to offend."

I wait until I'm done chewing, making Deborah sweat it out a little. By her eye roll, I can tell she's not impressed.

"He wore chaps," I finally say. When Deborah just cocks her head a little, I add, "A cowboy hat and chaps. That's it."

There's a beat of silence, and then my friend is laughing, her hand over her mouth. "Oh, Harrison," she manages to get out. "Don't you give that boy up."

I don't plan to.

She wipes a tear from her face. "Oh, I would've paid to see that."

"Not a chance," I shoot back. "He's all mine."

Deborah's smile turns soft. "So when's the wedding?"

I choke on my cookie, and Deborah laughs, patting my back. It's not until a good thirty minutes later that I'm finally leaving my friend-slash-coworker's house, a big grin on my face. The first thing I do when I get in my truck is grab my phone to text Sam that I'm on my way back—a good bit later than I thought I'd be. But my fingers freeze when I see the barrage of missed calls and texts from both Sam and my mom.

Pulse racing fast, I skim the notifications, but when I see the words "hospital" and "Winnie" in the same sentence, I immediately dial Sam.

He picks up on the first ring. "Harrison, I'm so sorry," he says in lieu of a greeting.

"What happened?" I ask, my voice shaking. My hands aren't much better. "Is Winnie okay?"

"She hurt her foot or ankle, but she's okay," he says quickly, and all those worst-case scenarios I'd been entertaining ease away, replaced by a far less terror-inducing concern. I close my eyes, blowing out a breath as Sam continues. "She fell climbin' down from the treehouse. We just arrived at the hospital"—he pauses to say something off-phone—"and your dad is checkin' her in now."

"Which hospital?" I ask, turning the ignition. My truck roars to life as Sam rattles off the info. "I'll be there in twenty minutes."

"Harrison, I'm so sorry," he says again, but I shake my head.

"I'll see you soon, okay?"

"Yeah, all right," he says.

I plunk my phone into my cup holder and pull out of Deborah's driveway, my heart racing the entire way to the hospital in Houston. I do my best to breathe evenly and remind myself that it's okay—*Sam said it's okay*—but my body doesn't seem to get the memo from my brain because I can't quell the disquiet, no matter how hard I try.

My feet feel heavy as I make my way inside the building from the parking garage. I follow signs to the ER, and when I get there, the receptionist informs me Winnie has already been taken back to a private room. I have to show my driver's license before she allows me through, but then I'm being directed down the hall to the third door on the right.

The moment I step into the room, I see Sam standing in the corner, wringing his hands. His gaze shoots to me, and his face, drawn tight in concern, shifts into something sadder than I've ever seen from the man. Sitting in a chair closer to the bed is my dad, and lying atop the small hospital cot is Winnie, an ice pack over her ankle.

"Oh, Pumpkin," I say, heading her way.

"The doctor thinks it's just a sprain," Sam says from behind me, speaking fast but not approaching. "He's orderin' an X-ray to make sure, but it doesn't appear to be broken."

I nod, lifting the ice pack gently to peek at my daughter's ankle. It's bruised and heavily swollen, but I'm relieved it's no worse.

"How are you feeling?" I ask Winnie, replacing the ice pack.

Her lip wobbles slightly, and her eyes are glassy, but she looks like she's doing her best to be brave. "I'm okay, Daddy. I'm sorry I wasn't being careful enough. I just slipped, and—"

"Hey, hey," I soothe, brushing her hair back. "Not your fault. Accidents happen. I'm just glad you're safe. Does it hurt?"

She nods. "Yeah, but not as much as before."

"They gave her a low-dose pain med," my dad puts in.

"Good," I say, closing my eyes briefly and breathing out. "Good. Will you be okay with Grandpa for a minute?"

Winnie nods, and knowing my daughter is okay, all things considered, I give my dad's shoulder a squeeze and turn to Sam. He's visibly shaking, his hands rhythmically twisting and his face pale. I stride his way, giving him a little tug toward the hall where we'll have some privacy. As soon as the door to Winnie's room closes behind us, Sam faces me.

"I'm *so* sorry," he says again, looking like he's readying for a lengthy apology.

I shake my head, bracketing his face in my hands. "Are you okay?"

Sam's mouth opens and closes, and he blinks at me, confused. "What?"

"Sammy," I say gently, my breath stuttering. The poor man looks like he's about to faint. I can't even imagine how terrifying it must have been for him, being the one there when Winnie fell. It was scary enough for me, even after hearing Winnie wasn't seriously hurt. It's *still* scary. I brush his cheeks softly. "Are *you* okay?"

His face falls, and I have just enough time to tug him in before he breaks.

"Shh. It's okay, love," I breathe, rubbing his back as Sam grips me tightly. His face is tucked against my neck, body wracked with his hushed sobs. A nurse passes us in the hallway, shooting Sam a worried look, but she doesn't stop. I'm sure the employees here see all manner of upset people on a daily basis. I kiss the side of Sam's head, doing my best to soothe him. "She's okay. It's okay."

"I should've been watchin' her more closely," he says, trembling. "It's my fault, Harrison. She's hurt because of me."

"Hey," I say, my own voice hoarse. "No. She's *safe* because of you. What happened when she fell?"

Sam eases back, his breathing evening out some. His eyes are wet, the brown pools looking big and endless and sad. "What?"

"Tell me what happened," I urge gently, wiping the moisture off his cheeks. "What happened when she fell?"

He swallows, blowing out a slow breath as he nods, as if readying his words. "I, uh... I got Winnie inside and took off her shoes, in case there was swellin'." He winces, and with Winnie in pain, I imagine that wasn't a pleasant process. "We got in my truck, and I had her hold an ice pack to her ankle where she said it hurt. And then I tried callin' you on the way to the hospital, but you weren't pickin' up."

"I left my phone in my truck," I say apologetically, nodding for him to go on.

"So, uh, I drove to your parents, 'cause I figured they'd be authorized to admit Winnie for medical attention. Your dad came with, and then you know the rest. The doctor took a look while you were drivin' over."

I nod, running my hands over Sam's shoulders and neck. "Sammy, you did everything right."

His breath catches again, and I go on.

"Winnie got hurt. An *accident*," I stress. "And you took care of her. You got her here, you got my *dad* here when I wasn't available, and...*fuck*." I tuck my face over his shoulder, and this time, it's me shaking. "*Thank* you. Thank you for taking such good care of my little girl."

"Harrison," he breathes, his grip around me like a band. "You're not...you're not mad?"

"No," I say firmly. "Of course not. I'm *grateful*, Sam. You're going to make such a good parent."

Sam inhales sharply, pulling back. His eyes ping back and forth between my own, so hopeful, so full of questions. But he doesn't get a chance to ask any of them before we're interrupted.

"Are you Mr. Bailey?"

Turning, I take in the doctor standing in front of Winnie's door and nod. "That's me," I say, giving Sam's arm a squeeze before I let go.

"Why don't y'all come on in, and we'll talk about gettin' Winifred patched up and sent home?" the doctor says.

"We'll be right there," I reply. "Thank you."

The man gives me a nod and heads into the room, and I turn to Sam, taking his hand in my own.

"Sam, I'm yours, right? That's what you told me."

He nods, and my eyes trace over his face. So beautiful, this man. Beautiful and breakable. He loves *so hard*. And yeah, maybe that makes him fragile, like me. But there's strength in that, too.

"I love you, Sam," I tell him. "And that makes you mine just as much as I'm yours. You belong to us now. To me and

Winnie. And I will never, ever be upset about you protecting your family."

Sam's breath pops out of him in little bursts, and then his hands are in my hair and his lips are on mine. The kiss is sharp and bright and full of promises, and I've never felt anything like it.

This. This is the strength of Sam's love.

Winnie and I are lucky to have him.

When we break apart, Sam's eyes are still wet, but the tension is gone from around them. I grab his hand, linking us together. "Come on, love. Let's get Winnie home."

★

"Comfortable?" I ask, tucking Winnie's bedding around her.

She nods, eyelids heavy already. I'm not at all surprised; it's nearly midnight. Luckily, the doctor confirmed Winnie only sustained a minor sprain, so ice and rest are in her future. I have no doubt she'll be back to running around in no time.

I give Winnie's forehead a kiss and reach for her book, but she tugs it protectively against her chest, eyes shooting to Sam, who's sitting on her other side.

"Um," she says, sounding uncharacteristically shy. "Could you read my book tonight, Sammy?"

Sam's eyes shoot to me, his chest rising with his deep breath. It's the first time Winnie has called him *Sammy*, and it's obvious I'm not the only one who caught it. I give him a smile, and Sam nods to Winnie.

"Of course," he says. "It'd be my honor."

"Pumpkin," I interject softly. "Would you like me to stay, or would it be okay if I bring Grandpa home? Either way is fine."

My dad won't mind waiting, but Winnie has been clinging to Sam ever since we left the hospital, and I know, as both my parents and Sam have pointed out, that I need to give Winnie and me more chances to be apart in small doses. I think it's something we're both learning: how to let others care for us.

Winnie thinks it over for only a couple seconds. "You can go," she says with a firm nod. My chest aches, but it's the good kind.

I give her another kiss before sliding off the bed. As soon as I'm out the door, I hear Winnie speaking, and I pause for just a second to listen.

"Sammy, we're best friends now, right?"

I can imagine Sam's responding smile. "The bestest," he answers.

"Well, I was thinking," my daughter says, "if you wanna call me Winnie, you can. I'd be okay with that."

There's a brief pause, and my eyes well. I look at the ceiling, blinking, as Sam replies, "Thank you, Winnie. That means a lot."

"You can read now," she says—more like *demands*—and I hold in my snort. Shaking my head, I pad down the stairs as Sam starts to read Winnie's book.

Fuck. This day has been something else.

"Ready to go?" I ask my dad.

He gives me a nod from the living room and rises, and we head out to my truck. My dad is quiet almost the entire ride back to my parents' home, but when I pull onto the street they live on, he finally speaks.

"He's special, isn't he?"

I glance over at him briefly, knowing he's talking about Sam. He *is* special, yet I can't help but ask, "How so?"

Again, my dad is quiet for a moment. When I park, he turns my way. "It's like he was made for you two, Harrison. I don't really believe in soulmates, but whatever pieces make up the whole of that man, they fit against you. Against you and Winnie. Seeing him with her today..." He shakes his head. "He's everything I'd hoped for the two of you."

I nod, my throat tight. "Yeah," I manage.

I'd stopped hoping. At some point in the past few years, I buried that little seed in my chest down deep. It was too painful, too raw to leave exposed without anyone to care for it. Numbness was easier. Resignation was *safer*.

Sam changed all that. He was so bright, so wonderfully warm, and that seed had no choice but to thrive again.

Maybe, in the recesses of my mind, I was ready for love. Or maybe Sam made it safe to hope. Whatever the reason, my dad is right. Sam is...*everything*.

"I haven't forgotten what you said," I tell him. "About being depressed. I'm going to talk to someone. I don't... I don't think I'm in that place anymore, but I don't want to slip back there, either."

And despite the fact that Sam makes me ridiculously happy, I know our relationship isn't a cure-all for my mental health. It's not fair to place that pressure on Sam, even inside my own head. At my core, I'm responsible for my own happiness, and that includes getting help if I start to flounder.

"Winnie, too," I add. "I think it's time we see someone so she can work through her feelings about her mom."

I wanted so desperately to be enough for my daughter. To prove I could be everything she needed. But those insecurities about measuring up are my own, not Winnie's to bear, and there's no shame in asking for help. In accepting it from others. I'm learning that.

My dad squeezes my shoulder, a serious but warm expression on his face. "I'm proud of you, Harrison. Your mom and I, we just want you to be happy. Both of you."

I nod, and my dad and I exchange a cramped hug in the cab of my truck. He heads inside—after reminding me Mom is surely going to want to come visit Winnie tomorrow—and I drive back home.

Tigger is waiting for me inside the front door when I arrive, and I let her out to do her business before the pair of us head upstairs. Much to my surprise, no noise is coming from Winnie's room, and Tigger squeezes right inside, likely settling herself at the foot of Winnie's bed. I find Sam in my bedroom, still awake.

"Hey," I say softly, closing the door behind me.

He shifts upright as I come over, shirtless with the covers around his legs. "Hey. She fell asleep while I was readin'. Prob'ly 'cause it's so late."

I nod, settling beside him on the bed. "Thank you, Sam. For all of it. I know today wasn't easy, but I'm really glad you were here for it."

He swallows, brows furrowed slightly. "Except she prob'ly wouldn't have gotten hurt if it wasn't for me."

"Hush," I tell him, grabbing his hand and squeezing. "I told you I was just waiting for Winnie to break a bone. I'm not all that surprised she fell. And hey, it was only a sprain. I'd say we lucked out."

He huffs, looking down at where our hands are tied.

"I imagine it was scary," I say softly. He doesn't respond, but his lips twitch. "I'm sorry, Sam. I wouldn't have wished that on you, but I *am* glad you were here for us today. I'm glad every day that you're here."

"Yeah?" he asks softly, a small smile gracing his face.

"Yeah. In fact..." I shift a little, pulling my leg up between us and facing Sam fully. My heart pounds, a nervous *thump-thump* inside my chest, but I power on. "I was wondering what you'd think about being here *every* day."

Sam lifts his gaze, and I can see it there, the hope that he heard me right. It makes it easier to say exactly what's on my mind.

"Sam, I want you here with us. And maybe you're not ready for that yet. If that's the case, that's fine. We can work up to it. But if you'd like to move in, I—"

I don't have time to finish my sentence before Sam's lips are crashing down on my own. He climbs over my lap, hands on my face and mouth doing its best to devour me. My surprise turns into a happy laugh, and Sam eats it up.

"Yes," he says, kissing me again. "Yes, I wanna be yours. Yes, I wanna move here. I want you and Winnie and Tigger and all the mess. Yes."

"It's yours," I say.

And then all I know is Sam's mouth on mine. The feeling of home.

Yes. A million times yes.

CHAPTER 30

✡

Sammy

"Well, shit," Carl sums up rather succinctly.

"Uh-huh," I agree, taking in the sight before us.

Carl and I responded to a call about a case of animal neglect after the landlord of an apartment complex had one of his tenants skip town. The renter disappeared five days ago, as far as anyone can tell, likely in an attempt to avoid paying the thousands he'd racked up in missed payments. The landlord let himself inside the apartment after hearing some suspicious noises, and what he found, in addition to a space cleared of all possessions and valuables, were two hungry animals. A dog...and a pig, of all things.

The pair are now both happily chowing down as Carl and I watch on. The dog, a hound mix with wiry gray hair, and the pig, much smaller than her companion, look surprisingly healthy. The tenant had been treating them well enough, but apparently, the two creatures didn't have sufficient value in his eyes to not be left behind like trash. *Dickweed*.

"Poor souls," I mutter, running my hand over the little pig. The thing is tiny still, about the size of my hand, and she's entirely pink under her layer of soft white fur, apart from a single black spot above her right eye. She wiggles as I scratch her back, corkscrew tail bobbing, but she doesn't yet pull her face from her food.

"We'll bring 'em with us back to Animal Control," Carl is telling the landlord. "Thanks for givin' us a call."

The man nods, grumbling about his lost money as he goes, but frankly, I think it could have been worse. At least there's no property damage inside the apartment. Remarkably, both animals seem to have been trained to use a litter box. It's far too full after five days of use, but hey, the guy doesn't have to clean urine from the floorboards.

"Good little piggy, aren't ya?" I say to the squirmy girl. She finally looks up at me, snout moving as she chews. "*Gah*. You're adorable." I boop her little snout.

"Oh boy," Carl says.

"What?" I ask, scratching along her back again. The hound was less receptive to attention, which is no surprise given the circumstances. Carl and I are giving him space while he eats.

"I know that look," my coworker says.

"What look?" I straight-up giggle as the tiny pig dances, trying to get my scratching nails just where she wants them.

Carl shakes his head as he walks away to collect transportation crates, but I swear I hear, "Of *course* with Sammy it would be a pig."

"I don't know what he's talkin' about, but you're a good little piglet, aren't you?" I coo, tugging my phone free. Luckily, I know a nearby vet who can examine our farm friend.

And come to think of it, that gives me an idea for the hound, too.

"We'll get y'all sorted," I assure the both of them. "Don't you fret."

———————★———————

Harrison's eyes, when I walk through the doors to his practice, are wide and amused. "Sam..." he says slowly. "Is that a pig in your shirt?"

I grin, running a couple fingers between the little pig's ears. She *is* snuggled inside my uniform, her head poking out above the undone buttons near my chest and her snout twisting about as she takes in the vet practice. My guess is she's been stuck inside that apartment for most of, if not all of, her life. She's been sniffing like mad ever since we left the building.

"Harrison," I respond. "This is Piglet. Piglet, Harrison."

I give him my most winning smile, and Harrison's eyes shut in an extended blink. He bites his lip, shaking his head a little, and I have no clue what to think of his reaction. But then he opens his eyes and smiles back.

"You named her Piglet?" he asks, closing the distance between us.

I nod slowly as Carl comes through the door, the hound on a leash in his hand. We've started to gather the attention of Harrison's coworkers—one woman squeals as she rounds the desk to get a better look at Piglet—but my eyes are on my boyfriend.

He licks his lips a little. "What are we going to need?"

My heart skips a beat. "Really?" I ask. "Can we really keep her?"

"Sam," he says softly. We both ignore the woman petting Piglet's head. "How can I possibly say no to you? Do you even realize the power of your face?"

I bark a laugh as Harrison smiles and lets Piglet sniff his hand.

"Do we know how big she's going to get?" he asks.

I grimace a little, looking down at the tiny thing. She's small now, sure, but... "Well, there's every chance she *is* a teacup pig," I hedge. "But I wouldn't put money on it. The good news, however, is that she already knows how to use a litter box."

Harrison sighs, but his smile never falters. "So we just adopted a house-trained pot-bellied pig?"

"Surprise," I say weakly.

Harrison laughs, hand coming up to squeeze the side of my neck. "And the dog?" he asks, looking over at where Carl and another employee—Tessa, I think her name is? I'm still learning—are crouched down near the hound a few feet away.

"Well," I mutter. Here goes the next part of my plan. "I wondered if maybe Abbott—"

"What's this?" the man himself asks, coming out from the hall that leads to the patient rooms. His brows are drawn in as he walks towards the congregation in the lobby, but as soon as his eyes land on the hound mix, his expression softens. *Bingo*.

"Heya, Abbott," I greet warmly. "We found these two on a call today. Figured we'd stop by to get 'em checked out before we bring that little lad"—I point to the dog—"back to Animal Control."

Abbott stops in front of the hound, who, although not Irish Wolfhound entirely, could very well have some in his lineage. The dog is tall—not by Irish Wolfhound standards, but tall nonetheless—and wiry. And if Abbott really has been feeling lonely, maybe a new companion is just the ticket.

The older vet examines the dog as Piglet squirms in my shirt. I give her a calming pet as I watch Abbott quite possibly fall in love. Harrison shakes his head in my periphery.

"Don't worry, Abbott," I say. "We'll clear out before long. Sorry for causin' a ruckus."

Realistically, I know Abbott isn't *in charge* around here—all the vets own shares in the practice—but I figured a tiny nudge might...

"You, uh." Abbott clears his throat. "You don't have anybody lined up to take him?"

"Not yet," I say with a smile. "But somebody will surely snatch him up quick. He's a handsome dog."

Abbott nods, and the hound sits regally as the vet pets his head. The older man looks around at his coworkers before clearing his throat again. "Perhaps he could come home with me? I have room, after all," he adds gruffly.

"Well, dang. You sure?" I say. "That'd be great, Abbott. The dog would be lucky to have you."

He looks pleased at that.

"I can help you with the paperwork," Carl adds, the perfect wingman. He leads Abbott and the dog over to the counter in front of Reception.

I turn back to Harrison, and the expression on his face bowls me over.

"Sam," he says simply, grabbing my arm and tugging. I follow Harrison into one of the exam rooms as the rest of his coworkers get back to work, and Harrison shuts the door behind us. He's shaking his head again, but then he smacks a forceful kiss against my lips. "You are the sexiest, sweetest, kindest person I've ever known."

My heart takes off as my grin stretches wide. "Yeah? Sexiest? It's the pig in my shirt, isn't it?"

Harrison laughs. "Sexy as fuck, Sam. You brought that dog here on purpose, didn't you?"

"I did," I admit, rubbing Piglet's head. She's calm again; otherwise, I would let her down. "I figured after what you told me, the man could use somebody in his life. Even if that somebody is a dog."

Harrison's hand lands on the side of my neck again, his thumb rubbing over my skin. I like it *way* too much, the way he's looking at me. The way he's touching me. But I push my want away for later.

"Sam, you have such a big heart, you know that?" he says. "I'm so glad it found its way to me."

My insides do a complicated pop and melt routine that reminds me of Winnie's volcanoes. "Even if said heart added a pig to your family?" I check.

"Even so. *Especially* so," he says, looking down at Piglet and sighing from deep within. "Welcome to the family, Piglet. I think you'll be right at home. Let's give her a check, shall we?"

Heart feeling oh so full, I pull Piglet out of my shirt and hand her over. She fits right in Harrison's palm. He's gentle and calm as he checks her over, completing a full exam and administering a few vaccinations against common bacteria that could harm our new little pig. We'll have to bring her back in two weeks for boosters, but then she'll be good to go for another year.

"All set," Harrison says gently, smiling down at Piglet, who's happily munching up a treat. I must audibly sigh because Harrison looks my way. "What is it?"

"I love these kind eyes," I tell him, stepping around the exam table and brushing my finger near his temple. My mind flashes back to that first day I met Harrison in Plum Valley, when we were working together with the sheep. "Y'know the first thing I noticed about you?"

"My kind eyes?" he asks with a smirk.

"Actually, no," I admit. "It was your ass."

Harrison barks a laugh, and I chuckle with him, one hand on Piglet to make sure she doesn't take a plunge off the exam table.

"Practically got whiplash when you walked by," I tell him. "But then you turned, and there they were. Those baby blues, all sweet but wary. I wanted to soften those eyes."

"You do," he says quietly.

I'm glad. So very glad.

"There was somethin' about you that always felt safe, Harrison," I say seriously. "Like, if I could just get you to look at me with those eyes, everythin' would be...okay."

"Sam," he says gently.

"And it is, y'know?"

He nods. "I know." After squeezing my arm, Harrison says, "I still have a couple more appointments this afternoon, but I'll catch you and Piglet at home?"

"You bet," I say, snagging one more kiss.

"A pig," Harrison mutters as we leave the room. "I can't believe we have a pig."

I wonder what Harrison would think about adding a few more dogs to the family.

I'm all the way across the lobby when I hear Deborah's delighted voice. "Oh my word. Is that a *pig*?"

Harrison's laughing when he catches my eye. "See you at home, Sam."

I shoot him a salute, return Deborah's wave, and head outside, Piglet tucked in my arms. Carl is waiting out near the truck, no hound in sight. I give him a grin, and he rolls his eyes.

"Yeah, yeah," he says. "You were right. Abbott adopted the dog."

"Knew it," I say, transferring Piglet into her carrier for the ride back to Animal Control. Hopefully now, the older vet will feel a little less alone.

Twenty-five minutes later, Carl and I are pulling up in front of Animal Control. I decide not to head back inside, instead wanting to get Piglet home and settled. Paperwork can wait until Monday.

"See you this weekend?" I ask Carl before he exits the truck.

We're having a cookout. Although it might be best to steer clear of pork products on the grill.

"Yeah," Carl answers. "I'll be there. Still think I should bring Rosie?"

"I don't see why not," I tell him. "If any of the animals have trouble gettin' along, we'll just split them between inside and out."

Carl gives me a nod. "All right, then. See you this weekend." He pauses, door aloft. "Oh, and Sammy?"

"Yeah?"

"I better be your best man at the weddin'." He gives me a wink before shutting the door and walking off.

I laugh, but damn if that doesn't make me grin so wide my cheeks hurt.

When I get home—*home*—I bring Piglet to the backyard. I can't imagine Tigger would have any issue controlling herself around the little pig, but just in case, I grab a leash before finding the dog waiting just inside the back door. I've no doubt she already noticed the new arrival.

"All right, girl," I say, clipping her leash in place. "You better be nice to your new li'l sister. She's smaller than you *now*, but she could very well outclass you within the year. Just keep that in mind."

Tigger wiggles her stub tail.

"Here we go."

Of course, there's absolutely nothing to worry about. Tigger sniffs Piglet politely, and Piglet—already used to being around dogs—ignores Tigger's curious nose. Piglet seems much more interested in rooting around, her little snout snuffling against the ground as she explores. I wonder if she's ever had the chance before, or if she's only been allowed to root around on carpet. Well, now she'll have plenty of chances to get dirty with Winnie and Tigger.

I let Tigger off her leash before long and sit down in the grass, watching the pair wander. The sun is out today, and even though the weather is getting cooler, I don't mind. I let the Texas sunshine soak me from above, eyes closing as the wind rustles the branches of the oak tree. I should probably change out of my work uniform and get cleaned up, but I'm in no hurry.

With a smile, my gaze shifts to the treehouse, the structure looking like it grew right from the tree. I didn't realize it at the time, but I think putting up that treehouse was the very start of me setting down roots. Yeah, I wanted Harrison on a baser level before then, and I was nearly desperate to see what we could become. I think I was more excited about him and all he had to offer than I was willing to let myself acknowledge. It was a feeling. That whisper of *home*.

But digging into the dirt with Harrison, seeing the way we worked together so effortlessly, the way Harrison so clearly desired me, too—it was the first time I thought I might truly get everything I wanted. For once in my life, maybe I *had* found the place I belonged. Maybe that man, that little girl, their dog, and their perfectly messy life...maybe they'd been waiting for me. I could be their dream come true. They were certainly mine.

I let out a sigh. I can't see the stars this early in the day, of course, but I flit my thumb over my hip, right atop the constellation etched into my skin.

What do I wish for now when everything is already as it should be?

"Holy fudge! Did we really get a pig? Oh my *God!*"

Winnie races past—her ankle long since healed by now—and skids to a stop a few feet away. She pivots, collides into me with a quick hug and an enthusiastic screech that might have burst my eardrum, and then she's off again, running toward where Piglet and Tigger are exploring in the bushes. She slows once she reaches them, waiting to make sure Piglet is comfortable, but then she's petting the little pink pig with the biggest smile I've ever seen on her face.

"I think that worked better than cake," Harrison jokes, taking a seat beside me.

I bump my shoulder into his. "Think so?"

He hums, eyes squinted against the sun as he watches Winnie, Tigger, and Piglet.

"And what about you?" I say, turning my head against his shoulder, nudging his neck with my nose. "What could I bribe you with?"

He swallows, pulse racing under my lips as I feather a kiss across his skin.

"Maybe you'd like to fuck me in that shed later," I suggest whisper-soft, thrilling at Harrison's sharp inhale. "You could pump me full of your cum and watch it drip back out while I finish myself off."

"Jesus," Harrison hisses.

"And then after you clean yourself off my skin, you can have the slice of chocolate cake I hid in the freezer."

Harrison grabs my chin, kissing me hard. "You," he says shortly, eyes on fire, "are the most perfect man for me."

My grin is swift, a happiness I feel down to my toes.

"Angel of cake and cock, at your service," I mumble against his lips.

Harrison laughs and then moans. There's another kiss. A single bark. The sound of a child laughing and running around. And somewhere, way up high above us, the stars are twinkling, waiting for their moment to shine.

But down here on Earth, Harrison's lips are curved against my own, and I know I'm home.

CHAPTER 31

※

Harrison

"Aw, fuck," Sam groans, hanging his head. His hands scramble at the tool bench in front of him, fingers leaving tracks against the dusty surface. The smells and sounds of sex are strong in the small shed.

"Don't come," I choke out, sweat beading down my brow. "You promised I could watch."

He grunts, his ass tightening around me, but he reaches down, staving off his release.

"C'mon, stud," he groans out. "Any day now."

I huff a laugh, forehead against Sam's shoulder as I fuck him from behind. His ass fits me like a glove, and every inch of the man in front of me is a dream come true. I easily could have come by now, but I've been holding off.

"What if I want to take my time?" I say, groaning as Sam's body squeezes me tight.

"Stud," he warns.

I can't help it; I laugh. Sliding my hands around to Sam's chest, I tug him upright, molding my body to his as much as humanly possible as I lose myself in this man. In the smell of him, the feel, even the taste as my lips find that sweet spot below his ear. He's my Sam. And there's simply no resisting him.

My orgasm hits me hard once I stop fighting it, a full-body rush that starts in my fingers and barrels through the very heart of me. It goes on—Sam moaning all the while as I grind against his ass—until finally, I'm all but slumped over his body as tingling aftershocks race across my skin. I take a moment to simply breathe. To feel the way Sam and I are connected. Feel the wet warmth of my release inside his body. Feel his heartbeat racing steadily beneath my palm.

"Stud," he says at last, voice hoarse. "I gotta come. I can't—"

I laugh again—*God*, the way he makes me feel—and pull out slowly as Sam breathes a sigh of relief. A trickle of my cum works its way down Sam's thigh as I watch, and I groan at the sight of it.

The first time we did this—fucked bareback in the shed—was almost a year ago. But *damn*, did I become addicted fast. It's not something we can do often, mainly because it's always a risk when Winnie's around. But she's with my parents tonight—at least for the time being—so Sam and I get to let loose.

I like our idea of romance. Sex in the shed. Cake and beer after Winnie goes to sleep. And what Sam now refers to as *Harrison ropin'*. I'm an especially big fan of that last one.

"Turn around," I tell Sam before he can start jerking himself off. I want him in my mouth tonight.

He doesn't need to be told twice. He spins, I drop down, and the moment his cock is in front of my lips, I suck him in. Sam slaps his palms back against the tool bench, his hips hitching forward, and it's all over from there. He stutters out a groan, his long-held-off orgasm detonating, and his release splashes across my tongue. I swallow him down greedily, holding tight to the firm globes of his ass.

"Fuck," he finally says, muscles relaxing and chest heaving.

I give his softening cock a gentle suck before letting him go. "Turn around," I tell him again.

He groans but does as I ask, turning and bracing his elbows on the tool bench. He spreads his legs without a word, and I trace my tongue up his thigh, all the way to his asshole, swiping up the cum running from his body.

He rumbles out another "*Fuck.*"

Christ, do I love making him purr.

I give his ass cheek a little nip before standing. "Come on. Let's go clean up."

He doesn't argue, and five minutes later, we're in the steaming-hot shower, washing the dusty, sweaty excursion off our skin. Sam is humming, which I find so adorable I can't help but grin in response. He squints his eyes open from underneath the shower spray when I give him a hand soaping up, and a smile lights his face.

"So, what's next?" he asks. "Are we breakin' into that cookie dough tube you hid in the vegetable drawer?"

I huff a laugh, spinning Sam so I can wash his back. "Not quite. I have other plans."

"Oh, you do?" he says, a suggestive edge to his voice I don't miss.

My heart rate kicks up, but I force a slow breath through my body. "Yep," I say, slapping his ass. "So let's go."

After Sam and I get dressed, I send a quick text to my parents, and then I lead him downstairs toward the back door. He looks confused as we head back into the yard, but he follows easily, Tigger and Piglet at our heels.

Piglet, as it turns out, is *not* a teacup pig. She's now eighty pounds and stands nearly as tall as Tigger's shoulders. But the pig integrated into our family with ease, and both she and Tigger have taken to spending nights in Winnie's bed. Winnie doesn't mind the extra company one bit.

It's fully dark when we all pile outside, and thankfully, it's a cloudless night.

"What're we doin'?" Sam asks as dog and pig take off running after bugs or shadows or who-knows-what.

"You'll see," I tell him, dragging him along to the treehouse. Sam chuckles when I head up the ladder, but he follows me without question. When I get to the top, I stoop inside Winnie's fort, reaching up to open the moonroof. I plant my back against the big trunk in the middle of the treehouse once I'm done and wait as Sam joins me. We've never come up here before, just the two of us.

We're quiet for a moment, Sam looking up out of the roof at the stars above. My pulse hammers in my ears as my fingers drift over the box in my pocket.

"Sam," I say gently.

He turns his head toward me, a small smile on his face. He looks delicate in the moonlight. Soft and beautiful.

"Do you remember that first night we went camping in the backyard, over a year ago?" I ask.

He nods, his eyes creasing at the corners. "Yeah, o'course. Why?"

"I never told you this," I say, my mouth dry. "But I heard you talking to Winnie that night. I heard you talking about wishes."

"Yeah?" he asks, looking more curious than anything. I wonder if he even remembers what he said. The words that have been stuck inside my head ever since.

"I like the starlight. It's like...hope. It's full of wishes. Those stars come out at night, and I look up at 'em and see my future. I see all the things I want my life to be."

"Yeah," I reply, swallowing. The crickets sound like they're chirping in time to my heart. "I hadn't wished for a very long time, Sam. Not until you."

"Harrison," he says softly, but his mouth clamps shut the moment I shift up onto one knee, and his eyes shoot wide in understanding.

Remarkably, all of my thoughts settle as I look at the man I love. At his big, brown eyes and expressive face. At the strength of his body, but, more importantly, the strength he carries inside. When I look at him, I'm certain he's the one, and my voice comes out even and true.

"Sam, you came into my life, and you were sunshine, so big and bright and beautiful. You were sunshine, but you were starlight, too. You woke me up, and you made me *dream*. You gave me hope for a partnership when I thought I'd lost that for myself. And now, all my heart wishes for is you. It's you, you, *you*, Sam."

He stutters out a breath, and I pull the ring box from my pocket. My hand is steady, and Sam's eyes drop, watching as I flick it open, revealing the onyx ring inside. It gleams dark under the starlight, but the constellation I had engraved along the surface shines silver and bright. Seven little stars.

"I was stuck before you came along," I say quietly. "I'd convinced myself no one could love me and all of my baggage. But I just hadn't found *you* yet. The way you love us? God, it's wonderful, Sam. It's huge and perfect and right. You belong with us no matter what. But I hope you'll do me the honor of becoming my husband. And Winnie's dad," I add carefully. "Because we don't want you to ever doubt that you're ours."

A single tear rolls down Sam's cheek. "You're askin' me to marry you?"

I give a start, realizing I never actually said the words. "*Shit.* We really do need to work on our romantic declarations, huh?"

Sam lets out a watery chuckle. "I dunno. Seems pretty perfect for us."

Yeah, it really does.

"Sam," I say again, drawing in a breath. "Would you marry me?"

He huffs out a laugh-cry-moan, swiping at his cheek and nodding furiously, and his adamant "*Yes*" is almost too quiet to hear. I laugh with him when he reaches for the box, and my hands begin to shake as I pull the ring free. I knew—I *knew*—what Sam's answer was going to be, but now that I've heard the words, it's hitting me in a rush.

Sam said *yes*.

He's going to be my husband. Winnie's dad.

Ours. Permanently.

Sam looks down at the ring as I slide it into place—a perfect fit—and then he's grabbing me behind the neck and tugging me forward. His lips meet mine, warm and insistent and bursting with joy, and it's all I can do not to cry. The good kind. The relieved kind. The kind that means forever.

"Did he say yes?" Winnie yells, and Sam breaks away from me, eyes wide once more.

"Yes, he said yes!" I call back.

There's a whoop from below and then the sound of Winnie's little footsteps climbing up the ladder. Her head pops into view first, blonde hair in disarray, and then she's scrambling between us, her star pajamas glowing softly in the light of the moon. Sam hugs her tight, so many emotions flashing over his face as his gaze finds mine. My parents call up their congratulations, Winnie starts gushing about how *I told Daddy you'd want it to be under the stars, and I was right, wasn't I? This is awesome.* But Sam doesn't say a word. He doesn't need to. I can see it in his eyes.

A glimmer of starlight. The future spread before us.

It's quite possibly the most beautiful thing I've ever seen.

"Love you," I whisper among Winnie's excited ramblings and the sound of the rest of our family celebrating below.

Sam's smile is like the sun. "Love you, too, stud."

EPILOGUE
TWO AND A HALF YEARS LATER

✦

Harrison

As Sam, Winnie, and I stroll leisurely past the brick-faced shop fronts on Main Street, Winnie keeps up a running commentary of everything she and Janey did at the planetarium field trip yesterday.

"And you should've seen Josh. I mean, gross. Everyone knows you don't stick food up your nose. He's still immature, though. Twelve-year-olds," she says with a snort.

Sam and I share a look over Winnie's head, and his eyes go wide. Right. *Twelve-year-olds*. Because Winnie is thirteen now. Officially a teenager.

Wonders never cease.

"Me and Janey ignored him, though," she goes on imperiously. "And the tour guide let us position the telescope *ourselves*, which was *so cool*. He said it was obvious we knew what we were doing, which is true. We've had lots of practice."

Because, in a turn of events no one saw coming, Winnie and her "difficult" classmate Janey became fast friends when they bonded over stars. Janey comes over often now, and she and Winnie spend a lot of time up in the tree fort, making use of the telescope Sam and I bought Winnie for her birthday last year.

The not-so-little-anymore girl is still going strong on her plans to become an astronomer.

"You had fun, then?" Sam asks. We didn't get a chance to talk much about the school field trip after Winnie arrived home last night. She was too tired, and then, this morning, she spent our entire drive over here with her face stuck in her tablet. Now, though, she can't *stop* talking about it.

"It was the best," she says, skipping once. "We found Andromeda, Cassiopeia, Cygnus, Auriga…"

Winnie keeps listing constellations as my eyes snag on the sign for Country Cones, Plum Valley's one ice cream shop. I stop, and Sam notices first, coming up beside me.

"Wanna go inside?" he asks, like it's even a question.

"Winnie, want ice cream?" I call out.

She stops, pivots on her heel, and rushes back over. "Uh, yeah."

Sam snorts and grabs the door, holding it open as Winnie and I pass through. A bell jingles overhead, and the kid at the counter looks up from his phone.

"Welcome to Country Cones," he says dutifully, sounding bored. "Home of the best dang ice cream in all of Plum Valley. Or somethin' like that."

I huff a laugh as Winnie steps up to the counter, looking at the ice cream choices. The shop is empty apart from us, and a fan whirs overhead.

"What'll you have, li'l miss?" Sam asks our daughter, reaching like he's about to ruffle her hair but pulling his hand back at the last moment. He shoots me a bewildered look that manages to convey his relief. The last time Sam messed with Winnie's hair, she about bit his arm off.

"Um," she says, hemming and hawing before finally deciding on a flavor. "Peanut butter cup."

"Cup or cone?" the bored teen behind the counter asks.

"Cone, thanks."

The employee scoops up Winnie's order, and she takes it over to a booth in front of the window as Sam asks for a cup of cherry chocolate. I get vanilla with sprinkles.

As Winnie gets lost in her phone, Sam knocks his foot into mine. We're sharing one side of the booth.

"How're you doin', husband?" he asks quietly, using his new favorite nickname for me. It still sends a shiver down my spine every time I hear it.

Unsurprisingly, we got married under the stars on a cloudless night. Winnie was our flower girl, and to this day, I get choked up every time I remember the ceremony. It was beautiful, Sam even more so.

That was over a year ago.

I give him a responding smile as I scoop up a spoonful of my ice cream. It's perfectly sweet, and the sprinkles add just the right bite. "I'm good," I tell him honestly after thinking over the question.

"You don't regret comin'?" he checks.

At first, I wasn't sure I wanted to come back here when Sam mentioned an animal he had taken on the task of transporting. The couple in Plum Valley was interested in the dog they found online, but because of their older age, travel wasn't an immediate option. Sam offered to drive the dog over from Houston for a meet-and-greet, which we did first thing when we arrived in Plum Valley. It went well, and the couple adopted the sweet old canine. It was a great fit.

But there wasn't a real reason for Winnie and I to be here other than the fact that Winnie wanted to come. Apparently, seeing the place her dads met was going to be *so romantic, Dad. Like something out of a fairy tale. Can we go? Please,*

please? I'm fairly certain Winnie's expectations were dashed when we drove for a solid five minutes in town seeing nothing but cattle. But she's been upbeat since we arrived, albeit that might have to do with whichever friend she's texting incessantly. Probably Janey.

"I don't regret coming," I tell Sam. "It's a beautiful day, and I have you, Winnie, and this ice cream. What more could I ask for?"

He gives me a smile at that, bumping his shoulder against mine. "Another dog?" he proposes, laughing when my face falls into a scowl.

"Sammy," I groan halfheartedly. "We already have three dogs and a pig."

"Uh-huh," he says breezily. "So why not make it an even five pets?"

I grab his chin, stealing a kiss that tastes of chocolate and Sam, and he rumbles against my mouth. "That doesn't even make sense," I tell him. He laughs again when I give his face a little shake and then push him away.

"I think I know a way to win you over," he mutters, going back to his ice cream.

Shit. He's going to break out the chaps.

My pulse fires, and I look out the window to distract myself. A few folks pass by outside, and I watch them for a moment, enjoying the simplicity of this day. The truth is if Sam wants another dog, we'll get another dog. There isn't much of anything I'd deny the man. Not when he gives so much to Winnie and me.

Sam's fingers land on the back of my neck before long. Not a teasing touch, just a grounding one. The kind he shares with me often, like he wants to remind me of his presence. Or remind himself of mine. I give his leg a squeeze.

"Can we drive by the place you met?" Winnie asks, her phone finally put away.

Sam snorts lightly, shooting me a little glance as he licks his spoon clean. "Suppose so," he answers. "But it was private property, so you won't be able to see much."

Winnie pouts at that. "What about where you had your first kiss?"

I cough, mind flashing back to the shed on Mr. Calhoun's property, and Sam rubs my back.

"Can't see that either, Winnie," Sam answers.

She huffs. "*Fine*. Can I at least take a picture of you two before we go?"

"Of course," I tell her, amused by Winnie's fascination with learning about this place Sam and I first met. I guess I get it. I mean, what are the chances Sam and I would find each other in this town four hours from home instead of in the city near where we both lived? We were twenty minutes apart for a decade, and yet our paths had never crossed.

If for no other reason, I can thank Plum Valley for that. For bringing us together.

Ice cream finished, the three of us pick up our trash and head out of Country Cones. The employee waves a goodbye without ever lifting his head, and the bell jingles once more on our way through the door.

The breeze rushes past when we step onto the sidewalk, kicking up a few small tumbleweeds. The sun is bright and high in the sky, and if I take a big enough breath, I can smell a hint of wildflowers and cattle. There's something to be said for the countryside.

"Come on," Winnie urges, giving my hand a tug. "Let's take the picture over here."

Dutifully, Sam and I follow our daughter. She plants us side by side on a small green space beside the road, angling us so the quaint visage of Main Street is at our backs. Then she fidgets with her phone for a solid minute before declaring she found just the right angle.

"Say cheese," she says.

"Cheese," I reply, just as Sam's mouth lands a smacking kiss against my cheek. He grabs my chin, holding me in place for the assault, and I can't help but laugh, wrapping my arms around him as his stubble pricks my skin.

"Perfect!" Winnie declares, rushing over to show us the finished product.

Sam gives my cheek a wipe, and I tug him close, brushing my lips against his. The simplest touch from Sam always feels like coming home.

When we part and I happen to glance off to the side, the smile on my face freezes. There, about a hundred feet away, is a man I'd recognize anywhere.

Wyatt.

He's stopped outside the aptly named Feed Store at the end of the road, clearly having spotted me, too. His hair is long, just like how I remember, but I can't make out much else from this distance. For a moment, we both simply stare. Then Wyatt's face breaks into a broad grin, and he lifts his hand in greeting.

I don't know what I was expecting—honestly, I hadn't much considered the chance of running into Wyatt again—but all I feel looking at my ex is...contentment.

I'm perfectly content—happy with the choices that led me here and grateful for all I have. There's no urge to run or flee, and the only feeling coursing through me directly related to my ex at all is a vague sense of sentimentality for the brief time we shared.

In fact, now that I'm standing in front of the man again, I have a sneaking suspicion it wasn't Wyatt I was running from the last time I was here in Plum Valley—that day when Sam dragged me into Mr. Calhoun's shed. I don't think my panic was about him at all. I think, perhaps, I was running away from myself. From the fact that, deep down, I *knew* something in my life had to change. I was sinking and alone, and I didn't want to be like that anymore. Seeing Wyatt was just a reminder I'd been hurt in the past. And I knew, if—*when*—I found the courage to try again, I could get hurt...again.

But then there was Sam. *Sam*.

Not a day goes by that I'm not ridiculously happy to have put my faith in Sam. He and Winnie—they're my family. And, of course, there's my parents, Deb, Carl and Tilda, and all of our fur-babies, too.

But this man with his arm around my waist, who's complimenting Winnie on her picture-taking skills—he chose me. He puts me first every single day, and I do my absolute best to make sure he knows he's cherished in return.

So, no. There are no more of those hard, brittle feelings lingering inside. No sadness. No wishing things were different.

I am loved. And I love. Fiercely. Madly. Wildly. Fully.

I wouldn't change that for the world.

"Stud?" Sam asks quietly, tightening his grip on my side. "See somethin'?"

A smile tips my lips as Wyatt's eye holds mine, and I raise my hand in response to his hello. For just a beat longer, that's how we stand. Then Wyatt gives me a nod and turns away, and that's that.

"Just an old friend," I tell Sam, turning his way and snagging his belt loops. Winnie is preoccupied once more with her phone.

Sam's eyes crease at the corners, a gentle display of concern, but he gives me a nod. "Anythin' else you wanna do before we head home?"

I hum. "I heard there's a new bakery in town."

Sam barks a laugh. "Why am I not surprised that you wanna get some treats to go?" He leans close, lips whispering across mine. "My husband's got the biggest sweet tooth."

"Guilty," I reply, a grin on my face as I step back and hold out my hand. Sam takes it as he tells Winnie we're going to stop by the bakery, and I glance over my shoulder one last time.

Plum Valley sits peacefully under the midday sun, tall grasses in the fields off of Main Street blowing gently in the wind. The land stretches golden, a few cattle dotting the landscape in the distance, and above is bright blue sky. It may not be home, but it sure is beautiful. I give it a quiet goodbye before turning my focus to where I know my heart belongs.

Winnie grabs my free hand, eager to visit the bakery, and Sam keeps a hold of the other. I give him a squeeze, feeling his ring brush against my skin, and he looks over at me, his smile beaming and beautifully bright. It's sunshine and starlight and my future rolled into one.

And I wish, I wish, *I wish*...

For not a single thing more.

———————★———————

The End

About the Author

Information about Emmy Sanders and her complete list of works can be found on her website. Subscribe to her newsletter, join her Facebook reader group, Emmy's Enclave, and connect via email or social media:

www.emmysanders.com

Find online:
www.facebook.com/emmysandersmm
www.instagram.com/emmysandersmm

Milton Keynes UK
Ingram Content Group UK Ltd.
UKHW021312171123
432758UK00025B/1053